THE CORONER

THE CORONER

JENNIFER GRAESER DORNBUSH

W🌐RLDWIDE

TORONTO • NEW YORK • LONDON
AMSTERDAM • PARIS • SYDNEY • HAMBURG
STOCKHOLM • ATHENS • TOKYO • MILAN
MADRID • WARSAW • BUDAPEST • AUCKLAND

To Ryan, who had the courage to marry this coroner's daughter despite the human organs in the basement freezer and the body bags drying on the lawn. I love you.

WORLDWIDE™

The Coroner

A Worldwide Mystery/March 2020

First published in 2018 by Crooked Lane Books, an imprint of The Quick Brown Fox & Company LLC. This edition published in 2020.

ISBN-13: 978-1-335-29968-0

This edition published by arrangement with Harlequin Books S.A.

For questions and comments about the quality of this book, please contact us at CustomerService@Harlequin.com.

Harlequin Enterprises ULC
22 Adelaide St. West, 40th Floor
Toronto, Ontario M5H 4E3, Canada
www.ReaderService.com

Printed in U.S.A.

THE CORONER

ONE

MEDICAL RESIDENT Dr. Emily Hartford did her best to shake off the mounting pressure that pulsed through her shoulders, up her neck, and throbbed into the muscles at the base of her skull. *Where was that train?*

The chondroplasty video looped through Emily's brain on continuous replay. She had already watched it sixty-seven times. And in ninety-three minutes, she would be doing it for real on a retired professional soccer player who had torn up his knee. Now, recently retired from the sport, he needed the agility and mobility to run after two very active twin toddlers.

Emily, a third-year doctor in her surgical residency, checked the platform ticker for a fifth time. A signal flashed on the overhead monitor. Her train would be two minutes delayed. That was two minutes too late. A warm rain pelted her hood and soaked her running shoes and the pant legs of her scrubs. It would take all morning for them to dry in the highly cooled operation room. Her feet would be numb, with no chance of thawing until lunch. She had forgotten to pack fresh shoes and socks—a deep source of regret.

Her long blonde hair, wound into a bun on top of her head, was hidden under a wool cap. Her long, lean figure stood a good head above most of the early morning commuters who littered the train stop. With hair down, heels, and makeup, Emily was always turning heads. This morning, in medical garb and hair pulled up, she blended agreeably into the soggy gray workaday world around her.

Standing under the platform awning, Emily cracked open her cluttered handbag to search for her phone and headset. Finding them twined around a small notebook and tube of lip gloss, she untangled them and, popping them into her ears, started to search her phone for that video. She wanted to revisit it just one more time.

As she scrolled through her phone to find it, a calendar reminder popped up. *Today's my birthday?* Emily tapped the calendar app to double-check the date. Had she really forgotten about her twenty-eighth birthday? September 19th. Sure enough. Day of her birth. Emily had been so busy picking up extra shifts and studying all month, she realized, she hadn't given a single thought to birthday plans.

The train whizzed into the station, and Emily stuffed her phone back into her handbag. As the train slowed to a stop, the mass of commuters shuffled toward the sliding doors that swooshed open, exchanging a trickle of disembarking passengers for the flock of waiting ones. Emily moved with the herd into the busy train and searched for a seat. A self-absorbed hipster wearing a black hoodie beat her to an aisle spot. She scanned ahead to the one remaining empty seat in the last row of the car but gave it up when an elderly Hispanic woman limped up behind her with a toothless grin and three overstuffed shopping bags. Emily pointed to the vacancy, and the diminutive woman nodded gratefully to her as she slouched into the hard plastic seat. One of the lady's bags lost its balance and tipped out of her grasp. Emily caught it before it fell, preventing a canned goods avalanche. The woman offered a thankful smile. *"Mucho gusto, senorita,"* she said.

"De nada." Emily settled grocery bags around the woman.

Grabbing a hand strap, Emily tried to block out the musty smell of body odor and rain by breathing shallowly through the bottom of her nose. It was a trick her father, also a physician, had taught her when they worked in the morgue together.

Blaring rap music entered the cab, disturbing everyone's peace. Emily did her best to ignore a vagrant man squeezing through the center aisle, irreverently blasting his handheld radio. Profanities from the lyrics accosted her and the other riders, many of whom darted dirty looks at the guy. One of the annoyed commuters took courage: "Hey man, turn that thing off. There are children riding."

The vagrant never even glanced up as he kept trekking toward the back of the car, crossing into the next car to besiege another unsuspecting group of commuters. This was city living. Dense. Unexpected. And fast. Twelve years in Chicago, and Emily was still not completely used to the pace of this world. Although she did love the energy of the city, she didn't feel the same ease here as her boyfriend, Brandon, did. But then, he had grown up here. Known no other place. They'd met when she was a sophomore and he was a senior in college. On their dates he took her to underground Chicago and exposed her to the real Windy City. The places and people that moved under the surface gave it its texture and toughness. The more he showed her, the more she had come to understand the mysteries of this place. His enthusiasm and loyalty to this city that he loved so much was one of the reasons she had fallen in love with him. He was a fearless explorer, even in his own backyard. There was always something new to see and experience. He approached life with vivacity, curiosity, and thoughtfulness. Which, of course, made him not only a super boyfriend but also a superb surgeon.

She missed him. His schedule as a new surgeon working at Northwestern University Hospital was even more taxing than hers as a resident, and in the past couple of months they had hardly been able to spend a moment together beyond rushed lunches and late-night phone calls. But she was sure he was cooking something up for her birthday. Quite literally, perhaps. He was a foodie and self-taught chef. In his spare time, of course. And when was that exactly? She wasn't sure. She swore he got by purely on catnaps in the doctor's lounge.

Emily yawned and looked forward to seeing what surprises Brandon had in store for her day. In the meantime, she needed to focus on prepping for surgery. She pressed "Play" on the video button on her iPhone.

"Create a small incision around the front of the knee. Insert the arthroscope," the clinical voice from the lecture on her iPod instructed. *"This will help you diagnose the problem better and maintain surgery safety protocol."*

The chondroplasty marked an important milestone in her journey as a surgical resident at the University of Chicago Medical School. She would be calling the shots in the operating room under the supervision of the lead doctor and her mentor, Dr. Claiborne, with whom she had been working for three years.

"Expand the joint by pumping fluid into it through the pump hose inserted in one of the incisions. Using

the arthroscope, inspect the joint to find the source of the problem, the damaged tissue." The monotone voice droned as the camera kept an extreme close-up on the procedure. *Did these producers purposefully hire monks to record the voiceover?*

Emily felt ninety-six percent ready. With this little early morning review, she could pass the surgery with flying colors. In less than two years, Emily would be an employable surgeon, ready to conquer appendectomies, tonsillectomies, or colon resections. She might join a practice or stay on staff at a hospital. She wasn't sure just yet. One day at a time. Brandon, on the other hand—always the visionary—wanted to open his own surgery center one day. He had also had his sights set on international travel for a few years with Doctors Without Borders. Emily wasn't sure how she would fit into these plans. But she trusted Brandon had it all figured out.

"With your surgical tools, remove the loose cartilage tissue, which is what causes the knee to lock or pop if it drifts into the joint," the lecture continued. *"Take off the small patches of damaged cartilage, and then smooth out the surface of the repaired cartilage."* Emily made a mental picture of the procedure. It wasn't difficult to imagine. She knew the human body better than most. By the time she was sixteen, Emily had dissected over a hundred bodies with her father, a medical examiner for Freeport County, where she'd grown up. Emily had expressed an interest in medicine since she was thirteen, and her dad insisted that helping with autopsies was the best way to master anatomy. Emily dove right in, assisting where she could, between homework, sports practice, piano lessons, and an expanding social life.

Emily's phone buzzed, cutting off the video. She reached down to silence the call. It was a familiar Michigan number. Cathy Bishop, mortician and life-time friend of Emily's family. She had seen this number come up hundreds of times on her family's caller ID. Cathy and her husband had owned Bishop & Schultz Funeral Home. It was the only funeral home in Freeport, and they had worked closely with Emily's father. But Emily had spoken to Cathy only a handful of times in the past decade since she'd left home at sixteen.

Emily let the call go to voicemail. She replayed the video, trying to concentrate. But a foreboding nervous-ness pricked at her like it always did before a surgery. Working on dead people was easy. What's the worst that could happen? They were already dead.

Keep it together. Today is huge. You need to pass this next step flawlessly. Concentrate. Focus. Listen to the boring monk voice. She notched up the volume and harnessed her concentration for four more stops until the train conductor called out, "Forty-seventh Street Station." The train jerked to a slow roll. Emily shuffled toward the exit with a couple dozen passengers also jockeying for the door.

Exiting the metro, she jogged down the street toward the university hospital. Her heart rate elevated, and her breathing quickened. Running took away the nerves. Pat, pat, pat, pat, pat, pat. The balls of her feet slapped the wet cement as she darted up the hospital sidewalk.

It was showtime.

TWO

As EMILY ENTERED the surgery center on the fourth floor, her mentor met her with a quick glance and handed her a stack of charts. He had been a surgeon for almost thirty years; he was a loving husband, father of three, a grandfather for the first time last year. She was lucky that he had chosen her from among the seventy-five other surgical interns, to study under him. They had worked together for three years now, and he treated her tough, but fairly.

"Good morning, Dr. Claiborne." Emily broke into a forced smile that covered her frayed nerves.

"Dr. Hartford. Scrub in. I need you in OR five immediately. We have an emergency appendectomy." He handed her a chart and started to take off down the hall.

"Wait. Dr. Claiborne. But what about my chondroplasty?"

"I'm giving it to Karen Connelly. Don't be disappointed. You'll get the next one. I promise."

"Aren't you coming in?" Emily said.

"No, it's just a simple appendix. You got this."

He scurried down the hall. Emily stood there stunned and unprepared for the sudden change of plans. Five minutes! She racked her brain for appendectomy procedures as she scanned the chart. Her rubber tennies squeaked as she picked up the pace to the operating room.

Everyone was already in the OR, prepping, when

Emily entered the dressing area and tossed her bag aside. A nurse was scrubbing in at the sink.

"Jan, is there any chance you could take care of my bag? Claiborne just informed me I have—"

"I know, I know. I got it. I'm assisting you today. Claiborne threw you for a loop, huh?" She smiled at Emily as she secured her face mask.

"Big time." Emily pushed up her sleeves and turned on the faucet.

"And on your birthday too. Nice gift."

"What? How did you—?"

"Jackie. The nurse admin. She puts all our birthdays on the master calendar. Happy birthday, Dr. Hartford. See you there in five." Jan marched off with Emily's bag.

Emily scoured underneath her fingernails. Her hands were shaking slightly. Nerves and adrenaline and no breakfast. *When am I gonna get over these pre-surgery jitters?*

Dr. Claiborne had repeatedly told her that her nerves were normal, but Emily thought they would have subsided by year three.

She remembered Dr. Claiborne's advice and drew in several long, deep breaths from the pit of her belly. As she suited up in her gown and gloves, her body began to relax. The quiver floated out of her fingertips. Through the glass windows, Emily could see into OR number five. The patient was already prepped and under anesthesia. As Emily stepped in, a nurse was calling out vitals.

"Let's go, people! Dr. Hartford is here." All eyes fell on Emily.

"Good morning, everyone." Emily scanned the room

and immediately relaxed. "Pleasure to be here with you. Are we all ready?"

Heads nodded and Emily gave everyone a reassuring smile before she slipped her face mask over her mouth. The team moved into position. Jan handed her a scalpel.

The cool metal in her hand triggered muscle memory. This was her realm. Dead or living.

The tip of the knife pressed into the patient's skin to make the small incision where the scope would enter. Emily could envision the entire system under the layer of flesh. Within a few minutes, she was traveling inside familiar territory.

She scoped the patient's lower abdomen. "I'm moving the scope to the bottom of the ascending colon. There. A little bit lower. The appendix should be right at the anterior cecum."

"Patient's blood pressure is dropping. Eighty-five over sixty," said a nurse, monitoring vitals.

"Hold it there and keep me posted," said Emily with her focus on the video monitor as she scoped for the tiny tissue. She was quiet for a few minutes, her gaze moving back and forth between the scope and the monitor.

"Everything okay, Dr. Hartford?" Jan cut the silence.

"I am—it's just I can't…it's not…" Emily glanced up in time to catch worried glances flicker among her team.

"It's not what? Do you need me to call Dr. Claiborne?" Jan asked.

"I think this little bugger is trying to hide from me." Only slightly thrown off, Emily continued her laser focus on the monitor, adjusting the scope. "I don't mean to step on anyone's toes here, but are we one hundred percent sure this guy has an appendix?"

"Medical history doesn't indicate any prior surgeries. And he didn't have any scars on his abdomen or navel that I could see when I prepped him," said Jan.

"Paramedics said he was complaining of severe nausea and had a high fever when they found him in the park. He passed out on the way to the hospital," added another nurse.

"Guess I keep looking, then." Emily glanced up with a playful wink and caught the concerned eye of the anesthesiologist.

"Dr. Hartford, patient is exhibiting masseter muscle contracture. Temp rising. One-oh-three-point-seven… one-oh-three-point-nine…" said the anesthesiologist. "He's going into malignant hyperthermia."

"Get Dantrolene. And ice packs. I can't get out of here just yet," said Emily.

Several more team members hustled in with ice packs to cool the patient's body. Emily's fingers gripped the scope as she bore on to the monitor with intense concentration. "Where are you, little guy? Don't be feisty. It's time to come out."

The anesthesiologist administered the Dantrolene, and it worked quickly, relieving part of the immediate danger to the patient.

"His muscles are relaxing. But body temp is holding at one-oh-four-point-one," said the anesthesiologist.

"That's too high. Get that temp down. More ice packs. I need one more minute to find this thing."

All eyes were on the monitor as Emily scoped. Meanwhile, the anesthesiologist tried to stabilize the hyperthermia situation when another medical calamity presented itself.

"Where are you at, Dr. Hartford? 'Cause things are not great up here," said the anesthesiologist.

"Still playing hide and seek. Tell me what you got," said Emily, never lifting her eyes off the scope.

"He's going into ventricular tachycardia."

"Heart rate?"

"One fifty…one fifty-five…" he replied.

"That's rising too fast."

"One sixty…"

"Prep for defib!" Emily deftly removed the scope in a single sweeping movement. Its thin, long wand reappeared from the patient's abdomen into Jan's hand. Another nurse shoved the defibrillation paddles into the anesthesiologist's hands.

"Everyone back. Counting. One. Two. Three."

Emily took a step back as the paddles jolted the patient. But the current didn't work. The patient's heart rate raced on.

"Once more! In three, two, one!" she shouted, and the team watched anxiously as the paddles activated their voltage across the patient's chest. The second shock worked. The patient's heart responded, and the heart monitor dove back into a normal rhythm.

"Heart rate normal. All clear," said the anesthesiologist.

"Nice work. Let's get back on track. I'm going back in. Scope." Jan handed her the freshly sterilized instrument, and Emily immediately slipped the wand back into the belly of the patient. She came at a different angle this time.

"Where are you going with that thing?" Jan asked.

Emily's intense eyes darted to the monitor. She carefully worked the wand into a new position.

"I think I've got it…yup, it's right…there. Yes. Recto-cecum. It's hiding behind the colon."

"How on earth did you know to look there?" asked the anesthesiologist.

"I need a smaller scalpel and suction." Jan was on it.

Emily leaned in and performed the tiny laceration, removing the offending tissue.

"Got it."

"Beautiful," said Jan.

"Now, let's get this guy stitched up and ready for recovery."

The team gave her a quick round of applause.

Emily left the operating room and went to scrub out. Jan followed her. The anesthesiologist and a couple of other nurses entered behind them.

"Doctor, come on—how did you know what to do?" asked the anesthesiologist again.

"I've never seen anything like that, and I've been a nurse for twenty years," said another attending nurse.

"A pretty impressive way to start off your birthday," said Jan.

"Hey. You don't have to tell everyone."

They finished scrubbing out and filed into the clerical station outside the OR. A nurse popped up from behind the desk, and the anesthesiologist raised his voice in a rousing first line of "Happy Birthday to You!" The whole team joined in by the second "Happy Birthday," belting out a discordant melody from muffled face masks. As if on cue, Dr. Claiborne entered, holding a small round cake flaming with candles.

"Happy birthday, Emily. You definitely earned this today," he said.

Emily shook her head, but her eyes expressed just how much she really loved it…and her team.

Dr. Claiborne held the cake in front of Emily. The candles were making their final descent into the frosting. "That move you just made in the OR requires some explanation."

"I saw the same thing once during an autopsy of a forty-six-year-old male who died from a burst appendix. They couldn't find it and get it out in time. He left behind a wife and three kids."

"Well, I'm very impressed, but not at all surprised, Dr. Hartford. Well done," he said. "Make a wish."

Emily closed her eyes. But the only thing she could think to wish, she knew, would never come true. A thousand candles all blown out at once would never help her reconcile with the pain she'd run from in Freeport twelve years ago.

Instead, she wished that Brandon would do something spectacular for her birthday. It was a safe wish. One she could bet on.

Eyes still closed, Emily drew in a breath and extinguished the candles in an exaggerated exhalation. The crowd around her broke into applause, and when she opened her eyes, all the candles were smoking.

THREE

Fifteen years earlier, on Emily's thirteenth birthday, thirteen smoking candles wafted up from her birthday cake toward the chandelier hanging over the Hartfords' formal dining room table. Hartford family birthdays were special occasions and were always celebrated with china and cloth napkins, a tradition Mary Hartford started when she and Robert were first married.

"So...what did you wish for?" said Mary, Emily's mother. Mary and Robert had declared that thirteen was a significant milestone birthday in the Hartford home, and Emily would be granted a special birthday wish. Anything she wanted. Within reason. Emily was usually very low-key and easy to please. She liked simple, practical things and rarely asked for much. She had decided on her birthday wish months ago, and she had been dropping hints to her parents: maybe she wanted a bike...or a Caribbean cruise...or a shopping spree to the outlets, like her best friend had gotten. Secretly, none of it was true. Emily wanted something much closer to home.

She was about to answer her mother when the land-line rang from the kitchen. Mary looked up at Emily as she dumped a large scoop of ice cream in a bowl, next to a piece of cake.

"Are you expecting a call from one of your friends?" said Mary as the phone rang a second time.

"No, everyone wished me a happy birthday at school."

"Could it be your mother?" Robert asked Mary.

"Grandma called me after school," said Emily, and the phone rang a third time.

"Then, that can only mean one thing," said Mary turning to Robert. "Never fails."

"I think my wish just came true," Emily said under her breath.

"What? What do you mean?" said Mary.

Robert rose on the fourth ring and rushed into the kitchen to grab the phone before the answering machine picked up the call.

"Dr. Hartford speaking," said Robert. Emily had one ear to the kitchen as Mary placed a bowl in front of her.

"I just hope he can stay long enough to finish your birthday dinner. You only turn thirteen once," said Mary.

Emily only heard this kind of frustration in her mother's tone when death interrupted family celebrations or holidays. And it always did. Without fail.

From the kitchen, Emily heard her father ask his usual round of questions: "What's the address? Uh-huh. Is that across from the Strongs' farm? Yeah. Dangerous corner there. Third accident this year. Okay. Are the police there? Okay. Have they cordoned off the area? I see. Okay. Give me twenty minutes."

When Robert returned to the table, a plate of cake and ice cream waited at his place, but he didn't sit. "I'm so sorry. I can't stay. Mary, can you wrap this up for me, please, and throw it in the freezer. You guys, don't wait for me." He slid the plate to her, and she took it back.

Emily hated that all-too-familiar disappointment that sucked celebration out of the room.

"What happened?" said Mary.

"Single-car fatality. Two victims."

"Anyone we know?" asked Mary.

"I don't have names yet."

"Meaning, you won't say."

"You know I can't."

"Was it someone from school?" said Emily.

"Why do you always assume it's someone from school?" said Mary.

"I'm just curious," said Emily.

"Morbidly so, I'm afraid," said Mary.

"Look how you're raising me. Can you blame a girl?" Emily said, and Mary gave her a small smile.

"I don't think it's anyone from your school." Robert said.

The vague nugget was enough to give Emily a silent sigh of relief. She was grateful that this call had not been one of the harder cases her father commonly investigated, like a suicide, house fire, or—worse—homicide. She wasn't sure she was ready to attend one of those just yet. From how her father had described those types of deaths, she knew she would definitely have to develop a stronger stomach first.

"We'll do this later. I promise, but right now there's a whole team of responders out there waiting. Not to mention the victims' families, who are probably wondering why their kids aren't home yet."

"Oh, Robert, it's a couple of high schoolers?"

Robert nodded. "It's gonna be a long night."

Emily eyed him. Now was the time. She needed to speak up.

"Aren't you guys wondering what I wished for?"

"Oh yes, we're brimming with eagerness to see how much you're gonna set us back," joked Robert.

"Dad!"

"I'm all ears if you can follow me to the office," said Dad.

"Can it wait until tomorrow, Em?" said Mary as she and Emily trailed him to the office on the other side of the house.

"No, it can't. It has to be now. Tonight."

"Wow, Em, you're not giving us a whole lot of warning here," Robert said, grabbing his camera equipment and a couple of new body bags from a box on the bookshelf where he stored them.

"What I'm asking doesn't involve any planning."

"Maybe not, but we still need time to make it special for you," Mary added.

"You can't."

"We can try."

"No, I mean, it's nothing you need to spend money on."

"I like the sound of that," said Robert with a wink.

"Your father has to get going." Mary said.

"I know. And I want to go with him," Emily said, eliciting a startled reaction from both parents. Robert looked to Mary.

"On a case?"

"Yes, I want to see what Dad does. And…and I want to attend the autopsy."

"Can she do that? Legally, I mean?" asked Mary.

"We're not dealing with a crime scene here, so as long as she doesn't get in the way, I don't see why not," said Robert.

"It's different than looking at the pictures you sometimes see on Dad's desk," said Mary, drawing a concerned look.

"I know. But Dad's always saying how it's the best way to learn anatomy. Which I'm gonna need to know if I'm going to be a doctor."

"She makes a good point," said Robert.

"These are real people. Young people. Not much older than you. How are you going to handle seeing them on that table cut up?"

"I... I... I'll try to think of it like the baby pigs we dissected in science."

"Except smellier," Robert joked. "And if at any time during this you don't feel good or it's upsetting you, you can leave. Just step out. Okay, honey?"

"Okay. But I'll be fine. I've thought about this," said Emily. "Mom? Can I?"

"It's not as surprising, I guess. Having grown up around all this," Mary said after considering it for a moment. "I'm okay with this as long as your father is. He's the one who has to watch you."

"Probably best you stay in the car while we're examining the scene," said Robert.

"Are you sure you're ready for this?" Mary asked, her brow still furrowed in worry.

"Completely," answered Emily.

"Okay. Wish granted," said Mary, planting a kiss on Emily's forehead.

And with that, Robert handed her two wrapped body bags. Emily was about to embark on her first death investigation case.

FOUR

AFTER SURGERY, Emily freshened up at her locker. She changed into jeans and heels, a welcome relief from dirty scrubs. As she pulled out her bun and brushed her long hair, she heard someone approaching behind her.

A sexy voice crooned, "I know what you're thinking in that beautiful, blonde head of yours, Emily Hartford. You're saying to yourself, 'It's lunchtime and I'm gonna skip the salad and go for the grilled cheese and chocolate brownie because it's my birthday.'"

"I would think that even if it weren't my birthday."

Emily smiled and turned to see Dr. Brandon Taylor, four years her senior, standing lean at six feet four inches in his scrubs and long black overcoat. As par for the course, he looked amazing. His wavy chestnut hair had a fingers-run-through look, and he smelled amazing, a warm, woodsy aftershave that smelled like fall lingering on his skin. She met his lips with a kiss. She wanted more, but another doctor entered, and she drew back.

"Hope you're hungry. I need a long lunch to decompress after this morning's surgery."

"I wish I could, Em. But Dr. Claiborne needed me for the afternoon shift, so I'm gonna head back to the hospital. I just wanted to drop by for a few minutes to wish you happy birthday. And say congratulations. I heard about this morning's game of hide and seek."

"Why, thank you and thank you," she said with a playful bow. "But it was just an appendectomy."

"Give yourself some credit. Dr. Claiborne said he had never had a resident make such an amazing appendix rescue before."

Dr. Claiborne was also Brandon's supervisor at Northwestern University Hospital. Emily's phone beeped as a text came in from Cathy Bishop. Emily shoved the phone into her purse.

"And did he also tell you he gave my chondroplasty away to Karen Connelly? I studied so hard for that," Emily said.

"You'll get your chance."

"I hope so. But Karen's done, like, six now."

"She probably needs the practice. Dr. Claiborne knows you're competent," said Brandon. "It's hard to keep up with someone who's been slicing open bodies since she was thirteen."

"Dead bodies don't count," Emily replied. Her phone buzzed. She glanced into her purse and saw a voicemail coming in from Cathy.

"Aren't you going to answer it?"

"Not when I only have a few minutes with you."

"Is it important?"

"It's Cathy Bishop. From back home."

"Okay, I remember that name. Remind me again."

"An old family friend. She and her husband, Hugh, sorta became like second parents after my mom died. I would go over to the Bishops' and hang out and have dinner, because Dad was always working."

"Sounds like she was someone important to you," Brandon said.

"She was. Yes."

"And you stay in touch?"

"Off and on. She calls when she's in town. We get together for dinner."

"Sounds like she's someone who cares about you," Brandon said. "When are you going to introduce me to these interesting people from your past?"

"It's just a happy birthday call," said Emily as she dug into her locker for her coat. Cathy had been an integral part of her old life in that last painful year in Freeport that Emily had wanted to block from her life forever.

"And I haven't really met anyone from your family," Brandon said.

"It's only my dad."

"Case in point. We've been together two years. When are you going to explain to me the real reason I haven't met him? Or why he hasn't come down to visit? And why you don't go up to visit him?"

Emily looked up at Brandon, who was smiling patiently. She knew he wasn't accusing. He was truly curious.

"Are we really having this conversation now? It's my birthday."

"I just want to know you...all of you."

"We come from really different walks of life, Brandon. My life in Freeport was boring."

"I just wonder why you won't let me in."

"Does my past really matter that much to you?"

"It might help me understand more about who you are," said Brandon smiling.

"What do you want to know?"

"Like, did you ever pull any crazy pranks on your teachers? Or who you dated in high school. Or why you keep a picture of your mother on your nightstand, but you never talk about her."

"I never pulled any pranks on teachers because I was too scared I would get into trouble. My high school dating life consisted of one boyfriend my sophomore year. And my mom was...perfect."

"And taken from you far too soon."

"Exactly."

"Why don't you ever talk about what happened?"

"You know everything I do."

"I doubt that, but I'll press 'Pause' on this for now." Brandon's expression grew serious. He pulled a square box wrapped in a purple silk ribbon from his backpack. She would recognize that box anywhere. Treat of all treats.

He met her lips with a kiss and handed the box to Emily. "Happy birthday."

"Violet's Cupcakes." She untied the purple silk and lifted the flaps to reveal a tan frosted cupcake inside. "Peanut butter and jelly."

"You ordered that on our first date."

"And you thought it was gross."

"Still do."

Emily brought the cupcake to her mouth.

"Emily, before you..."

She bit down, her teeth clinking on something metal in the frosting. She spit out her bite into her palm.

"Oh my gosh! There's something in it!" Emily said. "Something hard. I almost broke a tooth."

"Are you okay? Did you swallow it?"

Emily rubbed her tooth back and forth with her finger, trying to rub out the pain.

"What on earth was that?"

Then she looked down into her other palm. A two-karat diamond ring smeared with peanut butter frosting was staring back at her. "Oh. My."

She glanced at Brandon, who was now down on one knee. And it hit her. This was *the moment*.

"Emily Hartford, I love you and I can't imagine spending a single day without you. Will you please become my wife?"

Emily's mouth gaped as hot and cold pulses surged through her body. She took the ring, pinched between her fingers, and instinctively started licking off the frosting. Then she noticed the panic on Brandon's face as he watched her clean the ring.

"Emily? Emily! I'm asking if you'll marry me," he finally said.

The ring stuck around her tongue, Emily looked up at Brandon's expectant smile. Brandon was effortlessly sophisticated, well traveled, and cultured in a way her family never even desired to be. Before Brandon, Emily hadn't really lived outside university walls. She hadn't the funds or any idea where to even start. Brandon had introduced her to exotic sashimi, taken her to comedy clubs, and surprised her with a beach vacation to Indonesia. Until that trip, Emily had never even been outside the Midwest. Dating Brandon was like staying at the Palmer House, the classiest hotel in Chicago, and diving into those soft white cotton sheets they refreshed every day. Brandon had showed her how to find the best life had to offer. And even though Emily didn't always feel that she fit in to such a pampered life, Brandon made her believe she deserved it.

"Emily?"

"What? Oh. Yeth. Yeth, yeth, yeth!"

"Was that a 'yes'?" Brandon pulled the ring from between her lips.

"Yes, I will marry you!"

"Thank you," said Brandon as he slid the ring onto Emily's finger.

"Oh my gosh, it's amazing! This is amazing! I love you."

"Surprised, then?"

"Completely. Feel my pulse," said Emily.

"I'd rather do this." Brandon leaned in to kiss her. Emily's phone buzzed again from her purse. She ignored it as the kiss lingered. Finally, Brandon let up and said quietly, "I love you, Emily Hartford. Secrets and all."

"I love you too." She leaned in for another kiss. She held up her hand and, out of the corner of her eye, admired her ring in disbelief.

"Does your family know about this?"

"My mom helped me pick the ring." Of course, she did. His mom would want to make sure her son's fiancée's ring was the talk of her country club crowd.

"You both did a great job. I love it. I love you."

Emily's phone buzzed again as a voicemail dinged.

"You sure you don't wanna check that? Cathy seems pretty persistent to wish you a happy birthday." Brandon released Emily from their embrace. Emily dug for her phone.

"It's not Cathy this time. It's a Freeport number. But I don't recognize it. I can deal with that later," she said as she started to slide the phone into her pocket. A text pinged back at her, and Emily drew the phone back out to check it again.

Em, this is Jo. Pls call me ASAP.

"Who's Jo?" asked Brandon.

This was weird. "We were best friends growing up."

"Another friend I've never heard about. File this away in the secret life of Emily Hartford. You're very popular today."

"We haven't spoken to each other since I left Freeport." She looked at Brandon, who was raising his eyebrow in suspicion.

"That's odd."

Which part? Emily wondered. The part where they hadn't spoken to each other in twelve years or the part where she was calling today of all days? She dialed into the voicemail and pressed "Speaker" so Brandon could listen.

Jo's voice filled the room. "Emily? This is Jo. I'm calling from Freeport Memorial Hospital. I'm an ER nurse here. I'm calling because…well, your dad…had a heart attack. Please call me."

The voicemail clicked off. Shock and disbelief surged through Emily as the cupcake dropped from her grip.

FIVE

EVENING WAS CLOSING in as Freeport County Sheriff Nick Larson sat in his cruiser, mulling over the strange events of the past twelve hours. Most of his days were filled with long stretches of patrolling dotted with somewhat minor offenses like truancies, thefts, or domestic assault. But this day had begun with the mysterious death of Julie Dobson, a high school senior, local equestrian hopeful, and daughter of a state senator.

Within minutes of being called, Nick arrived at Premiere horse stables, the only equine center in the county. It sat on the outskirts of Freeport, about six miles from the city limits. The entire operation—barn, stables, training ring, performance ring, office building, and pasture—spanned a couple hundred acres.

Nick viewed Julie's body on the stretcher where the EMTs had laid her. It had looked like an accident, but he couldn't be sure because a farmer had discovered Julie's body and transported her from the scene to Premiere's stables. When the EMTs got to the stables, they tried routine resuscitation maneuvers on Julie. After a few minutes, they pronounced her dead at 7:56 am.

Julie couldn't have been gone for more than an hour because rigor mortis had not yet started in her extremities. Over his years in law enforcement, Nick had worked with Dr. Hartford, the county medical examiner, many times and learned the stages of decomposition. Just by observing the front side of Julie's body, she could tell that Julie didn't seem to have any exterior wounds. Of course, he wasn't by law allowed to touch her body, so he couldn't be sure what he might find on her back side. He'd have to wait for the medical examiner to turn her over.

Nick then took the dirt two-track from the barn out to the field, where the farmer told the EMTs that he'd found Julie lying face down in a small crick that ran across the northwest corner of the training fields, far out of sight of the Premiere's barns. Probably a good twenty-minute trot by horse from the stables. The form of her body was molded in the mud along the bank, and little puddles of water had formed pools where her head and legs had impressed into the ground. This disturbed Nick. What on earth could have caused this young life to be snuffed out so quickly? Had something spooked Julie's horse, Mercedes? Had Julie fallen off? Or had there been a medical condition that had flared and rendered her unconscious?

Mercedes had not fared well from the accident either. A farmer had found him lying along the fence of a neighboring farm, and called the stables. His front right knee was shattered; a death sentence for an equine. However, Nick didn't think the Dobsons would put him down. They had the means for surgery and rehab. Mercedes would never perform again as a show horse, but he would make for a good training ride.

Nick moved carefully about the scene, scanning the ground and brushing for any evidence. He then made the call to Dr. Hartford. When Dr. Hartford didn't answer the phone, Nick left a message and took the next half hour to shoot photographs of where Julie's body had been and the surrounding area.

Nick phoned Doc again and the voicemail picked up, but he didn't leave a message. It was highly unusual for Doc not to answer. He was always on call and near his phone. Nick asked the EMTs to wait with the body while he drove out to Doc's house, twenty miles away.

He soon discovered the unfortunate reason why Doc Hartford was not answering his calls. Nick found the doctor in his backyard, near a woodpile, slumped over and near death.

Because of the doctor's unnatural position, Nick was afraid he had a second body on his hands. A quick pulse and breath check relieved him. Doc was still alive!

Nick immediately dispatched a second ambulance to Doc's house, and he stayed with him the entire eight minutes and thirty-six seconds it took for the emergency team to arrive. By that time, Doc had regained consciousness but was slurring his words and claiming he felt woozy. And it took all of Nick's strength to keep the good doctor from moving about and trying to stand up. While they waited, Doc insisted Nick tell him about Julie's case. Doc gave Nick permission to turn over Julie's body to get more photographs, cautioning him to be careful to note any impact wounds. He wanted Nick to move the body to the morgue, where he would do the autopsy. Nick held back his skepticism that Doc would be up to performing it. He knew it was better to let the old man have hope that he would soon be well enough to resume his work.

Once Dr. Hartford was off in the ambulance, Nick returned to the scene of Julie's death and finished the investigation. He carefully rolled Julie over to a prone position, but he couldn't see any obvious causes of death, like a stab wound or bullet hole. An autopsy would reveal much more. Now he just needed to find someone to perform it, as a call to the hospital revealed that Doc was laid up in the ICU, recovering from a heart attack.

Nick had managed to quell his worrying for a good part of the day. But after informing the family and putting out an official press notice, he knew it would only be a matter of hours before the news media from Rock River, the nearest, larger city of half a million, would descend on Freeport to get their story for an early-morning news cycle the next day.

Nick realized the pain forming in his stomach was not stress, but hunger gnawing at him. He thought back to his last meal. Lunch from the day before. No wonder. A burger in his system would help organize his thoughts. So he drove his cruiser down to Orion's Belt, an all-night diner at the edge of town, and was greeted by a solitary waitress and a young couple on a late date, sharing a meal.

"Anywhere you like, Sherriff," the waitress, Loretta, called out. He took a seat near the front, and she dropped a glass of ice water in front of him. "Long day, huh?"

"Is it still Friday?" he asked.

"For a few more hours," she replied. "Know what you want?"

"Double cheeseburger, fries, small salad, vanilla shake, and coffee," he rattled off.

"Somebody's starving," Loretta said. "How do you want that burger cooked?"

"Medium."

"You got it," she said and sauntered to the kitchen.

Nick took out his notebook and tried to focus on notes he'd taken earlier from the scene of Julie's death.

The tragedy had rocked the close-knit community. Of course, the question on everyone's mind was the cause. Nick had checked out the location where the farmer had found her, but he hadn't noticed anything unusual or indicative of foul play. So, how did Julie die?

Nick had been racking his brain about it all day as he went to the high school and took statements from various teachers and friends who knew Julie. There seemed to be no apparent reason for a natural death. A conversation at the police station with her parents confirmed that she had not been sick or had any life-threatening illnesses. And he had a hard time believing it was a homicide. Julie wasn't a threat to anyone. There was no evidence to assume it was a teenage crime of passion. She had no boyfriend or jealous ex. Was it a random act of violence? He couldn't wrap his mind around that because there were no signs of rape or force. No defense wounds. At least from what he could see.

Here's what he knew so far. Circumstantial evidence pointed to the fact that she had been riding alone Friday morning. She was wearing her riding gear, and her horse, Mercedes, had been found in a nearby pasture, wearing Julie's saddle. But nobody had actually seen Julie riding that morning. Even the owner of Premiere, Gary Bodum, who'd arrived around 7:30 am, hadn't seen Julie. He stated that it wasn't uncommon for Julie to get a ride in before her first class period at school, which started at 7:45 am. When that was the case, Julie always left the stables before Gary arrived, so it hadn't occurred to him to look for her when he got to work.

From what her parents reported, Julie had been a clean kid. No drugs or alcohol. A superior equestrian. Honor Society student. Loving daughter and sister. His interview with a few friends from her school yielded no suspicions that anyone had anything against Julie Dobson.

The town first officially learned of Julie's death during a noon school announcement provided from the Dobson family. Shortly after, Nick had managed to tamp down the rumors, which had been circulating all morning, and quietly lined up a team of grief counselors at the high school for the afternoon.

Nick had stressed to anyone who asked that the case hinged on the medical examiner's report, which would take a little longer than usual, seeing as how the town's medical examiner had just suffered a major heart attack. After his examination, Robert's nurse, Jo, a good friend of Nick's, told him in confidence that she was uncertain that Dr. Hartford would ever recover enough to return to his position as medical examiner, and he would definitely not be able to perform Julie's autopsy. This gave Nick several options. They could send Julie's body downstate about an hour, to Rock River, where there were several forensic pathologists who could perform the autopsy. It would cost Freeport County four times Dr. Hartford's hourly rate, not including transportation fees. Or they could check with Michigan State University, which often accepted bodies for medical school students to practice on under the supervision of licensed forensic pathologists. Their fees were only double Dr. Hartford's rates, half of what Rock River pathologists charged. Of course, Nick would need to get Julie's parents' approval for this. That could prove challenging because the university was more than a three-hour drive from Freeport, and that meant even more transport costs.

They could always send for another medical examiner, whose fees would be five or six times Dr. Hartford's normal rates. And it might take up to a week to get on a traveling medical examiner's schedule. But at least Julie's body could stay in Freeport, which would lend a great deal of comfort to her family and the community. And to Nick. He trusted Doc. Everyone trusted Doc. It would be hard for Freeport to see one of their beloved young go under the knife of a stranger. Questions and suspicions would be raised, and the answers never fully accepted. That was just small-town mentality. It wasn't easy for them to trust outsiders.

Nick sighed as he ran all these options through his head. These thoughts soon became clouded with Nick's distress about Dr. Hartford's heart attack. Dr. Hartford was a brilliant ME, and he didn't believe in bilking the taxpayers. He charged a minimal wage for his work, and he lived within his means. Greed wasn't woven into any part of Dr. Hartford's fabric. Unfortunately, Freeport County had long taken Dr. Hartford's services for granted. They were used to a bargain. And Nick knew that before he could decide what to do with Julie's body, he would have to get approval from County Commissioner Beavon's office to release the additional funds. Beavon saw little PR benefit to spending money on the dead. He preferred spending on flashy causes like festivals, park renovations, and street repairs. These were visible ways he could show off his benevolent stewardship of county coffers to the people of Freeport.

Loretta returned with a tray laden with Nick's order and set each part down on the table. She glanced curiously at the notebook open next to Nick.

"Shame about Julie Dobson. She was a talented girl. Big loss for Freeport," said Loretta.

"It is. Quite a shock."

"She and her family used to come in every Saturday for breakfast."

"Is that so. Did you talk with her?"

"Sometimes. Just chitchat. You got any leads on how she died?" Loretta asked, fishing.

"You know I can't talk about that," he said with the burger stuffed in his mouth.

"But I'm still gonna ask." Loretta nodded with a wink and filled his coffee mug.

Then, Nick added, "How well would you say you knew Julie?"

"I dunno. I've been at Orion's for six years. So I guess I've known her since she was eleven or twelve."

"You notice any changes in her behavior lately?" asked Nick. Loretta thought about it for a second as Nick scarfed down a few fries.

"I noticed Julie didn't wanna talk too much to her family," Loretta said. "It was like she didn't really wanna be with them."

"Isn't that normal for teens?" Nick asked.

"Not for Julie," Loretta explained. "She used to be really talkative with them. Telling them what happened at school. Joking. Laughing."

"When did that stop happening?" Nick asked.

"I guess over the summer. Julie would come in wearing a sullen look."

"Maybe she was tired," Nick suggested.

"That look was planted on her face the whole breakfast. Every week," Loretta said.

"Did you ever ask her or her parents what was wrong?" Nick pressed.

"One time I asked her mom if everything was okay.

And she just shrugged and said, 'You know teens.' So I left it alone. 'Cause I do know teens. And they go through phases," Loretta stated.

"Well, from your experience with teens, what kind of phase do you think Julie was in?" Nick queried.

"Who's to say? Teens got a lot more to think about these days than they did back in my time. Lot more to distract them. They got access to a bigger world, Sherriff. Could be almost anything," Loretta concluded.

"Anything like drugs, alcohol? Do you know who she hung around with?" Nick asked.

"Not really. I only saw her in here," Loretta answered.

"You said she was depressed?" Nick asked for clarification.

"I wouldn't say depressed. Just annoyed. Like any teenager dragged to breakfast on a Saturday morning with their parents. I didn't read too much in it," Loretta added, taking Nick's empty salad plate with her back to the kitchen.

Almost anything, thought Nick. That's what it felt like. A broad chasm filled with endless options and questions. He needed that autopsy done. First thing in the morning. There was a town and media that would soon be muscling him for answers.

He paid his tab and hopped back to his patrol car. He wasn't on patrol anymore, but he didn't feel like going home. He wouldn't sleep anyhow. He wanted to hang around Freeport until the press rolled into town, which could be any moment. They were known to set up camp in the middle of the night to break their story at dawn.

Nick decided to take a slow drive around town. Driving was therapy. It always helped him find answers he needed.

SIX

I⊤ was almost 10:00 pm when Emily's Nissan Leaf zipped through the empty streets of Freeport, her hometown, north into the mitten of Michigan, about a four-hour drive from Chicago. She hadn't seen the town in twelve years, but honestly, things didn't look a whole lot different since she'd left. A few storefronts downtown were boarded up. Others were new to her. A yarn store. A high-end home goods store. A new coffee shop. What once had been her mom's favorite department store, Glassner's, was now a sporting goods and outfitters, oddly boasting the same name. Live bait, ammo, and hunting licenses were advertised in the front window.

Exhaustion etched in her expression, Emily sailed past the four downtown blocks, blowing the only stoplight at the center of town. She kept going for several blocks, oblivious to the flashing lights behind her. Finally, the police car trailing her sounded its siren. The cop at the wheel let it squeal for a few seconds, enough time to grab Emily's attention, and then shut it off so as not to disturb the sleepy town.

"Oh, come on," Emily said as she snapped out of her driving trance.

Jerking the wheel, Emily drew the Leaf to the side of the street. It coasted to a stop, and she turned the engine power down. Around her small town, silence prevailed as Emily shuffled luggage aside to get to her glove box for her papers. A beam of light from a flashlight blinded her as she rolled down the driver's window.

"Did you know you blew a red light back there, miss? License and registration, please. I see from your plates you're not from Michigan."

"No. Yes. Well, not anymore," Emily said opening her glove box. "I grew up in Freeport." She turned and shielded her eyes from the blinding beam, enough to get a glance at the man behind the badge. And then it hit her. "Nick?" she said.

"Sheriff Larson," he corrected as he tipped his light down to get a better look. "Emily?"

"Nick Larson?" She couldn't believe it.

"Emily Hartford?"

Emily caught a glance of her face in the rearview mirror and hoped for a second he didn't see just how sallow it looked. Emily thought Nick looked tired too. However, he was even more striking than he had been in high school. Her heart twitched a little.

"This is so not how I pictured seeing you after twelve years."

"Me neither," Emily said as she nervously dug through her glove box. The last time she'd seen him was leaving high school that September morning of her junior year. He had filled out more, and a few faint lines that creased his forehead erased the baby-face image she had of him at sixteen. "So, you're a cop now. Wow."

"Sure am. You don't ever check Facebook, I see," he teased.

"I don't even have an account," she admitted.

"Most people are curious about things like their former classmates and ex-boyfriends."

"I guess I've never been most people," she said, glancing up at him.

"True. You don't fit into any mold but your own," Nick replied.

There was an awkward pause between them.

Emily cleared her throat and asked, "If you're gonna write me up, could you do it quickly? I'm kind of in a hurry to see my dad." She handed him her registration papers.

"Oh yeah. Your dad. Good news. They moved him out of critical care about an hour ago."

"They did?" Emily had forgotten that small-town news traveled faster than a bullet train. "I wonder why Jo didn't call me," she said under her breath.

"He's doing much better," Nick offered. "I went to check in on him after dinner. Gave us all quite a scare."

"Well, I don't think he's out of the woods just yet," cautioned Emily. "So, how much is this ticket going to cost me?"

"I'm not gonna ticket you, Em. Just pay attention to the signs. Things have changed a lot since you left. We added another stoplight," he joked.

"Guess I missed that," she said. "So, I'm free to go?"

"On the condition I can escort you over there."

"I think I can manage." Emily was anxious to put an end to their awkward reunion.

"I can't believe running into you like this. Not exactly how I pictured it," Nick voiced as Emily noticed he held his gaze on her for what felt like just a little too long.

"You pictured it?" She was surprised Nick thought about her at all.

"Yeah, well, you... I was really confused when you just disappeared without telling me."

Nick let it hang there as he stood outside her car windowsill.

"I wrote you that note. You never wrote back," she said turning her gaze ahead, ruffled by his comment.

"What note?" He leaned down and rested his arm on the sill.

Emily looked at him, "It explained why I left..." She wanted to add, *And how much I cared for you.*

Nick shook his head. "Where did you put it?"

"In your locker. I slipped it into the slats."

Nick let out a burst of laughter. "Well, that explains it. Did you ever see the inside of my locker? Complete pigsty. At the end of the year, I took a garbage bag and shoveled everything into it."

"You didn't go through your stuff?"

"Nope. Soda cans, old lunches, notebooks. I didn't even bother returning my textbooks. Just threw them away with everything else."

Emily nodded.

"Your note was probably in that heap of stuff, huh?"

Emily heard a slight tone of regret in his voice. She had thought Nick would be upset after she left, but at the time she had been completely incapable of handling her emotional behavior. She had felt awful, but she'd expected him to reach out to her at some point. When he didn't, she had been really hurt, but then assumed he didn't want to continue the relationship. It had never occurred to her that Nick might still be upset at her ten years later. Had she meant as much to him as he had to her?

"Nick, I'm pretty tired right now. I need to see to

my dad." Her voice thinned with drowsy impatience. "I'm gonna go."

When she looked up at him, Nick was staring at her again, studying her with a slightly inquisitive expression. This time his look felt oddly comforting, like returning to a well-loved book or a private spot in the woods. When they were in high school, she and Nick had become close friends and eventually started dating.

"Yeah, let's get you to the hospital. Follow me," Nick replied and then turned to head back to his car.

Emily knew he would not be dissuaded from escorting her. She watched Nick return to his car with the characteristic swagger that she had seen him exhibit a million times on the football field in high school. It brought a fleeting smile to her lips. Same ole Nick. Sure of himself. Eager—no…*overly* eager to help. And still deeply sensitive. Emily knew it had been unfair to leave him like she had. No warning. She would have been livid and unforgiving had the tables been turned. Despite their deepening bond of friendship, she had struggled to verbalize to anyone the trauma of that fateful year after her mother's accident. By the time she'd finished high school two years later, that aching to hear from Nick, to return to her former life in Freeport, dissolved as she launched Operation Shutdown: default mode. Emily had told herself that Freeport no longer mattered. College was a new start. Only what was ahead could determine her future happiness.

Emily checked her rearview mirror and saw that Nick was waiting for her. She rolled up the window and put the Leaf in drive. Nick pulled around her, his squad lights flashing. Although they only encountered a handful of cars on their way to the hospital, Emily found herself appreciating Nick's thoughtfulness in carving a traffic-free path to her father. Then she glanced at her hands on the steering wheel and noticed how her new diamond caught the glow of strobe lights from Nick's squad. The glimmers bounced back at her. She took a deep breath as they turned into the hospital parking lot, and told herself that at this moment she had to perform her daughterly duty and see to her father. She was expecting it to be an awkward reunion, but knew if they could keep the conversation focused on medically related topics, it would be tolerable. And hopefully, as soon as he could, Brandon could find replacements for the next few shifts and meet her up here to help her settle things. Brandon's presence would keep her calm and rational as she dealt with whatever she would need to with her dad. They would take care of things effectively and efficiently. No big deal. And if things got too tense between her and her dad, she would just focus on the good life she had in Chicago, and soon she would be back there planning her dream wedding, finishing residency, and beginning a new chapter with Brandon as her husband.

SEVEN

SEVERAL TV NEWS vans and their crews were already setting up camp in the parking lot as she steered her Leaf as far from them as she could. Nick's cruiser parked alongside her, and he jumped out before Emily. The news reporters were rushing over with their camera crews.

Seeing the encroaching entourage, Emily leapt from her car and started for the hospital lobby doors. The reporters started to swoop in on Nick.

"What is going on?" she asked.

"Word's out. They weren't here before," said Nick as he hustled to her side. "You know, I was thinking on the way over about what I would say to you when I saw you again."

Emily glanced back to find a particularly aggressive blonde newscaster gaining ground on them, her Herculean calves and stiletto heels pumping toward them.

"Okay. But do we have to do this now?" Emily picked up her pace. "They seem pretty determined to talk with you."

"I may not see you again for another twelve years..."

"Nick, why are there reporters here?"

"The state senator's daughter, Julie Dobson, was found dead this morning near Premiere stables."

Emily's eyes flitted to Nick in surprise. "What?

Wow! I'm so sorry. Shouldn't you be working that case right now?"

"I am. I was. I was processing when you zoomed across my path," said Nick as the blonde caught up to them and pointed a microphone into his face. Emily dodged around her and kept moving toward the hospital doors.

"Tell us more about the Dobson case, Sheriff. We learned from sources that a farmer, Mr. Gibbons, found Miss Dobson's body and brought it to the hospital? Isn't that considered a disturbance of the crime scene?"

"Crime scene? No one's saying this was a crime. When Mr. Gibbons found the body, he had no reason to believe it was a crime scene. And we still don't have evidence to support that. Mr. Gibbons was acting out of concern for the victim, whom he believed at the time might still be alive," Nick responded as he tried to keep up with Emily, who was out of earshot and approaching the hospital's lobby doors.

"What if it is a crime scene? Is there reason to believe foul play was involved?" the reporter pressed Nick.

Emily glanced back at Nick. She couldn't hear his response, but she could tell from the way he faced the reporters with confidence and eye contact that he was holding his own. He had always been comfortable with the camera. Emily noted how he didn't waver from the spotlight, taking time to address each reporter's questions. It had been like that in high school too. Always the showboat when it came to post-game interviews. She turned back to the hospital doors and entered as Nick gave his last statement.

"We've decided to cordon off the area as a precaution. But there's a high probability that Julie Dobson's death was accidental. We'll be able to confirm that after we get the autopsy results and do further investigations. We ask that you respect our hospital patients and staff and remain outside."

Once inside the hospital lobby, Emily did a double take. It was familiar ground, but she hadn't been over this threshold for thirteen years. She shook off the flooding memories and took in the lobby area, which had expanded since she'd last seen it. The lighting was soft, not fluorescent. The stark white walls had been painted sea foam green, and live trees divided the room into sections. Long benches lined the walls, and oversized chairs dotted the center. The room that used to seat twenty could now occupy twice that number. Magazine racks overflowed with current issues of *Time, Newsweek*, and *People*. The centerpiece of the room was a water feature that sent calming rivulets of water down a thin waterfall into a rectangular stone basin. The reception desk was tucked behind a sliding glass window. She could see the night receptionist chatting with a nurse. Neither of them looked up when she entered. Emily walked a few feet to the double doors that led into the emergency room, and paused. She'd hoped she might find Jo in there. She wanted to get her assessment before seeing her father.

The last time she had stood before these doors, at age fifteen, her mother's waning body had been inside as doctors and nurses administered triage in an effort to save her life. Frightened, she had watched helplessly through the crack between the double doors. Emily remembered a lot of blood on her mother's body, the floor, and on the sleeves of the medical team. Glimpses of her mother's contorted face had lodged themselves forever in her memory. Her mother's face was badly bruised from hitting the steering wheel, she would later find out.

Emily had stayed at the door, too terrified to leave. Inside, her father tried to assist, but a male nurse held him back and finally called security to escort him out. Two officers dragged him out and blocked the door so he couldn't return. He looked at Emily, but no words passed between them. Emily felt that his eyes exposed the truth about the situation in the emergency room. It was hopeless, but the medical team was compelled to try to save her mother.

He'd pleaded with the officers to let him in to be with his wife. They were compassionate but resolute as they held her father back. Her father began to wail. It was this, more so than seeing the attempts to resuscitate her mother, which had impacted Emily the most.

When he was finally allowed to see his dead wife, her father darted past her, without so much as a glimpse in her direction, into the emergency room. A nurse with a gentle touch came to Emily and took her by the arm, leading her toward the ER, letting her know she could see her mother now. But Emily had turned ghostlike and started to back away. She ran to a janitor's closet on the second floor and hid in there for several hours, using a damp mop to cushion her bum. It soaked her pants and made it look like she had soiled herself. As she hid in the closet, thoughts drifted in and out of Emily's mind, but she could capture none of them. The sound of the door unlatching broke Emily's trance as she startled a cleaning lady arriving for her equipment.

The cleaning lady had talked to Emily, although she couldn't remember about what, and had somehow convinced her to say goodbye to her mother. Meanwhile, her father, who sat next to his wife, unaware of Emily's whereabouts, seemed shocked to see her when she showed up at her mother's side.

Nick shook Emily from her memory as they dashed through the hospital doors, trying to keep the hungry reporters at bay.

"Everything okay?" he asked, searching her sullen face.

Emily readjusted her thoughts. "Ah yeah, I just need someone to tell me where my dad's room is."

"Oh, well, I can take you up there," Nick said.

"Maybe just point me in the direction," she replied. At that moment, the blonde news reporter shuffled in from an adjacent hallway. She had gained illegal entrance through a back door.

"Sheriff Larson, just one more question," she started in. "When do you anticipate having autopsy results?"

"You haven't performed the autopsy yet?" asked Emily, drawing Nick aside.

Nick moved them a few more steps away from the reporter's prying ears.

"Well, no. Because, if you remember, our medical examiner suffered a heart attack today."

"Right. Of course. I'm going on very little sleep and extra doses of adrenaline," said Emily. "Wait—then, why on earth did you tell that reporter it was an accident?"

"Because it probably was. And I don't want a media craze."

"Nick, you shouldn't be broadcasting your assumptions," Emily said.

"A good portion of my job around here consists of controlling the story," he quipped as he saw the reporter doing her best to eavesdrop. "I'm trying to deflate the event. It's a very effective tactic."

"By creating a fib? Okay, suit yourself," said Emily, too tired to care. She set her sights on the direction where she knew the elevator was located. "Can you please tell me which floor my dad's on?"

"Third floor. Last room on the right," Nick said as he made a beeline for the newscaster who was breaching the emergency room doors.

"Oh no, no… Miss, you can't go in there… Hey!" Nick sprinted over and disappeared into the ER.

Emily pressed on, turned a corner, and headed toward a set of elevators. She was about to press the button, when the doors opened, and the curvy, five foot six Jo Blakely stepped out. Jo was Emily's best friend from high school. A gregarious extrovert and one of those over-achieving women you thought you might loathe, until you find yourself having the time of your life with her. Emily noticed that she hadn't changed a bit. Her natural curls, which usually hung in a long bob, were tied up in a stubby ponytail. Her curves were shapely, but hard to make out under the scrubs. She was as radiant and attractive as she had been in high school. The last twelve years had been very gracious to Jo.

It didn't take Jo but half a second to recognize Emily and throw her arms around her in a big hug. She talked a mile a minute, whisking Emily back into the elevator.

"Emily! You made it! Let me take you to your dad. He's doing somewhat better, and we were able to move him into his own room about an hour ago. I'm sorry I didn't call. I got busy on the floor." Jo barely took a breath between thoughts. "It's so good to see you. How was the drive up? You must be exhausted—not that you look it. You look amazing underneath those dark circles. No offense. We've all been there. Anyhow, we gave your dad his own room. You know doctors."

The elevator doors opened on the third floor, and Emily was sucked down the hall by Jo's endless energy. At a time like this, she was glad Jo had enough for both of them. Just like she always had. Jo was a schemer and a dreamer. The social director and party planner. Emily happily played along with her in her adventures, taking the part of the practical friend who enjoyed the attention and picked up the pieces when things started to get messy.

"It's good to see you too," said Emily. "Thanks so much for your call. How did you get my number, if you don't mind me asking?"

"Cathy Bishop. She asked me to give you a call when you weren't returning hers," said Jo.

"Yeah. I was…in surgery this morning. And I kinda thought maybe she was just calling to wish me a happy birthday," Emily said, wishing now that she had responded the first time Cathy contacted her.

"Oh my gosh. It's your birthday. Happy birthday, Em," Jo said, giving her a side hug. "Of course, September nineteenth. You know I always think of you every year, even though I never get around to wishing you a happy birthday."

"I haven't exactly done a great job at staying in touch either," Emily said.

"Don't worry. Life gets busy. And I'm sorry I had to leave that info about your dad in a voicemail. I know it's a really shocking way to learn about such sensitive stuff. It's been a bit hectic around here today."

"Yeah, Nick was telling me about Julie Dobson," Emily said.

"A horrible, horrible tragedy. We're all kind of in shock. She was supposed to take part next week in the state competition. And she was favored to win it and get a full ride scholarship. It's devastating."

"Seems really awful. Did you know her?" asked Emily.

"I did. My two oldest ride at Premiere, so we knew her from the stable. She was always kind to them and giving them riding tips."

"You have two kids?" Emily asked.

"Three, actually. I got married after nursing school, and then my three little ones started to pop out pretty soon after. Jeremiah is eight. Jessica, six. And Jaden just turned three. I work part-time at the hospital. And part-time as activities coordinator and chauffeur," Jo said with a jolly smile.

"I'm glad. You sound happy, and you don't look like you've gained an ounce," Emily said. She had no trouble imagining Jo organizing a bustling household of three, plus husband and career.

Jo stopped by the nurse's station to pick up a chart.

"Can you give me a rundown on my dad's condition before I see him?" asked Emily.

"Already a step ahead of you. I grabbed his chart to see what the night shift has updated," she said. "They're short-staffed up here, so I said I'd fill in."

"Oh, you don't work this floor?"

"No, I'm on the second floor. In the baby ward," she said with a satisfied smile, handing Emily the chart.

"So, looks like his blood pressure is still pretty

high. He's on a good dose of meds to control it. Over-
all, seems like he's pretty stable," said Emily.

"And we're working to keep it that way. His doctor ordered and ran all the tests for later this morning.
He'll be in around noon to give treatment recommen-
dations," said Jo.

"Anything preliminary they can report?" Emily
asked.

"Massive heart attack. Substantial blockage. That's
the rough picture," said Jo, delivering the hard news.
"I'm so sorry, Em. When was the last time you saw
him?"

Emily hesitated for a second as she thought about it.
"College graduation. He came down to Chicago for the
ceremony and dinner and then drove back to Freeport."

Jo briskly led them from the nurse's station through
a set of double doors that opened into the intensive care
unit, a new wing of the hospital. Again, gone was the
fluorescent lighting, in exchange for soft bulbs inset
along the walls. The same sea foam green led down the
corridor as soft classical music from invisible speakers
filled the space. There was nothing clinical about it at
all. It had a soothing effect that started to calm Emily's
frayed nerves.

"So, you're finally a doctor," Jo said. "I always knew
it would suit you."

"Yeah. Well, I'm in a surgical residency," Emily explained.

"Big city surgeon. We're all so proud of you," said
Jo. "Of course, a part of me always hoped you and Nick
might tie the knot and settle down in Freeport. Teenage fantasy. I just always pictured the two of us being

here, raising our kids together. Having lunch together at the hospital cafeteria."

"I see you still have an active imagination," Emily said with a smile. She was glad to see that she and Jo could pick up right where they'd left off.

"We should go out while you're here. If you have time. You have my number on your caller list. Give me a shout when you come up for air."

"Let me see how things unfold," said Emily.

"Of course. But I have a feeling your dad's gonna be up and at 'em in no time."

Jo stopped them in front of the last door on the right. Emily read her father's name on the white board hanging on the wall outside the door.

"Do you need to check in on him first?" Emily asked. Now that she was here, she felt a twinge of anxiety sweep over her.

"I can wait, or I can go in and break the ice," Jo said. Emily she knew was reading the concern on her face.

"He doesn't know I'm here," Emily admitted.

"Well, actually, Cathy told him you were coming," Jo said hesitantly.

"Oh. Okay." Emily readjusted. "Actually, maybe that's better. Surprises can be bad on the heart."

"He's anxious to see you."

"Did he say that?" Emily asked.

"Listen, if it makes you feel better, just put on your doctor hat and tell him you're here to ensure his medical welfare," said Jo, flashing a smile.

"He's going to tell me it wasn't necessary to come all this way," Emily replied.

"It'll be okay, Em. You're his daughter. He loves

you." Jo gave Emily's arm a squeeze and headed back down the hall.

Loves me? Somewhere deep down, Emily sensed it was true. She had felt it in her childhood. And in those teenage years before her mom died, when she and her dad were teaming up on cases. But she hadn't heard those words from him after that day in the emergency room. Emily's last visual memory of her father was as a robust, but overworked, graying man hunched over his microscope in their home office, unable to verbalize his grief or connect with her anymore.

Emily took a deep breath and stepped through the door.

EIGHT

On an early spring day six months after her mother's death, fifteen-year-old Emily found her father sitting on the back porch, staring into the woods. It was a place she often found him after her mother's death. He could sit there half a day without moving, eating, drinking, or answering the phone. Sometimes she would call out for him three, four times, and he wouldn't answer. Wouldn't even glance her direction.

She approached her father, tentatively holding a dirty blue slipper by her side.

"Dad? Do you have a minute?"

Her father didn't turn to greet her, his sallow eyes never diverting from something in the woods. Emily required his attention now and wasn't about to leave until she got it.

"Dad? Can you talk to me, please?"

A moment passed between them. Emily took another step toward him, positioning herself at his side.

"Don't move," he said in a hushed tone that startled her. "Look. There." He pointed listlessly toward the woods. Emily saw a family of deer wandering through the Hartford family's densely wooded back acres, bobbing their heads to the ground in search of foliage to nibble.

"What really caused Mom's accident?"

"We don't know."

"But how could she just drive off the road? Was she distracted? Maybe she looked down at her phone?"

"Police think maybe she was swerving to miss an animal in the road," Robert answered in a voice that revealed some torment within himself. Emily didn't like this quiver in his voice.

"Okay, but let's say someone ran her off the road. Hit and run."

"Police found no evidence to suggest malicious intent," was her father's clinical response.

"But what do you think?"

"Not every death is foul play." She could barely hear him.

"So, you believe the police report?"

Her father remained silent.

"Don't you ever have doubts? Do you ever wish you had investigated?" Emily prompted.

"I trust the investigators." This time his voice was emotionless.

"Did you ever visit the site?"

"Of course I did."

Glancing up, Emily noticed that the deer family had wandered closer to the house. They were only twenty feet away now and had reached the perimeter of the Hartfords' yard where the greening grass of spring was yet uncut and growing wildly. The mother deer kept craning her neck left and right with each step, as if to make sure it was safe for her two fawns to proceed. Neither Robert nor Emily moved as the small herd feasted on the lush green banquet.

"I went to the site today. Now that the snow's melted," Emily said quietly. "I found this."

Robert's eyes darted to his daughter inquisitively as she held the blue slipper close to her chest.

"Mom's slipper," Emily said.

"I don't think so. The police scoured that area."

"No, it's hers. It's the pair I gave her last Christmas," Emily insisted.

"It must belong to someone else," Robert replied without looking at it.

"No, it's the one with the pink and yellow embroidered flowers. I know it's hers."

"Those are department store slippers. Anyone around her could have that pair." Her father's face creased with ire.

"It's a size eight. Her size."

Robert eyed the slipper.

"It was hidden in a clump of bushes near the crash site. It would have been easy for the police to miss," Emily explained softly. "Why would Mom have been wearing slippers in the car?"

Robert's expression changed as some grueling emotion that simmered inside his soul took over. Emily took a step back, fearing he might act on it, but he did not. Almost simultaneously, his pupils glazed over and settled into a faraway look of dull misery.

"I know it's hard, Emily, but we have to accept it."

A noise outside startled the deer family, and they bounded from the yard back into the woods.

"The slipper doesn't make sense. Can you look into it?"

"You're going to drive yourself crazy trying to guess."

"You don't know that until you try. Why won't you at least try? Why don't you care?"

"Nothing we do now will bring Mom back to us. It

won't make us a family again." His voice cracked. He stopped speaking, rose, and left the room.

We're still a family! She had wanted to scream at him, to shake him out of his grief. *I'm still here. I still matter!*

Emily's gaze crossed the yard to the back acres. It was empty now. The deer family had disappeared. She looked down at her mother's blue slipper and noticed the impression of her mother's foot worn into the terry cotton padding. Tears brimmed her eyes. Her mother had never worn her slippers out of the house. And her dad never left any stones unturned. In that moment, Emily became convinced that her mother's death was not a random, undetermined accident. Her father was hiding something from her.

NINE

EMILY FINALLY ENTERED the room to find her father resting peacefully in his bed. He was thinner and grayer and more sallow than she remembered. She took a few quiet steps toward his bed as he slept, and stood there for a second, not knowing if she should wake him or let him sleep. Maybe she should get Jo back in here to wake him and check his status? Maybe she should come back later? She started to turn back to the door, when her father's eyes fluttered open.

"Emily?" he rasped.

"Yes, it's me."

"I thought I heard someone enter," he said. "You drive here?"

"Yes. I drove up from Chicago as soon as I heard."

"Oh, you shouldn't have done that. I had a little spell, but I'll be out of here and good as new tomorrow morning. Sorry you had to waste your time," he said, sitting up and adjusting his bed sheets.

"I think it was more than that, Dad. You had a heart attack. You know that, right?" Emily was concerned by his lackadaisical attitude.

"My heart's fine. Maybe you can even get me discharged tonight."

"Don't get your hopes up."

The ice broken between them, Emily relaxed a little.

She recognized that stubbornness and was glad to see his gumption intact.

"Do you remember much about when it happened?" she asked him.

"I was chopping wood in the back. I put one on the block, raised my axe, and that's the last thing I remember."

"Do you remember who found you? Or how you got here?"

Dr. Hartford thought for a second. "Nick. Nick Larson. That football player you used to date."

"Yes, I remember, Dad." Did he have to bring that up?

"He was stopping by to pick up some paperwork from a farm fatality last week."

Emily was immediately grateful and a little ruffled to learn Nick was the Good Samaritan. What if he hadn't come by? Would her father also be in the morgue right now?

"You're fortunate he was there." Emily was determined not to be unnerved in front of her father.

"I am. I am." Robert agreed. "What's going on with that Dobson girl?"

"She's in the morgue downstairs."

"I guess I'll see if I can take care of that tomorrow," said Robert.

"Don't worry about it right now. Is there anything you want me to take care of at home? Or bring you?"

"Oh no, no. I'll be back there tomorrow. No need to make a fuss."

"I don't think so, Dad. I have a feeling recovery's going to be really slow."

"Says who?" Robert asked.

"The entire medical profession."

"Okay, hot shot Chicago doctor. What would you prescribe?"

"Well, I haven't seen your charts or scans. But to start I would say, no heavy lifting or strenuous activity. Get used to being on heart meds the rest of your days. And change to a vegetarian diet," she said.

"I have a freezer full of red meat that disagrees with you."

Emily decided not to argue with that. She let her father take a moment to rest, and handed him his water bottle.

"You should drink this. Stay hydrated," she said as she stood awkwardly at the side of his bed, wondering what to do next. Robert downed a few gulps, when Emily saw Nick out of the corner of her eye, poking his head around the door.

"Knock-knock, Doc. Can I come in?"

Nick didn't wait for an answer. He bounded in past her and greeted her father with a warm handshake.

"Hey. Doc. I don't plan to stay long. I just wanted to say hello. See how you were doing."

"Sluggish. But grateful. Thanks for stopping by when you did."

"Good to hear. Glad it worked out that way," said Nick.

"Emily tells me you stopped by about a case?"

"Yes, Farmer Gibbons found Senator Dobson's daughter face down in a creek on Premiere's property."

"That's what Emily was saying." Dr. Hartford's interest was piqued. "Now, which one was it? Julie or the younger one, Sarah?"

"Nick. Dad needs his rest. Can you do this later?" said Emily, gesturing toward the door.

"The older one. Julie."

"Oh, you're kidding! My, my. Awful. Really awful news," Robert said, turning to Emily. "She was sort of a Freeport celebrity."

"So I've been gathering." Emily nodded, impatiently glancing over at Nick again.

"You didn't call in another ME already, did you?" Robert asked.

"Well, that's actually why I stopped by. I hate to bother you about this, but I was wondering if you have any referrals?" asked Nick.

"Seriously? You're serious right now? Your bad timing hasn't changed one bit," said Emily.

"Referrals? No. Keep her in the cooler, and I should be able to make it down there in a couple of days," Robert said.

"Absolutely not," said Emily. "You're not going to be up doing autopsies in a few days, Dad."

"I kinda have to agree with her. I really need to move on this one, Doc. Got the press hounding me. And the Dobson family is pretty much inconsolable," said Nick.

"Okay. I can see your point about the Dobsons. They want answers. I just don't know who I would trust to handle this delicate matter," Robert said, thinking about it for a moment. "What has your investigation yielded so far?"

"Unfortunately, not much. Gibbons moved her body before we got there. I took some pictures from the area where she was lying, and did a visual search, but no evidence turned up that would lead us to believe her death was a homicide," Nick explained.

"Well, we could send her down to Rock River, but those pathologists are gonna charge us three times what I charge. And then we have the extra transport costs. Good luck getting Commissioner Beavon to approve that."

"He's not going to have a choice," Nick offered.

"Maybe not, but he'll complain something awful and find a way to cut something out of your budget at the next city meeting."

Emily was incredulous as she watched the two of them banter. Her father was only six hours fresh off his heart attack. And Nick—no boundaries! Emily checked her father's monitors and IV, which were running low, and pressed the nurse's button. She needed Jo's intervention.

"The truth is, Doc, I hate having to take Julie's body out of Freeport. Being a high-profile case and all," said Nick.

"I understand. We could send for a private pathologist, but again, those guys charge big time. And it'll take at least a week to get on their docket."

"Again the problem with Commissioner Beavon and budget," Nick said.

Robert agreed but added, "This is a special case with extenuating circumstances, however, and the senator may be able to call up a favor from the state for additional funds."

Emily felt for her dad's pulse and realized it was higher than she liked to see.

"Dad, I've called for the nurse. Your pulse is rising and you need a fresh IV. Nick, don't stress him out anymore. We've got to keep his blood pressure low."

At this, Nick respected her request. "You're right.

I'm sorry to bother you with this, Doc. I'll figure it out. It's my problem now. You just rest so you can get on the next case."

Nick was started on his way out when Robert got an idea. "Emily can do it."

"What? No way," she said. Nick turned back into the room. "Nick, you can tell that Beavon guy he's gotta approve the cost for an outside ME. There's just no other way right now."

"He hates spending money on the dead," said Nick.

"Or the living," Robert added.

"Then tell him you'll have to delay the autopsy. I'm sure Senator Dobson will be happy to go on record to the press about it. Which will pressure Beavon into releasing the extra money," said Emily. "Problem solved."

"Emily, there's no reason to waste taxpayer dollars or cause any more trouble or suffering to the Dobson family. You're a qualified doctor, and you used to be my assistant," said Robert.

"Your only problem right now is to get better," Emily insisted.

"You remember how to do one, right? That's not a problem, is it?" asked Nick.

Emily took offense. "I could do it in my sleep. But I didn't come here to play coroner's daughter."

"If you don't do it, I'll have to either send Julie's body to a stranger or bring in a stranger. I want to make sure we keep this close to home with people we trust," Nick said.

"Emily, I'm asking you as the current active medical examiner. Will you please take on this case?" said Robert.

Nick looked at her, hopeful. Emily felt cornered between them, but she was reluctant to budge.

"Dad. That's not why I'm home," Emily said. "And have you thought about how this is going to look when the estranged daughter of the medical examiner swoops in and starts meddling in some local, high-profile case? Isn't that a bit odd to you?" she pressed, hoping he would just drop it. She was tired, stressed, and the last thing she wanted to do was spend her night in the morgue. Yes, she knew her way around human anatomy, but this was different. Evidence might be misleading or inclusive. Witness testimony was often unreliable. But the corpse didn't lie. What if she overlooked something? Some key piece of information about how Julie had died? This was already a high-profile case. It was a big responsibility to shoulder, especially with only two hours of sleep in the last thirty-six.

"Nobody's going to doubt you, your position, or your expertise," Robert said. "You may not know it, but the people here have always thought very highly of you."

His compliment caught her off guard. She hadn't ever thought that her former community took much notice of her, let alone had formed a favorable opinion about her.

"It's been a devastating day for Freeport," Nick said. "Please do this for your old town?"

Emily was reticent as she weighed her thoughts, mulling over the situation she had unwittingly stepped into. In Chicago, death investigation was a twenty-four-seven business. She understood that in Freeport, cases like these were the exception rather than the rule, and a certain small-town urgency did exist. She also found that the old familiar curiosity she fostered as a teen sleuth at her father's side was quickly bubbling to the surface. The Dobsons' emotional and mental future depended on her findings from Julie's autopsy. And if something was amiss, the justice of this case was at stake as well. Julie's family deserved to know the whole truth about how their daughter had died.

"Just a quick look. To make an assessment," Nick suggested.

"Emily, it's a small repayment to someone I owe my life to," her father said, referring to Nick. "And I'll rest a lot better tonight if you just go down there."

Emily didn't expect the comforting draw she now felt to revisit a place that had held many pleasant memories in her childhood. Here, alongside her father, she had learned the basics of anatomy and human biology. Her father had showed her how to unravel the riddles of death. And while so many were left mystified and fearful of dying, Emily wanted to peel back the layers and make sense of it. She liked being a part of how her father consoled loved ones by showing them how to comprehend tragedy. She had also inherited her father's zealousness for furthering justice. All of these feelings came rushing back to her after twelve years of default mode.

"All right. I'll take a look," she said decisively. Emily would make sure that what happened with her mother's death investigation would *not* happen to this family.

Just then Jo entered, holding a fresh IV bag, and took one look at the disparate trio. In her ever-cheery voice, she declared, "Well, looks like everything's going just great in here."

TEN

EMILY AND NICK traversed the long corridor of the familiar building toward the morgue in the basement level. The low voices of the night shift, the beeping of monitors, and the hum of soft lights were the only sounds echoing through the spa-like halls.

"The hospital has done a lot of remodeling since you were last here," Nick said, trying to make conversation. "They added a whole wing and upgraded the emergency room. And across the street is a brand new medical center. Big city stuff, huh?"

"Maybe even better. The hospital I work in was built in the seventies, with nineties updates," said Emily, unwilling to admit she was impressed, and a little envious, of the modern improvements. "But I like to think it's the quality of the staff and surgeons that make it a state-of-the-art medical facility."

Nick stepped into the morgue behind Emily, who moved methodically through the room, its familiarity harkening back to her first autopsy on her thirteenth birthday.

THIRTEEN YEAR-OLD EMILY reached the morgue door and glanced up at her father. He paused and held Emily back from entering, handing her one of his old sweaters.

"Put it on. It's going to be cold in there," Robert said, prepping her. "And it will smell bad."

"How bad?" Emily asked, pulling the sweater over her head.

"Like nothing you've ever smelled before. It's called decomposition. It's what happens to human flesh when it starts to rot. It starts in the gut first, when the bacteria begins to eat the stomach juices and multiply," he explained.

"Is that why bodies bloat up?" Emily asked him. "Because the bacteria create gas?"

"Exactly. They teach you that in school?" Robert teased.

"It's like yeast when it rises." Emily could tell her father was impressed.

He took out a tube of vapor rub from his pants pocket and smeared a thin layer of the ointment over his upper lip. Then he handed the ointment to his daughter.

"It'll help with the smell," he told her as she dotted her upper lip. "Breath shallowly through the bottom of your nose."

Emily slathered on the salve and practiced a few shallow breaths. The ointment made her upper lip tingle and heated her skin.

"Do you know what you're about to see?" Robert asked, continuing to prep his daughter.

"It's not the first time I've seen a dead body, Dad," Emily retorted.

"I know, but this is different than the pictures and videos you've seen of some of my cases at home," he tried to explain. "The body will be undressed, and the skin will look a little yellowish. There'll be a lot of dried blood on the body, and the victim's face is badly mangled." He paused to see how Emily would take this. She listened, unflinching, as he described it.

"We're going to have some company. I've told one of the ER nurses she can assist. She wants to learn how an autopsy is done," he continued.

"Will I get to help?" Emily queried.

"We'll see," Robert said as the ER nurse arrived.

Emily stood near her father while he and the nurse removed the first body, a male, from the bag. Emily couldn't take her eyes off the way the skin looked rubbery. It was the expressionless look on his face that she couldn't look at. During the procedure, her dad explained each step to her. Emily remained very quiet, and a couple of times when her father used the blade saw on bone, she found her dinner surging up her throat. She cupped her hand over her mouth and forced it down.

"Take three deep, deep breaths, and say the colors of the rainbow," said Robert.

"That's weird advice," said the nurse.

Emily thought so too. "Red, orange, yellow, green, blue, indigo, violet."

It worked. Emily soon returned to the table.

"Dr. Hartford, is it even legal for her to be in here?" the nurse asked as she placed the victim's kidneys on a scale.

"The state medical examiner's office has no rules, regulations, or laws pertaining to who observes or assists with autopsies. As long as I remain in keeping with chain-of-custody procedures, then we're all good."

Emily knew that tone. It was her dad's teaching tone, and it sounded authoritative and somewhat condescending. Emily knew it was a warning signal not to cross him. He used it at home when he didn't want to have to raise his voice.

This time, Emily was glad he used it. She resented

the nurse for treating her like a kid. Toward the end of the autopsy, much to Emily's relief, the nurse got called back to the ER. She was glad it was just her and her dad because she could ask questions more freely. And he dropped the whole professor act.

Robert returned the victim's organs to the body cavity and showed Emily a large needle and thread he was going to use to stitch the body back together. Emily watched him sew a few stitches. "I could do that. I know how to sew."

"No harm in that, I guess. We've already recorded everything we need for the investigation." Robert handed her the needle.

"Yeah, I mean, it's not like I can do any more damage," said Emily, trying her hand at the gallows humor her father used so often around the house.

"Guess we'll see if your mother's sewing lessons paid off," he said, volleying the humor back at her.

"The skin is tough. It's not like fabric. Put some force behind it," Robert coached. "Start about an inch out from the incision."

Emily slid the needle into the flesh on one side and brought it through to the other side, completing a tidy, straight stitch.

"Good. Now, keep the tension and try another one," Robert said. But Emily was already a step ahead of her father. In just a few minutes, she had completed the job expertly.

DAD USED TO keep the protective gear in the bottom drawer under the counter," Emily told Nick as she went over and pulled open the drawer. It was stacked with sterilized vials and containers. "That's strange. They're not in here."

Nick went over to a tall cart, unlocked it, and opened the top drawer.

"He moved it to this locked cabinet because things kept disappearing." Nick pulled out two gowns, gloves, and goggles and handed a set to Emily.

"Someone was stealing aprons and masks?"

"Apparently a hot commodity. We never caught the thief. Or thieves."

"How do you know your way around here so well?" Emily questioned.

"I help out from time to time," said Nick. "Want me to slide the body out?"

"Please," Emily said. "When was the last time you attended an autopsy?"

"Just a couple months ago. I worked on a triple-vehicle fatality with Doc—I mean, your dad. Between the three cars, there were seven bodies," Nick said. "The driver of the third car was drunk. Killed everyone and walked away from the scene."

"An all-too-common story," said Emily as Nick rolled Julie's body out and transferred it onto a gurney.

"I can help you get her out of the bag," Emily said, pulling on a pair of gloves.

Together they wiggled and tugged the bag from Julie's body. Nick let the bag fall to the floor and pushed it over to the wall with his boots.

"Yes. Thank you." Emily took a cursory look while Nick stood nearby. She positioned Julie's body on the table and started with a careful external examination. As she worked, she dictated notes on the condition of the body into her iPhone.

"Julie Dobson's shirt and pants are damp. There is a rip in her jeans over the right knee. No abrasions on her hands or arms, indicating that she did not try to stop herself from a fall. No defense wounds on her hands. From where the jeans are torn, there seem to be cuts on her knee. Julie's hair is damp, and there is a significant gash on her forehead. The flesh is cut, revealing bone underneath."

Emily lifted Julie's head to reveal blood-matted hair on the back. She then smoothed back the hair to uncover a large gash.

"Anybody get X-rays of her skull yet?" Emily asked.

"Not that I'm aware of. The ER doc just sent her to the fridge as soon as she arrived."

Emily noticed that Nick was hanging back, much like she did her first time. Not sure how to help.

"Should be a camera in here," said Emily. "I need to photograph everything first."

"Doc installed one overhead," said Nick pointing above her.

Emily looked up. "Oh. Wow. That's actually a great idea. Can you make sure the batteries in the flash are charged?"

"Yeah, sure." Nick brushed her hand as he reached above her for the camera. It sent a tingle up her arm. *How can he still do that to me?*

"This is so weird, huh? You here. Me here. Like no time has gone by."

"I guess." She wanted to play it off and leave it alone.

"When you first disappeared, I tried really hard to try to understand why you just up and ran away and didn't tell me," said Nick.

"I didn't disappear. I went to live with my aunt,"

Emily said, making a note of the size and location of the head wounds on Julie's skull. "In all fairness, I did write you a note."

"Yeah, I know that now," said Nick with a smile that disarmed Emily.

"Looking back, it wasn't the best plan I've ever executed, but I was sixteen, and I just needed to get outta there. I never wished for things to play out that way," she said, adjusting Julie's head. "It wasn't personal."

"Yeah, I figured that out later. Grief is a strange animal." Nick replaced the old batteries in the flash.

"How's that flash coming?"

"We're all set." Nick held up the flash, and Emily stepped aside so he could click it back into place on the camera without brushing into her.

"Great. I'm going to start by taking some photographs of the body clothed. I need you to turn her so I can get everything. Okay?"

She reached up for the lens and readied the camera and caught him staring at her.

"What? Is something wrong?"

"No. It's just…you did it. You've become that brilliant doctor you always talked about being," he said in a thoughtful voice. "It's really impressive, Em."

"Thanks." She didn't know what else to say. So she stood there for a moment, adjusting the focus, her fingers trembling slightly under the latex gloves, hoping he didn't notice. *How can he unnerve me so fast? It's a compliment. Read nothing more into it. You're tired and stressed.*

For the next thirty minutes, Emily snapped pictures as Nick rotated Julie's body so she could report on all angles of her person. Except for Emily giving Nick directives on how to position the body, they worked in awkward silence.

"I'm going to prep the X-ray machine so we can take a look at her skull," Emily stated. "Can you get her on her stomach?"

After being dead for under twenty-four hours, Julie was still rigored, and her stiff limbs worked against him at every turn and angle. Emily was glad he was there to help. How would she have done this by herself? In the hospital, she had nurses to help her move patients.

More uncomfortable silence ensued as they moved Julie's body into position for the autopsy. As Emily selected the instruments she would need, her mind started racing with curiosity about Nick's life for the past twelve years. With several hours of autopsy ahead of them, she decided she might as well just ask him directly.

"So, I know you're the sheriff and that you saved my dad's life, but what else have you been up to the last twelve years?"

"I'm coaching football at the high school," he said.

Emily looked up at Nick. "That's nice. And so...what happened to *your* football dream?"

"Oh wow, you really have been out of the loop," he said, grinning. "Let's see, so senior year I tore my hamstring in the final game of the season, and that was it. I was damaged goods. Thankfully, my grades got me into Michigan State University, and I studied criminology. A position opened up in Freeport, and I figured why not?"

"Freeport? Why not Lansing? Detroit? Traverse?"

"Okay, you got me. There was a girl."

"Ah-ha! Anyone I know?"

"Remember Katie Fisher? No, wait. Of course, you

wouldn't. You were already gone. She was a freshman when we were seniors."

"What happened?"

"We dated all year. Then I went off to college. We kept dating. We dated all through her high school and my college years. After her graduation, she went to cosmetology school. I graduated MSU a semester early to take a job here. To be with her."

"And then…you got married? Had a couple kids?"

"Well…she decided she wanted those things…but with someone else."

"Oh gosh, I'm sorry," she said. "Who?"

"A client. At her first salon."

"Ouch."

"It's okay. I'm fine. They moved outta state, so at least I don't have to see them. One big, happy family." Nick laughed, but Emily could tell that Katie had hollowed out some part of him. A thought flitted through her mind. Had she done the same when she left Freeport?

"So why didn't you leave after that? Hit the big city? Spread your wild oats."

"I was settled in. Had bought a place. And, hey, I've always loved it here. And I love my job," he said.

"Fair enough." Emily had to remember that not everyone in the world wants to run screaming from their small hometowns. "And what about the other loves in your life?"

"Not a whole lot of selection up here," Nick said.

"Try online?"

"Disaster. The whole process seems kinda badly choreographed. Enough about my love life. What's that huge object bulging out of your glove?"

"What? Where?" Emily glanced down at her left

hand and realized he was referring to her ring. It hadn't even been twenty-four hours since Brandon had put it on her finger. "Oh yeah. I just got engaged. Today... I mean, yesterday. Morning."

"Congrats. Details?"

"His name's Brandon. He's a general surgeon who works at Northwestern. He went to U of C on a soccer scholarship. During breaks he goes down to Honduras to volunteer in the hospitals there. He's planning to open his own surgical practice one day." Emily stopped herself when she realized she sounded like she was reading his bio. This is how she had always introduced him. Brandon was really good on paper. And in Chicago, in Brandon's circles, that's how he always introduced himself. It was important to impress. But here, in Freeport, people were more interested in what kind of person someone was, not a bullet-point list of accomplishments.

"Where is he?"

"Who?"

"Brandon. Why isn't he here? With you. And your dad."

Emily looked at Nick as if he had just asked her to solve a nuclear crisis or stop world hunger. "Well. He had to work."

"I see," said Nick.

She jumped in with her list of defenses. "They set out his schedule three months ahead. So, it's really hard to get someone to switch with you last minute. Especially since he's the new guy. No clout."

"*No one* was available to switch with him?" Nick said.

"He's coming this weekend."

"Good. 'Cause it seems like you could use a little support right now."

She had never questioned Brandon's support, but just now a tiny doubt sprouted in her. Had he even tried to get someone to switch with him? She wasn't sure.

Emily pulled up the X-ray results on the monitor and studied the images, with worry growing on her brow.

"I have no idea what I'm seeing here, but your face is getting all funny. Something must be wrong," Nick said.

"It's a spiderweb fracture over the back lobe." Emily drew a line with her index finger along the fracture on the screen.

"Did she do that when she fell off her horse?" asked Nick.

"No. It's not from a fall. See how there are two sets of fracture lines? The second set intersects but then stops abruptly at the first set."

"Yeah. I see it. What does it mean?" asked Nick.

Emily looked up at Nick with all seriousness. "These injuries are not consistent with an accidental death. If it were a fall, there would only be one set of fracture lines," said Emily.

"I hear you, but I'm still not sure I understand what you're saying," Nick said.

"She was struck on the back of the head," said Emily.

"You're absolutely, positively, cross-your-heart sure?" Nick asked.

"Anatomy is anatomy. It doesn't lie," Emily said.

Emily moved Julie's head to the left so she could get a better look. She positioned a lamp over the skull. Emily fished through Julie's hair and gently rubbed her thumb along her skull. "Feel that." She pressed Nick's finger to Julie's skull. "Feel it?"

Nick pulled his hand back. "Yes. But how…with what…what do you think caused it?" he stammered.

She redirected him to the images from Julie's X-rays again and traced the fracture pattern with a grease pencil. "There's a pattern here and here and here," she said as she circled three identical areas of trauma to the skull. "But from what instrument or object, I'm not exactly sure."

It took Nick a second as the news soaked in, but he finally formed the words.

"Wait, Emily, so what you're telling me is that this is a homicide?"

"Yes, I believe so. Julie Dobson was murdered," Emily said. "The manner is clearly blunt force trauma to the head."

Nick stepped back, eyes going wide.

"You okay?"

"We haven't had a murder in Freeport in over two years.

"If we don't have a murder in two days in Chicago, we're doing good," Emily joked. Nick didn't find it humorous. Emily noticed his face was draining of color.

"Nick, you don't look well. You need some water? Sit down?"

"I'm begging you, Emily Hartford—you're gonna finish this autopsy, right? We need you. And you promised your dad you would help out." Nick's face was getting red and sweaty. Whatever he was feeling was more than nervousness. He paced the floor, radiating with anxiety and panic. "The press is waiting outside. And the killer…he could be anywhere. All this time that's gone by since she was found… I've gotta get a jump on the press. And the Dobson family—how am I going to present this to them? Oh God, they're gonna be devastated. How long can you hold off on the autopsy report?"

Emily felt an electric charge zip through her body. Standing in the same place she had as her father's teenage assistant, she was no longer a student. No longer an observer. She held the power to help solve this case.

"Don't worry, Nick," Emily said. "I know how important this is. I'm not going to do anything to jeopardize this case. I'll have the report in the morning for you."

"Thank you. You have no idea how much this means," Nick said, grabbing his hat and keys and heading toward the door. "Oh, I said I would stay and help."

"No, Nick—go. It's okay. You've got some big fish to fry. I can take it from here," Emily said.

"Thank you."

"I'll email you a preliminary report in the morning. It'll give you something to present to the Dobsons," Emily said. "You won't have tox results for another week or so."

"Yeah, that sounds like a plan. Just be extra, extra vigilant in your work. There's a good chance this'll end up in court once we catch the killer. I can't afford any mistakes," he said.

"You forget who you're dealing with," she said, feeling a yawn sneaking up on her.

"I think someone's gonna need a cup of coffee. I'll grab one for you from the cafeteria before I go."

"No. Go."

Nick was one foot out the door.

"You sure?"

"I'm sure. Are you wearing that to talk to the press?"

Nick looked down at his gown and quickly stripped it off. He tossed it into the laundry bin in the corner and slipped out the door, with a fresh smile for Emily.

"See you in the morning."

"See you." Emily smiled back.

As Emily grabbed a small electric saw and plugged it into the wall, she glimpsed down at the bulge of her ring. She thought about it for a second and peeled her gloves off. It would be best to remove the ring so it wouldn't get in the way or be damaged while she was doing the autopsy. She remembered that her father had always done the same with his wedding ring. She slid the bulky diamond in her front jeans pocket.

Music. There was always music in the morgue. Emily found her father's radio in a drawer and tuned it to the jazz station. She liked how few commercials they played in the middle of the night.

She calculated that she had been up for twenty hours straight, with at least another five hours of work before she could hit the bed. But for some reason, standing at the autopsy table, the blade of justice in her expert hands, she suddenly felt very, very awake.

ELEVEN

THE SKY WAS brightening to dawn when Emily pulled into the long, winding drive of her childhood home that lay on a ten-acre spread four miles due east of Freeport. She had meant to book a hotel room at the Pennington Inn, Freeport's only hotel, but by the time she left the hospital, it was late, and no one was on duty at the reception desk. She decided she would crash at her dad's home and deal with lodging later. Pulling into the driveway, she could tell that not one thing had changed about this place since her thirteenth birthday. She crawled toward the large, brick two-story, noticing a light on downstairs. There were two cars parked in the drive: a pickup truck she assumed was her father's and a four-door sedan she thought was probably his spare car.

She sat in her car for a moment, preparing herself for what she might find on the inside of the house. Would her dad have changed the paint? Remodeled? What had he done to her room? Would it look like some sad shrine? And what about her mom's stuff? Would it still be there? Had he kept anything? Over the years, there were moments when Emily wished for some memento of her mother's, but bitterness toward her father had kept her from inquiring.

Emily shut the car's engine down and stalled some more. In her mind, she ran through the layout of the home, visiting each room, nook, and cranny. She could recall every wall color, every knick-knack, every piece of furniture. She traveled the house in her mind's eye, putting herself in the best hide-and-seek spots, playing Ping-Pong opposite her sister in the damp basement. In her mind, she rummaged through the old toy box that her mother had kept, even years after she and Anna had outgrown playing with toys. Under her bed was a box of Barbie dolls she had left behind. In the closet she kept a plastic bin of trophies, ribbons, and memorabilia from special events. At the bottom of the box were several childhood journals she hadn't laid eyes on in twelve years, remnants of life before suffering. A whole 'nother life lay inside that she felt forced to revisit under the circumstances.

Emily glanced to the front window of the house and was startled to see a hand draw the curtain away. Who on earth was here? A shadow moved through the living room. Panic pulsed through Emily. A face appeared in the corner of the window, but Emily couldn't make it out in the dim early morning light. Then, the curtain bounced shut. Was it a burglar? Should she call Nick? The eyes appeared for a second. Then they were gone. The porch light flashed three times. Clearly, the entity inside was trying to get her attention. An intruder would never do that. The situation now seemed a little less threatening. But wouldn't her father have mentioned someone being here?

Emily waited a few more minutes, trying to figure out her best course of action as her breath steamed up the front windshield so she could no longer make out the house. She was wiping the steam off the window when suddenly the passenger door opened, wafting in a stiff breeze of cold, autumn air. Emily jumped.

"You coming in?" A woman hopped in, shutting the door behind her, and gave Emily a squeeze.

"Oh my gosh. You really startled me," Emily said, realizing the woman was Cathy Bishop. She looked the same as Emily remembered her. She wore short brown hair neatly styled, with modest makeup and simple jewelry. She was a busty woman with a trim waist and thin thighs, who liked to accentuate her assets, but always in a stylish, conservative manner. She never looked dowdy, even when she was out for groceries. Perhaps it was a consequence of her profession. As the town mortician who ran Bishop and Schulz funeral home, Cathy needed to present a professional appearance at all times. Even now, in the middle of the night, here was Cathy, sitting in Emily's passenger seat, wearing a sleek pair of black slacks, a fitted sweater, and a silk neck scarf.

"I'm beginning to wonder if you planned to come in at all," said Cathy.

"I wasn't expecting anyone home," said Emily.

"I see. So, your dad didn't mention I would be here?"

"No, he didn't." Emily shook her head with a grin. "But I'm glad it's you and not a thief."

"I was at the hospital earlier, and when they moved him out of critical care, I told your father I would tend to a few things for him at home and make sure the house was ready for your arrival. How did it go with him?"

"Okay, I think," Emily said, not wanting to dwell on it. "Thanks for calling me. I'm sorry I didn't get back to you. I was in surgery, and then later Jo called, and I didn't get a chance to return yours."

"It's okay. What matters is that you're here," said Cathy. "Do you think your dad'll be okay?"

"He doesn't think he's that sick," Emily started, "so

the first hurdle will be trying to get that through his thick skull."

Cathy laughed. "When I first saw him in the hospital, he told me it was just a little indigestion from a bad piece of meat he ate. Total denial. Thinks he's invincible."

"He's gonna need to slow down his life considerably," said Emily. "Maybe cut back on work. Change his diet."

"Like that'll happen." Cathy laughed. "But I'll see what I can do."

"You're not responsible for him, Cathy," Emily said.

"But I feel that I am," she said gently, and Emily detected a touch of intimacy.

"You're a great friend to all of us all these years. I probably never thanked you enough."

"Your family has always been a joy to me. And I hope we get to spend more time together in the future under better circumstances," she said.

"Perhaps." Emily left it at that. It seemed a strange comment to make after all these years, but Emily skirted around it and said, "He even thought he was strong enough to tackle an autopsy tonight."

"What? The Dobson girl?" Emily nodded. "That stubborn man," said Cathy. "I heard about it today, but I didn't mention anything to Robert. I knew it would only stir him up."

"Well, it did. But I made it clear he couldn't get involved. Instead, I got roped into it," said Emily. "That's why I'm arriving here so late."

"Classic Robert. But no better choice than you," said Cathy. "Terrible tragedy. What was the cause of death?"

Emily glanced at Cathy. "Cathy, you have to keep

this just between you and me because I haven't even told the family yet."

"Promise. Confidentiality is my bread and butter," she said.

"Homicide. She has a fracture to the skull."

"Did you tell Nick?"

Emily nodded. "He was there. And I sent him the official report an hour ago."

Cathy shook her head sadly. "This is going to be tougher than I anticipated. I'm meeting with the Dobsons tomorrow to make funeral arrangements. But don't worry—my lips are sealed.

"Does Nick have any leads on suspects?" Cathy asked.

"I don't know," Emily replied. "He said he had an investigation under way."

"It's kinda scary to know there's a killer out there," mused Cathy. "I wonder who would want to hurt that poor girl?"

Emily's thoughts raced to the community of Freeport who didn't know yet that they had a killer in their midst. This was the kind of place where people left their cars unlocked and their front doors unbolted. Emily made a mental note to keep both locked while she was here.

"So, I guess I'm crashing here for the night...or rather the day. I didn't get a chance to book a room," she told Cathy.

"No worries. I already made up a bed for you," Cathy said.

"Oh, that's sweet, but I don't want to dirty fresh sheets. I can just use the couch. I'm only crashing for a couple hours before I head back to the hospital," said Emily.

"Your dad wanted me to stress that you're welcome to stay here as long as you want."

"I don't think we're quite on that level just yet," Emily said, strumming her fingers over the top of the steering wheel. Her two-karat engagement ring caught Cathy's eye.

"Emily Hartford. Are you engaged?" Cathy exclaimed, snatching Emily's hand to get a better look. "Does your dad know?"

"Not yet," said Emily. "I was too busy trying to keep him from fleeing his hospital room for the morgue."

"I kinda feel privileged that I get to hear about it first," Cathy said with a smile. "Spill it. I want all the details." Cathy was wide-eyed for her story.

"His name's Brandon. He's a general surgeon at Northwestern. We met in med school at U of C, where he was on soccer scholarship and…" Emily paused and bit her lower lip slightly. She was doing it again. What could she tell Cathy about Brandon that wasn't on Brandon's LinkedIn page? She thought for a second and then said, "And he introduced me to sushi on our first date, took me to Thailand for Christmas break, and he wants us to do international medical missions in South America once we retire."

"Wow. Some catch. When are you getting married?" asked Cathy.

"Not sure," Emily responded.

"Here? In Freeport?" Cathy asked, hopeful.

"Oh, I don't think so. He's never even been here." She knew how it sounded as soon as it slipped from her lips. "His family's all in Chicago."

"I see."

"I don't know. It's all pretty fresh."

"Well, there's time for all those plans. I have to say, if this isn't the path to your father's recovery, I don't know what is," Cathy said with a growing smile.

"What do you mean?" Emily asked.

"Your happiness means everything to him. It always has," Cathy said. "And his happiness means everything to me. Another wedding in the family. How wonderful."

Emily looked confused. "Another?"

Cathy read her puzzled look and then realized. "What? He didn't tell you at the hospital? I told him he needed to tell you now."

"Tell me what?" Emily shook her head in disbelief.

"He called you two months ago. Do you remember?" Cathy said.

"Yeah, I think so. I know I got a message from him recently. But I never…"

"You never returned it," finished Cathy. "This needs to stop. He's your father."

"I… I… What did I miss?" She felt fifteen again under Cathy's scolding.

Cathy held up her left hand to reveal a simple platinum band.

"Your father and I got married a month ago," she said. "It was a small ceremony at church with just a dozen or so friends. He wanted you—*we* wanted you to be there."

"But my aunt Laura…she never said anything," Emily said.

"Your father instructed her not to say anything to you. He wanted to see if you'd return his call."

"I see." Emily cringed, feeling guilty. "Well, congratulations."

"Thank you. And likewise. I won't say anything to

Robert about your engagement. It's your news to tell," Cathy said.

The two sat in silence for a moment. Eventually Cathy spoke. "I'm really happy to be a part of your family, and I hope you'll accept that...accept me. Maybe this is part of a new start for all of us?"

Emily gulped back the lump in her throat. "Maybe. It's just a lot to take in at five in the morning."

"Understandably. It's been a pretty full day, so I'll let you get some rest. Welcome home, Emily. And happy birthday," Cathy said.

Emily grabbed her bag, locked the car, and followed Cathy inside. By habit, she turned left once through the front doors and padded up the staircase to her old bedroom on the second floor. Plunking down her things on a chair, Emily dropped into bed. She was exhausted and overwhelmed by the events of the past twenty-four hours. Sleep would help. She would need a renewed state of mind for whatever was coming at her with the break of this new day. Thankfully, Cathy was now in play to make health decisions for Emily's dad, and the Dobson autopsy was done. With any luck, she might be able to sail out of here in another twenty-four. She could be back in Chicago in time for Brandon's weekend off. Her stomach growled, but she was too fatigued to get up and go to the kitchen. What was the last thing she'd eaten? Oh yes, frosting. And as Emily drifted asleep, she thought about that PB&J cupcake from Violet's on the floor of the doctor's lounge. Freeport didn't have anything even close to Violet's Cupcakery. Her drowsy brain resolved to remind Brandon that he owed her another one.

TWELVE

EMILY ROSE AROUND noon and found a note in the kitchen from Cathy, informing her that she was at the hospital. She grabbed a piece of fruit from the basket on the counter and made a cup of coffee while she flipped on the TV to see if news of Julie's death had touched the noon news cycle. She caught the tail end of a local ABC affiliate broadcast from downtown Freeport last night, where they'd captured Nick leaving the hospital at midnight and giving a short statement saying the case was under investigation and "no further questions." Emily could tell the woman was not satisfied with Nick's answer, or maybe wanted to boost ratings, so the reporter interjected her own speculation that it was possible "Julie's death might be more than just an unfortunate accident." On that tag, the station went to commercial break, and Emily shut it off. She checked her phone. Nothing from Brandon. He was probably in surgery.

She finished her coffee and drove into Freeport to take a walk around and clear her head for the challenges of the afternoon ahead. Downtown Freeport was only three blocks in length, and the businesses were operating at their usual small-town pace. Emily snugged her sweater across her chest. She looked up at a gray sky that threatened storms. A light frost had tinged the tips of the grass and edges of the leaves. September 20. It seemed too early for frost, and she wondered if it were going to be an early autumn.

Emily walked one side of the street and then crossed it to cover the opposite side. She passed a total of three people. When in Chicago could she ever walk around a single city block and encounter so few people? Never.

Halfway down the block, Emily found herself standing in front of an odd window display in Glassner's Sports Shop. Inside, a happy deer family grazed on fake turf, completely oblivious to a mannequin hunter pointing a shotgun behind them. Emily found it ironic that this hunter was hoping to feed his family with theirs. It was an odd juxtaposition, much like the one she had stepped into last night. Trouble brewing beneath the surface of her hometown, and no one knew it was there. Yet.

This little window dressing scene spoke deeply to Emily about the underlying condition of threats in the world. *Aren't we all just trying to survive the best we can, but in the end, won't we all succumb to some hunter not of our choosing?*

Her thoughts turned to Julie. *Who was hunting Julie? Who wanted her dead? Why did they want her dead? Why her? And why now?*

It was the same set of questions Emily asked about any untimely death or disease. Especially her mom's. When her mom left the house that long-ago morning, she was a perfectly healthy woman in her late thirties. Happy home. Happy marriage. There were no indications that the Grim Hunter was pointing his rifle her way that day. Emily had never believed the story the cops gave them that her mom was swerving to avoid hitting an animal. Her mom knew that stretch of road was treacherous, and she was a good driver. Her dad had impressed on both of them that hitting an animal on that dangerous section of curve was better than trying to swerve to miss it. Yes, it went contrary to instinct, but swerve and you'd end up over the embankment. Dead. Hit the animal: animal dies, but you live.

Emily left hunter and his prey and traveled down the sidewalk. Her phone buzzed as she passed Tina's Hair & Nail Salon. Emily scrambled to find it in the bottom of her purse. Brandon's name flashed across the screen. "Hey, you okay? I just got out of surgery and panicked when I saw you still hadn't called," he started.

He knew her so well. "Yeah, I'm so sorry. I'm fine."

She had completely forgotten to call him last night and let him know how her dad was doing and that she had made it safely.

"What's going on up there? I opened up MSN on the 'L' this morning and saw your picture on the regional news link. Did I see this right? You actually performed an autopsy?" he said with a touch of worry in his voice.

"What? You saw it where?" What else had Nick told those reporters? She wished she had seen the whole news report. "Ah, yeah, I did," Emily said, her lips turning up at the sound of his voice. "You sound concerned?"

"Of course I'm concerned. What happened?"

"I can't really say over the phone because I haven't released the autopsy reports yet. The victim is a state senator's daughter and sort of a local equestrian celebrity," said Emily. She moved from Tina's and crossed at the stoplight. Across the street she could see Brown's Bakery, where her mom used to take her after school for the bear claws and cinnamon rolls. *All right, Brown's. Let's see how you stack up to Violet's.*

"So, I'm still a little fuzzy on something. How exactly did you end up doing an autopsy?"

"They suckered me in," Emily said, realizing how all this must sound to him. Less than a day ago, he had been proposing to her. Now, her name was appearing on news reports, and she was becoming consumed in a drama completely contrary to her normal life.

"Who is *they*? And are you okay with this? It just sounds so…well, very surreal."

Emily explained how it had all gone down, but left out the part about how Sheriff Larson was that one boyfriend she'd had in high school.

"Sounds like some odd but exciting stuff, I have to admit. All I did yesterday was a knee replacement," said Brandon. "How are things with your dad?"

"He's denying that there's anything seriously wrong with him. But I'll talk to the cardiologist today and see where we're going from here. Will you be able to come up?"

"I should be able to make it up there by the weekend," said Brandon.

"Meaning Saturday?"

"Probably Sunday. But only for a night."

"Any chance you can get someone to switch shifts and come up sooner? Or stay longer?"

Brandon paused on the other end. "I don't know, Em. I have four surgeries scheduled in the next three days."

"I thought you wanted to meet my dad?"

"I do. I do. Especially since he's going to be walking you down the aisle soon."

"Who says I'm going to ask him to do that?"

"Em, come on. I don't know everything that went down in the past between you two, but what are the chances you can patch things up while you're there?" he coaxed.

He had no idea how deep this rift ran. And she couldn't blame him. He had tried to pry it out of Emily several times during their dating life, but she wouldn't let him. Her secrets were a sore spot between them. Brandon didn't understand family secrets. Because she and he had none. They were transparent. They told each other everything.

"Em, are you there?" Brandon said.

"Dad married Cathy without telling me," Emily blurted out, changing the subject.

"*The* Cathy Bishop? The family friend and mortician?"

"Yes. I haven't talked with him about it yet," Emily said. "She told me when I got to the house."

"Wow. Big news. How do you feel about that?" he asked.

"I feel… I like Cathy."

"But what?"

"I never pictured another woman in my mom's home," said Emily.

"I'm sorry, Em. Just try to be happy for them," he said, but the tone of his voice dropped, and Emily could tell he was multitasking. "Hey, guess what? Dr. Claiborne asked me to cowrite a journal article and present it at the surgical convention next month."

"Congratulations. What are you doing over there?"

"What? Nothing."

"No, you're looking at something. I can hear you clicking on the keyboard."

Out of the corner of her eye, Emily saw a news van rolling onto Main Street. She checked her watch. 12:23 pm. The press were trolling town, no doubt waiting for the autopsy report to drop.

Emily gave in to her craving for a Brown's bear claw. She crossed the street, not noticing a white van slowing up to the curb a few yards behind her.

"Brandon, are you there?"

The van was trailing Emily now, and she picked up the pace. Emily walked a few more paces, landing in front of Luisa's Bridal Store.

"Yeah, I'm here."

"Do you need to go?"

"You caught me. I'm looking at wedding venues on-line," Brandon admitted as she glanced up at the towering white gowns on spindly mannequins in the window. "Have you thought about a wedding date?"

"I was hoping to bask in the glow of being newly engaged for at least another day or two," she joked.

As Emily looked into the street display window, she saw the reflection of the van in the glass.

"It's just…my mom's already bugging me," said Brandon "She has a venue picked out. She wants to reserve her country club."

"In Rolling Hills? That's the suburbs," said Emily.

"Yeah. I know we always talked about a city wedding, but she can get a good deal, and all their friends are out there," Brandon reasoned.

Emily picked up the pace and narrowed in on her escape route as a reporter and a cameraman got out of the van.

"But everyone we know is in the city," she said.

"People like to get out of the city for something fun," said Brandon.

Behind her Emily could hear the click-click of the reporter's heels gaining ground. She was just feet away from the bakery.

"Excuse me, Dr. Emily Hartford?" said the voice on her tail.

She felt a hand touch her shoulder. Emily turned to face a leggy, bottle-blonde reporter with chalk-white teeth and black-cherry lipstick that made her look a little zombielike.

"Can I ask you a few questions about Julie Dobson's death?" the woman pressed, sidestepping around Emily. Emily froze up.

"You are the doctor who performed the autopsy on Miss Dobson, right?"

Emily couldn't get away now. As she glanced at the camera lens in her face, all she could think was how she hadn't put on any makeup today. Not even a stroke of mascara.

"Brandon—hey, can I call you back?"

"Yeah, sure. Everything okay?" he said.

"Um, yeah. Call you later."

"What should I tell my mom?" he said.

"I don't know. Figure it out," Emily said faintly and then slipped her phone into her purse, never letting her eyes off the microphone positioned six inches from her gaping mouth.

"How did Julie Dobson die? Was it accidental?" fired the reporter.

"I can't comment on that right now. The report will be made public later today."

"Are you taking over the ME position for your father? What are your plans for the ME office now that your father has stepped down?"

"What? No, he hasn't stepped down. He's in the hospital, recovering," Emily said.

Out of the corner of her eye, Emily saw she was standing in front of the bakery door. She felt behind her for the door handle as the reporter loomed over her. *If I go in there, will she follow me, or will I be trapped?*

"Is it your opinion that Julie's death was an accident?" pressed the blonde reporter.

"I—I cannot comment right now," Emily stuttered.

Suddenly, the bakery door swung open, and a woman's voice barked, "Back away. You're interfering with an official police investigation." An FBI badge flashed and sent the reporter, bristling, to the edge of the sidewalk.

Emily, who had her back toward the door, couldn't see who the woman was. She had no time to react as she felt a firm grip around her arm. Before she knew it, she was yanked inside and backed into a corner. The woman then hastily bolted the bakery door and drew the privacy shades over the storefront window.

THIRTEEN

"NOW, WHAT CAN I get you? Cinnamon roll or bear claw?" said the friendly kidnapper, turning to Emily with a huge smile. It took Emily a second.

"Delia?" Emily found herself staring at the petite red-haired woman whom she now recognized with relief and great appreciation.

"That badge still comes in handy sometimes," said Delia Andrews with a full-bellied laugh. "Oh my. Look at you. You're the spitting image of your mother," she continued, embracing Emily.

Emily was taken aback by mention of her mother but quickly brushed it off, as she knew Delia meant well. Delia was a close family friend and former FBI agent who had sometimes consulted on her father's cases. Never married. No kids. Delia traveled the world with the FBI, always bringing Emily trinkets from exotic places like Malta, Mumbai, and Madagascar. Emily was pretty sure all of Delia's international gifts were still in alphabetical order in shoe boxes in the back of her closet.

"So which is it?" said Delia, slipping behind the donut counter and grabbing a small plate and tongs. "Bear claw or cinnamon bun? Or both! Go crazy."

"Bear claw?" Emily noticed that Delia was wearing a Brown's Bakery apron. "Delia, do you work here now?"

Delia nodded. "Retirement was boring. People

shouldn't retire, Emily. Remember that. They should just move on to something new. Besides, this place gives me a chance to keep up on the local gossip and do a little sleuthing for the cops. Shh. Don't tell anyone."

"I won't," Emily said, grinning with teeth full of pastry. Delia always had a plan up her sleeve.

"Shame on those media hounds, chasing you down on the street."

"Thank you for rescuing me. I was really getting up a creek out there." Emily sunk her teeth into the fresh, warm bear claw. She had forgotten how these melted in the mouth. Was there anywhere in Chicago that even came close? No. Not even Violet's. Brown's was still the best. She had just forgotten.

"Just sit for a spell. They'll get tired of waiting. You want coffee with that?"

"I'd love some. I need some. I've only been up an hour."

"Sit, sit. I'll make you a latte."

Emily sank into an uncomfortable wire chair and marveled at Delia's tireless spirit. If only she had an ounce of Delia's energy.

"When did you retire?"

"Last year," Delia said. "Toward the end of my service with the FBI, I was away more than home. At first, it was nice to be home. I must have slept twelve hours a day, catching up for the past thirty years. Then, when my sleep pattern went back to normal, I burned through a hundred and seventy-two issues of *Reader's Digest* and crocheted thirty-nine blankets for the neonatal unit. Finally, I landed here. But I admit, I have been struggling with wanderlust."

"Is there anywhere you haven't been?" said Emily as Delia set down a frothy latte in front of her.

"Can you believe, Fiji? Yes, Fiji. Not a lot of crime there."

"Sounds perfect. Maybe you should plan a trip." Emily brought her lips to the rim of the mug and inhaled the caffeinated aroma. She took a small sip.

"Ouch! Hot!" She clicked her tongue against the roof of her mouth.

"Let it cool a second. There's no rush."

Emily nodded and set the mug on the table. *I'm always in such a hurry in Chicago. When was the last time I actually sat with a cup of coffee?*

"I was sorry to hear about your dad. How is he?"

"I'll soon find out. Cardiologist was stopping in about noon." She checked her watch. "He should have already made his visit."

"I suppose midnight autopsies with former sweethearts isn't exactly what you thought you would be doing on your first Freeport visit in twelve years, is it?" Delia said.

Emily chuckled and shook her head. Small towns. There was no such thing as people minding their own business. She could get mugged in broad daylight on the South Loop, and maybe someone would stop to call 911. But here. You couldn't so much as get a splinter removed without half the town speculating on the best way to take care of it. "Brown's really is the perfect place for you, isn't it? And Nick was never a sweetheart."

"Oh, yes, he was. You just couldn't see it at the time, Em. With your mom…" She trailed off.

Emily tried her coffee again. This time it was cool enough to drink.

"I just think that destiny...fate, providence, kismet, karma, the universe—call it what you will—it comes for us and has its way with us."

Emily wished to put a stop to all this speculative nonsense, so she elegantly held out her hand for Delia to see her diamond. "I'm engaged, Delia."

"Well, I'll be. You could knock a person out with that rock." Delia gazed at the stone, turning it over in the light. "Lemme guess. He's a doctor. Probably a surgeon. A few years your senior. Handsome, of course. Born and bred in Chicago. A good man with fine taste. The kind you don't find around here. He has a family with pedigree."

Emily looked at Delia in amazement.

"You got all that from my ring?"

"I've been reading people for a living for over thirty years," Delia said with a wry smile.

"Spot on." Emily stuffed her mouth with another bit of bear claw. There was something annoying about how well Delia could still read her after all these years. And something comforting. She wasn't sure which one to give in to at the moment.

"His name's Brandon Taylor."

"Mrs. Brandon Taylor. Has a good solid sound to it," she said, smiling.

"Dr. Emily Hartford-Taylor," Emily corrected.

"Much better. Forgive me. I'm the old guard. Never had to deal with that name-change nonsense."

There was a knock at the front door, and Delia peeped behind the shade. Recognizing the person on the other side, she unlocked the door, and a teenage girl entered.

"Good morning, Sadie. Emily, this is Sadie. My barista in training. Sadie, this is Dr. Emily Hartford. She used to live here in Freeport."

"Hi," said Sadie with a small voice. "Nice to meet you."

"You too. Is this your first day?"

"Third."

"You'll do great. Delia's a lot of fun."

"Don't give her the impression we don't work around here," Delia teased. "Sadie, let's get you settled. Come with me." Delia ushered Sadie into the kitchen, which gave Emily a moment to quickly check her news app for any more leaks on the Dobson case. She searched for her name. A video link popped up from just minutes before in front of the bakery. Relief washed over her when she saw that they had assembled her comments in a fairly harmless manner. But Emily was mortified to realize how unattractive she had looked on camera, and vowed to be more vigilant about combing her hair and slathering on a coat of lip gloss before she went out in public. While she was waiting for Delia to return, it suddenly struck her: Sadie was in high school. Did she know Julie?

After a moment, Delia returned from the kitchen with Sadie. "Okay, make two espressos and an Americano. Go."

Delia hung back at Emily's table.

"She's a quick learner. Thank goodness. Some of these kids from Gen Z are absolutely helpless. And clueless. All stems from that helicopter parenting." Delia shook her head.

"Delia, can I ask Sadie some questions about Julie?"

Delia smiled. "See what I told you about this job? Window to the world."

Emily stepped up to the espresso maker. "Sadie, so what year are you now?"

"Junior."

"Did you know Julie Dobson?"

"She was a year ahead of me."

"Sure. Did you have any classes with her?"

"We had computer class together."

"Did anything seem wrong with Julie lately? Was she depressed or acting differently?"

"What? Why? Did Julie kill herself?" Sadie asked, darting her eyes up at Emily.

"Oh. No. That's not what I'm implying. No. I just mean, had anything big changed in her life lately?"

"Well, she broke up with her boyfriend, David."

"Do you know why?"

"Everyone knew why. Her father hated David."

"That's why she did it?"

"I guess so. Everyone's saying her father forced her to break it off. But I kept seeing them at school together, so I don't know."

Delia smiled and raised her cup to Sadie. "These are delicious, Sadie. Try a latte this time. Remember, one-third steamed milk. Em, you need a refill?"

"No, thanks. I gotta get going. A lot to tackle today."

"Tell your father I said hello and that I'll stop by later today to visit," said Delia.

"I will."

Emily slung her purse over her head and reached into it for her lip gloss. She swabbed the wand over her lips with a deliberation that expressed she was ready to forge battle with outside media forces should they attack. She started for the front door.

"Em, back door."

"Oh, yeah." Emily turned and saw Delia pointing through the kitchen.

"Here, I'll show you," she said.

Emily followed Delia through the kitchen, and Delia unlocked the back door that led into the alley. She peeked outside through the peephole. "Coast looks clear."

Emily grabbed the door handle and turned the knob. Delia set her hand over Emily's.

"Have you forgiven him yet?"

Emily rubbed her bottom lip over her top one, smearing the gloss above the upper lip line. Underneath, her teeth were clenched together. Why was Delia bringing this up?

"Maybe now's a good time?" said Delia, raising her hand off Emily's. "Don't wait too long."

"Did he ever consult with you on her case?" Emily said.

"No."

"Roads were clear. Visibility was clear. No other cars around. Nothing wrong with the vehicle. Didn't you ever question—"

"Of course. But accidents do happen. I've seen it hundreds of times. And there's nothing your dad could have done to change that."

Emily handed Delia a twenty-dollar bill.

"The bear claw was amazing, Delia. Make sure Sadie gets a good tip, okay?"

She pushed the door open and stepped out of Brown's Bakery, disappointed to know that Delia was just one more person that swept it under the rug.

FOURTEEN

THE NEWS VAN had vacated, so thankfully, Emily was able to steal back to her car two blocks away, unnoticed. Before heading to the hospital, Emily wanted to make sure she could get a room for the night, so she drove a few miles down Main Street to the Pennington Inn and checked in. The Pennington had a homey, country-inn feel and was the only hotel in Freeport other than a skeezy track motel that attracted hunters and truckers and rent-by-hours.

She dragged her luggage up to the second floor and collapsed into the soft down, king-size bed. She craved more sleep. But as soon she felt her eyelids droop, she forced herself up. *Come on. Keep going. Pretend you're making rounds. You can do this!*

Emily splashed cold water on her face, brushed her teeth, and jumped in her car, arriving at the hospital ten minutes later.

She requested her father's chart from a nurse and stood outside his room reading it. In the last twelve hours, her father's health had showed little improvement. If he wanted to get better and live longer, his whole life would have to change. Medications and diet changes would stabilize him. Several months in a rehab facility would strengthen him and return him to a semi-full life. But strenuous work like investigating deaths and doing autopsies was definitely out of the question.

Forever. Dr. Robert Hartford didn't know it yet, but he had just entered a forced retirement.

Emily made her way into his room and saw that he was perched up in his bed with a spread of newspapers. A TV news report coming from the wall-mounted flat screen held his attention.

"Good morning," she said.

"Hello. Shh," he said, pressing his finger over his lips.

"What's so important that—"

"Shh... It's Nick." He pointed to the screen.

Emily turned her attention to the monitor. On screen, the news station ran footage from the previous night when Nick was fielding questions from the hospital parking lot.

"In follow-up news from the untimely death of Freeport equestrian star Julie Dobson, we learned last night, through Freeport County Sheriff Nick Larson, that it is likely her death was accidental," said the reporter.

Why is he speculating like that? Is he trying to mislead them?

"We're awaiting an autopsy report from Dr. Emily Hartford, who is apparently filling in for her father, Dr. Robert Hartford, Freeport's medical examiner, who recently suffered a severe heart attack."

"They tried to come after me at Brown's Bakery."

"Vultures," Dr. Hartford muttered, clicking off the TV. Emily noticed a stack of reading material in front of her dad.

"Did Cathy bring you all this?" she asked.

"Yeah, so I wouldn't get bored. I told her I'm gonna be outta here this afternoon. There's no time to get bored," he said.

"You think so, huh? What did your cardiologist say?"

"He hasn't been by yet, but I expect him anytime," replied her father.

"You don't look very rested," she said, noticing the dark rings under his eyes.

"Who sleeps well in a hospital?" he said. "You don't look so wide-eyed either. Cathy said you slept at the house last night…or rather this morning."

"I did. But I got a room at the Pennington for tonight," she said.

"No need to waste your money."

When her dad started talking finances, Emily knew it best to change the subject. He was a spendthrift and ran his entire practice and the medical examiner business this way. He didn't believe in overcharging patients or bilking county taxpayers for coroner's office expenses. One thing was for sure: they had definitely never been one of those wealthy doctors' families like she met in Brandon's circles. She had never thought much about money, and quite frankly, dwelling on it made her uncomfortable, especially when Brandon talked boldly about what kind of salary expectations he had and the diversity of investments he wanted to make in his future. He was bent on making a fortune and being generous with his fortune. There was nothing wrong with that, of course. She just didn't have experience with the kind of wealth Brandon was used to.

"I ran into Delia. She says she's stopping by to visit later."

"She'd better hurry."

"Dad, prepare for the fact that you may be stuck in here for a little while," she said as Robert noticed his chart tucked under her arm.

"Everyone keeps telling me that, but based on what proof? Let's wait for the test results before you condemn me to a hospital bed."

"The EKG confirmed your heart attack. The other tests are just going to tell us how bad it was and what you need to do from here," Emily said.

"What does that file say? The one you're trying to hide there," he replied.

"I'm not trying to hide anything. Don't worry about it for now," Emily answered.

"May I see it, please?" Robert asked.

"Your doctor will go over it with you when he gets here," said Emily.

"Emily Ann Hartford, give me that file," Robert said. "And my reading glasses."

First and middle name calling was a serious matter, so Emily passed over the file and the glasses. There was no use trying to fight him. She would have done the same thing if she were in his shoes. There was no putting the wool over a doctor's eyes.

Robert glanced over the file with an emotionless expression. After he had digested the entire chart, he passed it back to her and took off his glasses. He rested his head against the pillow and stared across the room. Emily saw some of the life drain from his face. It was upsetting to see him grow a little older right before her eyes.

"What are you thinking?" Emily finally asked him.

"Lunch and vitals, Dr. Hartford!" said the day nurse, barreling in with a tray.

Emily kept silent as she did her job.

"Your cardiologist is running a bit behind. Should be here after three. Enjoy your meal. And ring me if you need anything, okay?" She returned the blood pressure machine to its place on the wall and marched out.

Robert took one look at the dry turkey slice, soupy mashed potatoes, and melting jello and pushed the tray aside.

"Shut the door."

Emily did so.

"What did you find on that Dobson girl?" Robert asked.

"Brain trauma, fractured skull," Emily replied.

"Yeah, that's consistent with what I found too," he said.

"What do you mean?"

"I snuck down to the morgue last night," he said.

"You did *what*?"

"Did you notice the double fracture lines on the skull?"

"Dad, you shouldn't have gotten out of bed."

"Freeport has a homicide on its hands," Robert said. "What's being done about it?"

"Nick's got this. You need to rest."

"I remember that Dobson girl. She rides this magnificent creature named Mercedes. She's been riding him since he was a colt. They grew up together, you could say. I just don't have any idea who would want to kill her. It doesn't make sense. Does Nick have any leads? Any evidence?" asked Robert, his brow furrowing.

"I'm not sure. I haven't talked to him since I gave him the autopsy report."

"Have you been out to the scene?"

"What? No. Of course not," she said. "I've barely even had time to sleep since I got here."

"I want you to head over to Premiere stables and do

some scene recreation so you can be sure your estimations of the attack will hold up in court," he said.

"But I wouldn't even know where to start,"

"I'm sure you remember more than you think. And I can coach you. It's of utmost importance that you comb the area for any missed evidence."

"Nothing I find now will be court admissible."

"Maybe not, but it'll give you and Nick some more clues as to the person who did this," he said.

"Oh no," she corrected. "I've done my job. Nick can do his."

"I'm asking you, as consulting death investigator for my office; will you please look into this a little more?"

"Dad, this isn't why I came to Freeport."

"You came to help me, right? And this is what I need," he insisted.

"The sheriff's department is taking care of it." Emily couldn't state it more plainly.

"Nick's got great instincts, but let's face it. How many homicides do we get in Freeport County? Visit the scene," said Robert.

Emily sighed as a text came in on her phone. It was Nick.

Arriving hospital in five. Pick you up by emergency doors.

"It'll take you fifteen minutes max to go over there and check things out," Robert said.

"Dad, it's not doing your health any good to work yourself up about this," Emily said.

"Emily, soon the Dobsons will be pleading with you: 'Who did this to our daughter?' And you'll have to ask yourself, 'Have I done everything in my power to give them justice?'"

Emily paused for a moment as his words tapped into a deeply seeded pain between them.

She wanted to push back: *Why didn't you do everything you could for Mom's case? And since you couldn't do it yourself, why didn't you hire an investigator?*

Emily managed to hold back, but her thoughts came out instead as "I don't think you're going to have a future as an ME anymore. You need to consider moving into a rehab facility."

"Is this your assessment or my doctor's?" Robert's voice sounded pinched.

"But I can tell by your charts that—"

"I have my own rehab plans," Dad said. "Cathy."

"So I understand," said Emily.

Robert's eyes flickered up to meet Emily's. "I called you a month before the wedding. I wanted you to know. But what was I supposed to do when you never called me back?"

"You could have left a more detailed message. Something along the lines of 'I'm getting married,'" she said.

"I don't need my daughter's approval."

Robert's neck started to turn red, and Emily worried that her conversation with him was raising his blood pressure. She certainly didn't want to be the cause for sending him into another heart attack. She took a deep breath and went into calm, detached doctor mode. She needed to treat her father as she would any one of her patients. "Look, bottom line is that you need professional rehab therapy in order to achieve a greater level of recovery. Cathy cannot provide this for you in the home.

It's best if you start off in a facility better equipped to handle cases like yours."

"Emily. Stop. I know what you're doing." He sat there for a moment, collecting his thoughts while Emily felt like she was twelve again and about to get a chiding for speaking out of turn.

Why had she expected this to be easy? Her dad was as stubborn and strong-willed as he had been twelve years ago. She would speak to Cathy about this. It was no use arguing with him.

"When do I get to meet this fiancé, Mr. Brandon Taylor?" Robert asked. Emily looked up, surprised by the abrupt turn of conversation.

"Don't worry. He'll meet with your approval. Not that I'm asking for it," Emily said.

"I trust your judgment on the matter."

"He wants to meet you."

"When's the date?"

"I'll keep you posted," Emily said.

"I suppose you'll get married in Chicago?" he asked.

"Yes."

"Church wedding?"

"We're not really church people," Emily said.

"You used to be," Robert said. "I'd like to help pay for it."

"Thanks. We don't need…we can afford it," she said.

"You're my daughter, and I want to help," he said. Emily sighed and looked away. "Don't shut me out of this. Please."

While Emily felt her father still owed her a great deal, it wasn't a debt that could be paid, or bribed away, through a wedding gift.

"What exactly did you have in mind?" she asked.

"I guess fathers typically pay for the reception, right?"

Emily nodded. "I'll talk to Brandon about it."

"Are you interested in having your mother's dress and veil?" Robert asked her. It jabbed her in the gut. She had never considered it. It seemed so intimate. She hadn't even known the dress still existed.

"I don't...know" was all Emily could muster.

"Well, it's yours if you want it," Robert said. "I've been saving it for you."

At that moment, Cathy entered, carrying a brown paper grocery bag.

"Emily, hey. I missed you this morning," she said as she removed the hospital tray and started stacking food items from the grocery bag in front of Robert.

"I'll leave you two alone so you can enjoy your lunch," Emily said, rising and grabbing her coat.

"We wish you'd stay," Cathy pleaded. "There's plenty here for three."

"Nick's waiting for me downstairs," said Emily.

"Emily, remember what I said. Premiere. Take a second look. That's all I'm asking," said her father, digging into a fresh deli sandwich with enough mayonnaise dripping down the sides to clog an artery.

FIFTEEN

As Nick and Emily pulled into the Dobsons' long driveway, Emily saw that now several news vans had re-
located to the street in front of the Dobsons' house.
Apparently they had been tipped off that the Dobsons
would be receiving the official autopsy report this afternoon, and this had alerted more media outlets to camp
out. They were stretched out along the sidewalk in front
of the Dobsons' historic Tudor when Nick's patrol car
carved a path into the Dobsons' driveway.

"So, you ready for this?" said Nick.

Emily realized that she couldn't still her quivering
hand. "Actually, now that I'm here… I've never delivered this kind of news, Nick. Dad always did this part."

"Just be straightforward. Like you're giving a diagnosis. That's all you have to do. I'll take care of the rest."

Emily nodded and looked to the front of the house.
The Dobsons had hired two security guards, one sta-
tioned near the front door and one standing off by the
driveway, waiting to escort them inside.

As soon as Nick placed the car in park, the media
descended onto the lawn.

"Stay put a second," Nick said, exiting the car. He
rushed around to her side to open the door while the
bodyguard shielded them from the pressing reporters.

Nick led her past the probing microphones and camera lenses onto the Dobsons' front porch, where the re-

porters were not allowed to be. The bodyguard followed them in and led them down a hallway and into an empty drawing room. They were seated and told that the senator and his wife would be arriving shortly.

A housekeeper entered after a few moments and delivered a tray with coffee. They thanked her, and both downed the liquid adrenaline. Upstairs, they could hear the creaking of the family's footsteps, but no utterance of voices could be discerned.

"My hands won't stop shaking," Emily said under her breath.

"You'll do fine," Nick replied and sent her a confident smile.

"I was at Brown's this morning, and I found out something interesting," Emily said, noticing how professional Nick looked in his smoothly pressed uniform, his hat in his lap.

"The barista said Julie had just broken up with her boyfriend, David," said Emily.

"Breakups happen all the time. You know high school," said Nick. "Relationships are fickle at that age. Right?" Emily detected a touch of sarcasm that she was pretty sure was aimed at her, but she let it go.

"I'm just saying, maybe you should talk to her. Her name's Sadie. Apparently, she knew Julie from school. Unless you have a better lead?"

"Em, you did the autopsy. That's all you need to do. You don't need to go dredging up leads. I'll do the detective work. Got it?" Nick said.

"I can't help what I overhear."

"Or what Delia tells you?"

"I bet you get a lot of good leads from Brown's."

"I swear the population of Freeport exists on baked

goods and gossip," Nick said, grinning. "And while the baked goods are solid, most of the gossip isn't. Besides, you have your dad to focus on. How is he?"

"Stubborn."

"That's a good sign."

Emily heard the Dobsons descending the staircase. She followed Nick's lead and politely rose to greet them. Senator Dobson entered with his wife, Gloria, clinging to his arm. Emily noted how well put together they looked. If she hadn't known the occasion, she would have guessed they were on their way to a luncheon. Both were dressed in business attire. Coat, tie, shoes shined. Dress, hose, heels. Gloria's hair was done, and her makeup did a fairly decent job of masking her swollen eyes.

"Welcome to our home. Please have a seat," Gloria offered as the senator placed her tenderly in an armchair. "Can we get you anything? More coffee?"

"No, thank you, Mrs. Dobson," Nick answered.

"I'm fine, thank you," Emily said. "You have a beautiful home."

Emily immediately regretted adding that. This wasn't afternoon tea.

They all sat awkwardly frozen while Nick made small talk and expressed his condolences. She was wondering when she should speak, when Nick nodded at her and she took this as her cue to give her report.

"Mr. and Mrs. Dobson, I am very sorry for your loss. If you don't mind, I'd like to just get right to the point and discuss the findings of your daughter's autopsy."

The Dobsons nodded. "We think that would be best," said the senator. "It seems like there's some speculation running around, and we'd like to set things straight as soon as possible."

"Of course. To get to the point, my autopsy revealed the cause of Julie's death to be blunt force trauma to the head. I found several fracture areas in the skull, which led to hemorrhaging of the brain. This is the official cause of death."

"So it was an accident?" Gloria interjected. "She fell off her horse and hit her head?"

Emily glanced at Nick, not sure what to do. Nick was about to intervene, when Senator Dobson said, "She didn't fall. Julie's a strong rider. She would never fall during a trail ride. That beast bucked her off. He's been skittish and distracted all summer. I'm having him put down immediately."

"No. Please don't. It's not Mercedes's fault. Julie didn't fall and she wasn't bucked off. I'm afraid it's much worse than that," said Emily as both parents looked at her. "I'm ruling the manner of Julie's death a homicide."

"My daughter was murdered?" Senator Dobson formed the words carefully.

"Somebody killed Julie? Are you sure?" said Gloria, her voice pinched.

"The pattern of the fracture lines indicates several intentional blows to the head. There is no scenario in which this kind of fracture is caused by a fall."

Senator Dobson noticed a cameraman pointing a lens into the picture window, which was draped with a thin lace curtain. The security guard quickly shot over to close the shades. Then, he disappeared into the hall, and Emily could hear him on his two-way radio, communicating with the outside security guard.

"Mr. and Mrs. Dobson, do you have any idea who might have wanted to harm Julie?" asked Nick.

"Absolutely none," said the senator.

"She made friends easily. Everyone liked her," added Gloria. "I mean, she wasn't super popular or anything. But she kept a few close friends and never made any waves."

"She has no enemies," the senator affirmed.

"No, but you may," Nick said. "Anybody you can think of who might do something like this to get back at you or send a message?"

The senator shook his head fervently. "I know there are people who dislike some of the things I stand for. But to kill my baby... I can't think of... It's not reasonable," he sputtered, choking back tears. Gloria shot him a mistrustful glance.

"You have enemies, Gabe. And if you know of anyone who might have done this, you need to speak up. Now."

"Gloria, I swear I don't know," he said.

"You hired two security guards. That says something about you," said Nick. "What are you afraid of?"

Emily wondered if this was part of Nick's tactics. Was he trying to push the senator? See where he might crack?

"Can we please stop wasting time on this?" said Senator Dobson. "What leads do you have?"

"Have you ever received any death threats? Threats on your family?" asked Nick.

"No. Never. And I've never bribed anyone or accepted a bribe, or mishandled funds, or cheated on my income tax! I don't have those kinds of enemies!"

"What kinds of enemies do you have?" said Nick.

"The normal kind. The kind who write me nasty emails because I voted against allowing a medical marijuana facility to set up shop here."

Nick waited for a moment to let the senator calm down. "Have either of you been unfaithful?" said Nick.

"No. Of course not," said Gloria, looking to her husband. "Gabe?"

"Gloria. Darling. No." He went to her side and took her hand.

Gabe's answer seemed to pacify his wife. Still, Emily was curious to see where Nick was going with this line of questioning.

"Okay, let's just go back to yesterday. When was the last time you saw Julie?" Nick asked them.

"I was the last to see her," the senator said. "I dropped her off at the stables on my way to the office."

"What time was that?" Nick asked.

"A little after seven," the senator replied.

"Mrs. Dobson, how about you? When was the last time you saw Julie?" Nick questioned.

"I saw her the night before," Gloria told him. "She was at the kitchen table doing homework. I kissed her goodnight, told her I loved her, and went upstairs." Gloria started to tear up. Emily reached over and handed her a tissue box from the coffee table. Gloria took one and gingerly dabbed away the mascara smudging under her eyes.

"Anything unusual about her behavior recently? Anything out of the ordinary? Was Julie depressed, unhappy, stressed, acting out, or being overly secretive in the past few weeks or months?" Nick went on.

Emily observed how expertly Nick handled the victim's parents. He leaned in when he spoke. Maintained eye contact with them. Let them breathe when they needed to. He knew how to handle people. It had always been his gift, she remembered. And now he was putting it to noble use to serve justice.

"She was stressed about some things," Gloria sniffled.

"What kind of things?" Nick asked.

"College applications. Scholarships. The upcoming state equestrian match," Gloria said.

"Sounds like normal senior-year stuff," Nick replied. Gloria nodded.

"Can you give me the names of anyone else you think I should talk to?" Nick asked.

"Gary Bodum. He owns the stables and does most of the riding instruction. He knew Julie pretty well," said Gloria.

Nick jotted down the name. "How about friends? Teachers?"

"You can find a list of her teachers from the school," said the senator.

Emily found it odd that Senator Dobson didn't know the names of his daughter's teachers and friends. He seemed to be an attentive father, taking his daughter to riding lessons, but perhaps it was part of the politics of being seen in a favorable light.

"Friends?"

"She didn't bring them around here," said Gloria. "At least not when we were home."

"Anyone else come to mind?" Nick asked.

"There was that David Sands fellow," said the senator. Emily side glanced at Nick as if to say, "I told you so."

"Tell me about David," said Nick catching Emily's look. "Did she bring him around?"

"Oh no. They dated last year for a time. We didn't like him from the start. Once they got serious, Julie stopped hanging out with her friends. Her grades dropped. She even started skipping riding lessons," said Gloria.

"Sounds about right for two kids in love for the first time." As Nick said it, a memory flashed into Emily's mind. She and Nick ditching school to go ice fishing. It was the first day the lake was completely frozen over. Nick's dad had built an ice shack for two, complete with stools, a lantern, radio, and six-pack cooler. She sat with Nick all afternoon, drinking hot cocoa from a thermos and catching nothing on her line. It didn't matter that she was shivering the whole time or that she didn't like fishing. It was enough just to be with him. "What about David didn't you like?"

"He was pushing Julie to get married. We wanted her to go to college first. Pursue her riding. Get her degree. Meet other people and have bigger experiences," said Gloria. "We didn't want her tied down at eighteen."

"That seems reasonable to me," Emily said, and Nick shot her a look.

"How did she respond to that?" said Nick.

"She rebelled. So we asked her to stop seeing David. And when that didn't work, we grounded her and forbade him from coming over," the senator said.

"But they didn't stop seeing each other, did they?" asked Nick.

"We know she was sneaking around some," said the senator. "But eventually, things changed."

"Can you explain?" Nick asked.

"Julie lost interest when David started seeing another girl," said Gloria.

Of course, Julie would be depressed, thought Emily as she saw Nick jot down the words *Loretta, Orion's* in his notepad.

What does that mean? Who's Lorretta? She would ask him later.

"I don't want this murder thing going public just yet, Sheriff," the senator said. "I'm asking you to keep this out of the news and protect our privacy until we get some real answers."

"I understand your concern completely. But I can't make any promises," Nick stated. "I don't control the press, and they're practically beating down your door."

"I'm required to make an official registry of cause of death with the county," said Emily.

"How long can that wait?" said the senator.

"Tomorrow?" replied Emily.

"We would appreciate that."

"I'll wait to release the official police statement until six pm tonight," said Nick. "I want you both to know that we will be working tirelessly to find out who did this to your daughter."

Gloria then turned to Nick. "We prefer to control the story when it breaks. If you can just give us a little time. Gabe will call his press secretary to help draft a public statement."

"Of course, that's the right thing to do, dear," said the senator, pressing her hand into his.

"Is there anything else?" said Gloria.

"Do you mind if I take a look around in Julie's bedroom?"

Gloria motioned to a sweeping staircase. "Upstairs. Last door on the left. And if you'll excuse me." Gloria rose and left for the kitchen. Nick headed upstairs, leaving Emily alone with the senator. Her hands had stopped quivering, but she felt uncomfortable in the silence between them.

"Dr. Hartford, thank you for stepping in for your father," the senator said. "We wish him a full and speedy recovery."

"My pleasure. And again, my sympathies on your loss," she replied.

"Security will see you out when you're finished," said the senator as he left the room to join his wife.

Emily stood up and paced the room. She didn't know if she should stay in that stuffy room and wait for Nick. Or just wait in the foyer with the security guard. That would be weird. Or go back to the squad car. Not with all those press out there. Curiosity got the best of her, and she bounded up the stairs to find Nick examining photographs hung in the hallway.

"What are you doing up here?"

"I don't want to sit down there all alone. It feels… sad."

"Fine. But please don't touch anything. Put these on." He handed her a pair of latex gloves. She followed Nick down the long hallway. There must have been eight bedrooms on the second floor.

"They seemed really composed for just learning their daughter was murdered."

"People react in different ways to bad news," said Nick. "Or maybe it's the whole politics thing. They've been under the public eye for so long that they go into robot mode when bad news hits."

"Maybe." She thought they kind of reminded her of Brandon's parents. Good news. Bad news. Always the same stoic look.

"Who's Loretta Orion?" she asked Nick.

"Waitress. She works at Orion's. Told me the Dobsons came in there regularly and that Julie had been acting depressed for a few months."

"I guess that's confirmation," said Emily. "Did she say why?"

Nick shook his head.

Nick and Emily went to the last room on the left. The door was open. They entered, and Emily's eyes traveled to an impressive wall plastered with Julie's equestrian trophies, ribbons, clippings, and awards.

"Wow. She was accomplished," said Emily. "Not that I know much about the equestrian world."

While Nick was rummaging through Julie's dresser drawers, Emily's attention was drawn to a scuffling noise from inside the room. She walked toward it, but Nick pulled her back and drew his gun, moving slowly toward the closet and, putting a finger to his lips, motioning for Emily to be quiet.

Nick threw open the door, training his weapon on a tear-stained and bewildered teenage girl sitting on the floor, clutching a photo album. She let out a little scream when she saw the barrel of Nick's gun pointed at her. Nick immediately lowered it, and Emily jumped over to see who was in there.

"Hello? Sorry to startle you. We didn't know there was anyone in here. I'm Dr. Emily Hartford. And this man is Sheriff Larson."

Emily stepped between Nick and the girl as her diminutive figure shrugged a half-hearted hello. "I'm Sarah. Julie's sister."

"We're really sorry about Julie," Emily said.

"Sarah, I'm gonna have to ask you to please step

out of the closet," said Nick. "Emily, could you take her into the hall?"

Emily reached in to help Sarah up. "Sheriff Larson just needs to take a quick look around. Okay?"

Sarah nodded and Emily led them into the hallway. They took a seat on a wooden bench between two bed-rooms.

"Pictures of you and Julie?" said Emily, pointing to the photo album wrapped in Sarah's arms.

Sarah shook her head and cracked the book open so Emily could take a look. It was a brag book of Julie's equestrian conquests. In most of the pictures, Julie wore the victor's ribbon. Sarah flipped through the pages as Emily made small comments.

"Who's that guy next to Julie? I keep seeing him," Emily said, pointing to a newspaper clipping of Julie with a first-place trophy and a young man standing next to her and holding up a second-place trophy.

"That's Vince. He and Julie have been competing since their freshman year," said Sarah.

"Looks like Julie does most of the winning," Emily said with a comforting tone.

Sarah nodded and turned the page to a picture of Julie sitting proudly atop Mercedes.

"So, I'm just curious, what happened to your sis-ter's horse?"

"Mercedes went to the vet's ranch to Dr. Lillen. I'm afraid my dad will put him down," said Sarah.

"I hope that doesn't happen," Emily answered.

"Me too. He doesn't deserve it. It's not his fault," said Sarah.

"What's not his fault?" Emily was curious to know what Sarah had been told.

"Her accident."

Emily remained silent.

"You were the doctor who looked at my sister, right?" Sarah asked.

"Yes, I was. I did," said Emily.

"Did you find out why she had an accident?"

"I did. Probably best for you to talk with your parents about it."

"They won't tell me the whole truth," said Sarah.

"They won't? Why not?"

"They don't think I'll understand."

"How old are you?"

"Fifteen."

Emily could relate. She wished someone had sat her down after her mom died and told her the truth. Her father hadn't. Or couldn't. No police officer or family friend ever broached the subject with her. And when she tried, they dodged her questions. And there were so many unanswered questions that still hung in the balance from that early fall day of her mother's accident. A surge of anger ripped up in Emily.

In that moment, Emily decided that she needed to level with Sarah. She wouldn't trust the Dobsons to do it. Parents could be overly protective to the detriment of what was actually good for their children. She would not run the risk of allowing Sarah to endure years of emotional torment like she had.

"Julie was killed because somebody struck her."

Sarah blinked and kept calm. Too calm. For a second, Emily wondered if Sarah might freak out. What would she do? She hadn't thought that telling Sarah the truth might backfire on her. But instead, Sarah just looked at Emily with remarkable maturity as it sunk in.

"Did it hurt her?" she asked.

"Probably a little. But only for a second until she blacked out."

Sarah glanced down at the photograph of her sister. Then she looked up at Emily, "Who would hurt my sister?"

"That's what we're trying to find out."

Sarah looked up at her with the empty eyes of a confused fifteen-year-old whose world had just been shaken to the core. The yearning to provide Sarah with some answer that would ease her agony swelled in Emily. A simple trip home had mushroomed into something bigger and deeper, touching on places of Emily's life that she hadn't examined for a long time. But there were no coincidences; Emily believed this. So why now? Why Sarah? Why Emily? There was no uncertainty about whether this was meant to be; Emily was meant to help Sarah through this.

Nick came out of the room, snapping his gloves off. "I'm all set. Thank you for letting us intrude, Sarah."

Sarah responded with a doleful look as Nick headed toward the stairs. "I thought of a few more questions for the senator," he told Emily. "Meet me downstairs when you're done."

"Okay. I'll just be a minute," she responded and turned to Sarah. "I know it's hard to believe right now, but it won't always feel this awful and raw. I promise."

"It hurts right here." Sarah put her hand in the middle of her chest. "Like my lungs are going to collapse."

"I know. Just keep getting up every day. Talk to her. Like she's here. It helps."

"Dr. Emily, did Julie have her bracelet on?" asked Sarah.

Emily was unsure. Had she missed something during the autopsy? "Can you describe it?"

Sarah held up her wrist to reveal a gorgeous silver bracelet loaded with charms.

"Like this. We had matching ones. Different charms, of course."

"I'm sorry, I didn't see anything like that," said Emily. Disappointment spread over Sarah's face.

"Can you find it? Please?"

"You're sure it's not in her room? I can help you look."

"It's not. I looked a million times," Sarah said.

"Have you checked the stables?"

This caused Sarah's gaze to go to her feet. She choked back a few tears. "I can't go there. Please. Julie never took it off. Can you look for me?"

"I'll tell you what. I'll have Sheriff Larson send an officer out."

"No, I want you to do it."

Emily was impacted by Sarah's woeful insistence. She couldn't deny that she connected deeply with Sarah's heartache. In these past few minutes, she and Sarah had formed an inexplicable bond. A silent pact. If only someone had been Emily's advocate during the time of her mother's tragic passing. Perhaps her life and her relationship with her father would look a lot different than it did now.

Emily felt her father's request to revisit the scene gnawing at her. She knew it was the right thing to do, and she wanted to find that bracelet for Sarah. Did she need to tell Nick that she wanted to look at the scene? She didn't want him to think she was going behind his back. He might not understand, and she didn't want to cause a row. He had enough on his plate right now. He didn't need to be traipsing around the countryside looking for a lost charm bracelet. And really, it wasn't like she would be stepping into the territory. She wouldn't be questioning anyone or handling any interrogations. The scene wasn't cordoned off. Anyone could go out there. It was fair game. And if she did find anything out of the ordinary, she would call Nick immediately.

"Sure, I'll take a look for you," Emily told her.

Immediately, Sarah's arms encircled Emily in a hug. "I miss her so much."

I get it, thought Emily. *I so get it.*

SIXTEEN

EMILY EXITED HER car and wandered through Premiere Equestrian Center stables toward the office located at the back of the large barn. She hoped the owner, Gary Bodum, would be able to escort her to the site where Julie's body had been found.

She reached the office and found the door closed and locked. On Bodum's desk was a half-eaten breakfast sandwich and a glass of soda, bubbles fizzing up the sides. He was here. Or had been here recently. Emily took her time strolling through the barn and scanning the area for any sight of Julie's charm bracelet.

Up ahead she noticed a stall adorned with flowers, ribbons, handwritten notes, and candles. It belonged to Julie and Mercedes. She stopped to admire it and noticed some of the newspaper clippings were the same ones she had seen in Julie's album.

"You here to pay your respects?" said a deep male voice from behind her.

Emily turned to see a man in his forties approaching with a long, thin tool in his hand. He was looking inquisitively at her.

"I'm Dr. Emily Hartford."

"Gary Bodum. Owner and trainer," he said.

"Just the person I was looking for."

"You're Doc's daughter," he said.

"Yes, that's right," she replied.

"I thought you ran away to Connecticut or something, like, ten years ago?"

"Chicago. I went to live with my aunt in Chicago."

"I heard your old man suffered a heart attack. How's he doing?" Gary asked.

"He'll pull through."

"He took a big hit," Gary said. "Tell him I said hello and wish him a speedy recovery."

"Do you know my father well?"

"As well as anyone does here in Freeport. Run into him at the Farm and Feed from time to time."

"I see."

"And a couple years ago he did an autopsy on one of the horses that died suddenly."

"He did?" Emily had no idea her father's business extended to the animal kingdom.

"Was hit by a fast-attacking viral disease, and because of your dad's findings, we were able to treat and save the rest of the stable."

"That's a happy ending," said Emily. "Nice memorial you've got set up here."

"I didn't have much to do with it. People kept bringing things. I'm not really used to strangers just dropping by, but I think it's important for folks to be able to grieve," said Gary.

"You trained Julie, didn't you?" she asked.

"Since she was ten."

"I'm sorry for your loss."

Gary lowered his gaze and fixed it on the empty stable.

"So, was it an accident?" said Gary.

"I can't really comment on that just yet," Emily said.

"I understand. Let me know if there's anything I can do," he said.

"There may be something. This may seem like a weird question, but you didn't happen to find a silver bracelet with a lot of charms?"

"I know which one you're talking about. Julie never took it off. But no, I haven't seen it."

Emily glanced toward the pasture behind the stables. She surmised that the site of Julie's demise lay somewhere in those fields. "Do you mind telling me how to get to the scene of the...the accident?"

"I can do better than that. I can take you out there," said Gary. "You ride, don't you?"

Emily nodded slightly, "I've ridden. Before." Which was the truth, but it had been years.

"I'll saddle up one of my older, gentler ones," Gary said, noting her apprehension.

"That sounds good," replied Emily. She followed Gary into the stables.

"After Farmer Gibbons found Julie, we went out looking for Mercedes and found him about a quarter mile from Julie's body," Gary said.

"Was he okay?"

"He was injured. Couldn't get up to walk."

They reached a stall marked "Laney." Inside was a beautiful brown mare with jet-black eyes and a light brown mane. Emily reached out her hand, and Laney nudged it playfully.

"I called Dr. Lillen, the vet, and she rushed over, gave him something to calm him down and loaded him into her horse trailer so she could bring him back to her ranch."

Gary strapped a blanket and saddle onto Laney. As

he snugged up the saddle, he took one look at Emily's slim black dress pants and heeled boots.

"I got some extra sets of waders hanging up by the office. You might wanna put on a pair. It can be pretty mucky out there, especially down by the creek, where Julie was found. You can slip 'em right over your own boots." Emily looked down at her prized Italian leather footwear, which she had saved up for and purchased on a vacation to Milan the year before. They were coated in sawdust. She turned up the bottom of her right heel to discover a small patch of matted manure on the sole.

"I'll take you up on that. My footwear is more familiar with asphalt and concrete."

Gary pointed her toward the office and told her he would meet her in the riding area with Laney. Emily found her way back to the office, where there was a line of waders hanging from wooden pegs along the wall. They seemed to all be about the same size, so Emily grabbed the nearest pair and pulled them on over her boots and pants.

Emily waddled out to the ring in her waders, which were three sizes too big. Gary was already there waiting with Laney. He boosted Emily onto the old mare and gave Emily a quick riding refresher. Soon they were off, with Gary leading out of the ring toward the pasture beyond.

"So, you were the only one here that morning?" Emily called up to Gary, who steered them onto a dirt trail.

"Yeah. I was the first employee in here. Got here about eight," Gary replied. "Tim is supposed to come in around seven and get things opened up. Feed the horses. Exercise them."

"Tim?"

"My stable hand and groom," Gary said. "He cares for all horses in the barn."

"What time did he arrive?" she continued.

"He was late that day. Came in about eight thirty. I was livid."

"Did he say where he had been?"

"Home," said Gary. "Vehicle trouble, I think, or some such excuse."

"And was anyone else here that morning?" she asked.

"Not that I know of, and I really doubt it. But in all fairness, the horse owners all have keys to the stables so they can have access to their horses at any time," Gary said.

"And when did you notice something was off?" Emily asked.

"I was saddling up my horse to take a ride when Jack Gibbons from the farm just north of my pasture pulled up in his pickup with Julie's body in the back."

"So, help me understand this: Why did he remove her from the scene?"

"Thought there was something that could be done for her. There isn't any cell service out there, and he didn't want to leave her," Gary said.

These people have no idea how much they screwed up this case, Emily thought, pursing her lips to keep her exasperation from slipping out and giving anything away.

"Gary, for the future, it might be helpful for you all to know that it's illegal to touch a dead body before the medical examiner does," she said.

"Thank you for the pointer, but I hope I'm never again in a position to remember that," said Gary.

Emily knew this one misstep could throw a monkey wrench into the investigation, especially once it got before a judge. There was a chance it might be dismissed altogether if it was ruled that evidence had been tampered with.

Gary's horse trotted up ahead, leaving Emily and Laney to lag a little behind in a steady pace that allowed Emily time to think. For the rest of the way, she rode silently along the trail running along the edge of the pasture. She found she had nothing to distract her. No iPhone. No texts. No surgical procedures to prep for. No annoying passengers on the "L." It was refreshing, like a burden lifted, and she felt lighter. She relaxed into the atmosphere, drinking it in with all her senses. The sky was heavy with thick, gray, billowy clouds that held the promise of rain. The smell of the musty ground rose up. The grasses were browned and rustling in the wind. It was the only sound.

She had forgotten how quiet the world could be without the constant roar of trains, horns, sirens, people yelling. She breathed in and out. In and out, each exhale releasing notch by notch the tension she continually carried with her. By the time they reached the outskirts of the scene of Julie's homicide, Emily discovered she had completely given herself over to the country. She didn't have to fight off the hundred distractions that were usually coming at her in the city. She was simply focused, calm, and clear headed. It was the best meditation she had experienced in years.

Gary stopped his horse, and Emily did the same. Gary pointed north, "Over there, under that grove of trees by the stream. That's where she was lying."

"I think I'll just slip off my horse and walk in from here," Emily said.

"If you give me a minute to tie these guys up, I can go with you," Gary offered.

"No, thanks. I'd like to preserve the scene as much as possible," Emily said. "Please. Just stay here."

"All right, then." Gary grabbed Laney's reins as Emily dismounted.

"Have there been a lot of folks out here since her body was found?"

"Not that I'm aware of."

"Sherriff Larson?"

"He and his crew came for half a day. Cordoned off the area. Did their photographs and searches, then cleared it."

"Yeah, it's difficult to prevent animals and weather from intruding on what's theirs by nature."

Emily strode over the small crest that led to the stream. She was careful to watch her steps and the ground below her feet for any remaining shreds of evidence that might have been missed. It was not that she didn't trust Nick. She just knew, from many experiences returning to scenes with her dad, that even in the best circumstances, no one is perfect, and police resources are limited and the force overworked. Sometimes, things got overlooked because they were hidden in the first place, under soil, leaves, branches. These pieces of evidence weren't necessarily useful in court, but they might prove helpful to the case in some other way. Like her father had always taught her, you had to stay open to possibilities and think outside the box. Criminals often did things, and left things, without thinking.

She stopped about thirty feet from the stream and took in the entire scene, trying to recreate the murder in her mind. A few small, wild shrubs gathered here and there along the trail, big enough to shield an adult from view. If the killer were on foot, he would have to traverse the narrow path into and out of the stream. Julie would have heard and seen him coming. She would have had time to change course or turn around. That is, if she suspected danger.

What if the killer was someone she knew? Maybe someone from the stables? Another rider? A horse owner? A trainer? A local who knew the back trails between the farms?

Emily crept her way closer, scanning the ground. She started to spot numerous shoeprints crossing the scene in all directions, realizing quickly they belonged to Nick and his police team. And probably a set to Jack Gibbons and Gary Bodum.

Emily padded toward the stream. She could easily identify the spot where Julie's body had lain. In a small area near the edge of the stream, the weeds and river grass were matted to the ground. As she drew closer, she could see an imprint of small geometric impressions in the mud. Curious, Emily studied it a little longer, soon determining the impressions were from the charms of a bracelet. A tiny horse. A horseshoe. And a heart.

SEVENTEEN

Nick learned from the secretary at Freeport High School that David Sands had been absent the day Julie was found dead and hadn't been back to school since. So he drove to David's home and found him sitting on the front porch, a distant, apathetic look on his face.

"David Sands?" Nick inquired.

"Yeah, I'm David."

"I need to talk with you. Do you have a minute?"

"I guess so," he said.

"Are your parents around?" Nick asked as he approached. "It'd be nice to have them present for this."

"Why? Am I in trouble?"

"No. Not that I'm aware of. I just want to talk with you about Julie Dobson," explained Nick. Nick had looked up David's birth date and knew that he had turned eighteen two months ago. He was legally an adult, and it wasn't required that his parents be present if Nick wanted to question him. But Nick felt it was always better to get parental support when possible.

"They're at work," said David. Nick couldn't wait.

"I'm Sheriff Nick Larson." Nick asked, "David, I wonder if you could tell me where you were yesterday morning?" Nick saw he had David's full attention now.

"Home. In bed. I overslept."

"What time did you get up?"

"My dad woke me up on his way out to work. So

maybe eight thirty?" David said. "He got me up and told me I had to get to school."

"So did you go then?"

"Nah, I slept another hour, and then I got up and was eating some breakfast when my buddy called about Julie…he had heard she was found…"

David started to break. Nick gave him a moment to compose himself. He understood how the death of someone you know could be upsetting, but David's reaction seemed normal for someone who had been close to the victim, even if he was an ex.

"It's okay. Take your time," Nick offered.

"Do you know how she died?" asked David.

"We're still investigating that," Nick said. "I was under the impression you two had broken up and gone your separate ways. I don't mean to pry, but you seem really broken up about her death for an ex-boyfriend. You must have really loved her."

"I do…did…love her," David said, fresh tears welling up his eyes.

"The Dobsons said Julie lost interest when you found a new girlfriend and moved on," said Nick.

A brief smile touched David's lips, and he wiped the wet from his eyes. "I guess it worked then."

"What worked?"

"Her dad made us break up. He hated me. We snuck around for a while, but then he started having his security guard spy on us. So Julie thought maybe we needed to cool it," said David. "I started fake dating my friend Jenny to get them off our backs," he said.

"So you never really broke up," said Nick.

David shook his head. "We were planning to get married," he said. "As soon as she graduated and turned eighteen."

Nick made a note of it. Scorned lovers defying parental odds. It was a tale as old as humanity. He had to give them credit for their ingenuity. They had fooled her parents, Sadie the barista, and the whole high school.

"Was there anybody Julie had an issue with? Or disliked?" Nick asked.

"Why are you wondering that?" said David, curiosity rising in his tone. "I thought it was an accident?"

"I'm just trying to rule things out. Please don't read anything into the question. It's part of the investigation," said Nick, playing it down. "Anyone she had a beef with?"

"Not really. She was on good terms with pretty much everyone. But you know, Julie didn't have a lot of time for a social life. Most of her friends were from the stables."

"What was life at the stables like for her?"

"Mostly good. Like a family. Except lately she was really angry with Bodum."

"Tell me about that."

"There were bad things happening at the stables and Bodum wasn't doing a darn thing about it," David said.

"Bad things? Like what?" Nick asked.

"To Mercedes. Someone was coming in at night before the competitions and tying up his head so it would drop more in the ring. She also found dye on his coat, which gave him skin rashes. And she suspected his tail was being deadened so it would lie still during competitions."

"Did she tell Bodum?"

"Yeah. She wanted Bodum to install video cameras

so they could catch the person doing it. Bodum said he couldn't afford it. Julie even begged her dad to pay for it."

"Did he?"

"No. He thought she was crazy. Said she was making those things up in her imagination."

Nick jotted these things down. He had heard about such things happening at barns, but never suspected mistreatment at Premiere.

"What did Bodum think?"

"None of the other horses were bothered, so he thought maybe Julie's dad had a point. Julie was really protective of Mercedes. He told Julie he would have the grooms keep an eye out for anything unusual," said David.

"But this was clearly abuse," Nick said. "Why didn't she report it?"

"We talked about it. But we knew that would cause Gary and Premiere to go under investigation, maybe have his barn shut down. Gary's the best trainer in the state. He's been with Julie since she was eight. Julie didn't want to lose him in her senior year."

"What about an anonymous call?" Nick asked. "Did she or you ever think about that?"

"Nothing's anonymous. Mercedes was the only horse being hurt. She wouldn't. She thought it would raise too many red flags, and she might be disqualified from competing. Julie did what she could to protect Mercedes, short of sleeping at the stables. The stress was really making her performances suffer. I was worried it would jeopardize her scholarship chances. And that scholarship money was her freedom ticket."

"What do you mean? Julie was headed to college either way, right?"

"Yeah, but a scholarship meant she could break financial ties with her dad."

"It was that bad?"

"They're controlling. You've met them."

"They seem like normal, concerned parents to me."

David didn't respond. Nick mulled all this over in his mind. There was nothing about Julie disliking Bodum that pointed to motivation for murder. Bodum may have been irresponsible in turning a blind eye to the abuse or siding with the senator, but would he want Julie dead? It was almost impossible to draw the connection. Nick had gleaned all he could for the time being.

"Thanks, David. Let me know if you think of anything else," Nick told him. "I'm really sorry for your loss. I know it doesn't feel like it now, but your life's not over. There will be good moments again."

"But not with her," David noted. "She was the one, you know?" David kept his gaze on the front yard, and all Nick could think was, *Yeah, I do know*, as he walked back to his patrol car, wishing he had taken the time to sort through his locker on that last day of junior year.

EIGHTEEN

EMILY DROVE FROM Premiere straight to the police station and waited for Nick to return. She was standing in the lobby when he arrived through a back door. She could see him bustling to his office with a worried look on his face.

"Surprised to see you here," said Nick.

"You have a minute?"

He motioned for her to follow him to his office.

"Learn anything new since our visit to the Dobsons?" she asked.

Nick told her about his conversation with David and that he felt that Gary had no real motivation to kill Julie Dobson. Emily thought it was odd that Gary was so unwilling to stop the abuse on Mercedes.

"Did someone threaten Gary to keep quiet? Who would be abusing Mercedes like that? And where was Gary Bodum when Julie was being killed?"

"I know. I have the same questions," Nick replied.

"Nick, I went to the pasture this afternoon," said Emily. "Just to take a second look."

"Okay."

He didn't seem surprised or upset about it.

"Sarah asked me to look for something of Julie's. A bracelet. Bodum said Julie always had it on."

"Did you find it?"

"Well, not exactly. I found this, though."

Emily took out her phone and pulled up pictures she had snapped of the charm impressions in the mud. He paused for a moment as his brow furrowed, and color rose in his cheeks.

"I can't believe I missed that. I combed through that area a dozen times."

"Well, you didn't exactly know that you were supposed to be looking for it," said Emily.

"Did Sarah really tell you about this? Or did your dad ask you to do this?"

"It was Sarah," she said. "And a little bit my dad."

"I knew it. He doesn't trust us cops to do our job."

"Don't take it personally. It started a long time before you became a cop."

"Look, Em, when I first arrived on the scene, I wasn't even aware that her death was a murder. Her body was gone. I had nothing to go on. We all thought it was an accident. And truth is, that whole area was compromised the moment Farmer Gibbons stepped in and removed her body. It was a huge guess just trying to figure out what was within the scope of the scene and what wasn't," Nick defended. "I'm still not entirely sure."

"I know. I'm not blaming you. It was a tough situation," said Emily. "I was just trying to… Nick, I didn't come to Freeport to try and usurp your job. I just really feel for Sarah. I want to do everything I can." The whole thing seemed so surreal. Thirty hours ago she had been in Chicago, saving lives and getting engaged. Now she was standing in the Freeport Sherriff's Office, helping her high school sweetheart solve a murder case.

"The question now is, where is that bracelet?" said Nick moving on.

"I scoured the field and the stables and didn't see it. My next thought is to check with Farmer Gibbons. He was the first person that we know of who saw Julie after she died."

"You think he took the bracelet? What would he want with it?"

"I don't know. But I looked this up. It's a Pandora and they're worth a lot of money. Hundreds. It would have been an easy steal."

"I have a hard time believing Farmer Gibbons is a grave robber," said Nick.

"Probably not. Maybe it fell off her wrist and some curious person trolling through the field found it after your investigation? Or maybe the killer took it? Just find out if Gibbons noticed the bracelet was on when he found Julie."

Nick sighed, "I've already questioned him, but I'll pay him another visit. And I'll put a search out at the local pawn shops."

"Thank you. That bracelet means a lot to Sarah."

At that moment, Emily's and Nick's phones pinged simultaneously. An incoming text with an attached video link from Jo was coming through: Have you seen this?!

Emily clicked on the link to a YouTube video with the title "Find This Man Who Killed My Sister."

"Oh no. Sarah, what have you done?" said Emily as she touched the "Play" icon.

The roughly shot video came from a GoPro camera that seemed to be attached to the inside of a horse pen at thigh level. The video captured the horse's legs, which looked sleek black and muscular; as the camera lens tilted up, they could see the horse was male. After a couple of moments, a shadowed person wearing men's jeans and work boots entered the stall. Mercedes whinnied and stamped his hooves at the ominous presence, as if he knew something bad was about to happen to him. Swinging from the man's hand was a tool that neither Emily nor Nick could fully identify because of the poor lighting conditions. What they could see was that the man grabbed one of Mercedes' legs with one hand and used the tool in his other hand to score the horse's legs. The beast whinnied in pain and tried to wriggle free. The man managed to steady Mercedes and continue the horrible abuse, but in the process unknowingly knocked the GoPro off its mount. The camera tumbled to the floor in a blur, landing at a slightly upright angle that caught a darkened image of the horse's head. The camera caught just enough light to reveal that the horse was Mercedes. After a moment, all was still. The sound of the man's boots faded away. Mercedes shook his mane and restlessly stamped his legs against the sides of the pen, jostling the GoPro to face the floor. The video went black and ended.

"How did Sarah get this?" Emily glanced at the number of views. "This video has over 25,378 hits. And counting."

Nick moved the "Play" button back a few seconds and hit "Pause" when the man's boots came into view, freezing the image.

"There's your killer. Not a lot to go on."

"But more than we had two minutes ago."

Emily locked looks with Nick. The stakes had definitely changed.

"Who do you think did it?" a parent piped up from the benches.

"We are currently interviewing a number of people who may have information. But I can't reveal the names of any suspects."

"What about that monster in that video?" shouted a father dressed in a business suit. "You need get your hands on him."

"You are right, sir—that's a very troubling video. And we are currently investigating its source."

A mother stood up and pointed at Nick. "I wanna know if my kids are safe. Do we have a serial killer on the loose here?"

"Oh no, no, ma'am. I wouldn't jump to that conclusion. This seems to be an isolated incident. However, I would always advise that you keep tabs on your kids and know where they are and who they are with. Let's continue to act with common sense and safety in our community. Let's watch out for one another like we always do. And if you hear of anything or see anything, please contact the sheriff's office."

The questions of unease and paranoia went on for another twenty minutes. Nick did his best to quell any rumors and conjectures before the principal dismissed the students and teachers back to class. As parents trickled out of the auditorium, Nick overheard the doubts of many of them. How could this have happened to one of their own? Was no place safe anymore? Maybe they needed a more competent police force? Was Larson really equipped for this kind of terror in the community? What if another dead body cropped up? What if the killer was another student? Was the video really real? Or just a publicity stunt the senator had arranged? Little arguments sprung up between exiting parents. Tensions were mounting before his eyes and would soon spread out into the community.

The only thing left for Nick to try was damage control via media. He led the journalists outside the school property to willingly answer a few more questions for them. He kept the sound bites neutral and diplomatic.

Yes, the Freeport Police were doing everything in their power to find Julie's killer.

Yes, he had employed the help of the state police who were sifting through the dozens of tips coming in each day.

Yes, each tip was being carefully recorded and explored.

No, he could not comment on whether or not the tips had revealed anything significant to find the suspect or suspects.

No, he could not say with certainty whether there was just one suspect or multiple suspects.

No, he was not aware that Julie was not cheating in the ring.

No, he was not aware that the senator was not buying off her competition wins.

No, he did not feel responsible for Gibbons moving the body from the scene.

No, he did not believe the scene had been compromised by Gibbons removing the body.

Yes, he had been properly trained in crime scene investigation.

Nick kept a straight face and even tone as he told them he was through taking questions. He politely excused himself and drew back into the school to find Emily. She was waiting on a threadbare tweed couch

NINETEEN

AFTER THE VIDEO DROPPED, twice the number of media descended instantly upon Freeport and landed at the high
school where Sarah Dobson was in class. Nick called
Emily to go with him to the school so she could talk
to Sarah, as they had formed a bond over the missing
bracelet. Once they arrived at the school, Emily was
directed to the teacher's lounge, where Sarah was waiting. Emily found her standing at the window, chewing
the corner of one of her nails.

"Sarah, how are you doing?" said Emily.

"I don't know."

"Do you need anything to drink?"

"No."

"You want to tell me what happened?"

Sarah turned and faced Emily, and she could see
that Sarah had been crying. Emily could tell by her
eyes that dark thoughts were swirling around in Sarah's
mind. She remained patient and professional, hoping
that Sarah would open up to her. The click, click, click
of the second hand moving around the face of the large
clock on the wall marked the passage of thirty seconds.
It seemed like a lifetime to Emily. Finally, Sarah spoke.

"Everyone thinks we're this perfect, happy family.
But we're not."

"All families have secrets, Sarah."

"Not like ours."

"You'd be surprised. My family has secrets. Did you know my mother died in a car accident when I was fifteen?" Emily saw that Sarah was engaged with her now. "It happened one early fall morning. Perfect weather. Great road conditions. Nothing wrong with her vehicle. After the investigation, no one could tell me what really happened. Even my own father."

"Why?"

"Exactly. That's a 'why' I've been living with all my life. And I want to make sure you don't have to live with any *whys* or secrets. Can you help me?"

Sarah nodded.

"Do you know anything about what you saw on that video?"

"I don't. I hardly ever went to the stable. That was Julie's thing."

"Do you have any idea who it is in that video?"

"If I did, I wouldn't have posted it." She was sounding defensive...and scared.

"I believe you.

"Is there anything you can share with me that would help us find out who killed your sister?"

Sarah's eyes darted across the room, then back to Emily. Classic aversion. *She knows something, and she's not gonna spill,* thought Emily, who did not let up her compassionate gaze on Sarah.

"Did you find the bracelet?" asked Sarah, fidgeting with the zipper on her sweatshirt.

"Not yet. But I won't give up. Promise."

"Am I in big trouble?"

"Well, you certainly stirred things up," said Emily.

"I thought posting it would help you find out who killed her."

"I understand." Emily paused to choose her words carefully. "But Sarah, do you realize you interfered with a police investigation here?"

"Did I ruin it?"

"I don't know." Emily had to be honest. "Hopefully not. The police are grateful to have another lead in the case. But you should know, for the future, that in criminal investigations there are pieces of evidence, like this video recording, that should be held back from the public until the police can puzzle it out, put it all together, and a proper arrest can be made. Does that make sense?"

"You must hate me?" Sarah squeaked out.

"I don't hate you. No one hates you."

"I'm so sorry."

"I know you are. I know you were just trying to help."

"My parents are gonna kill me."

"I doubt that. But if there are any secrets you want to share, you can come to me. Or Nick. Anytime. Okay? It's always best to get them out in the open."

Sarah nodded and Emily gave her a hug. At that moment, the lounge doors flew open. Mr. and Mrs. Dobson charged in, ready to devour their one remaining daughter.

TWENTY

MEANWHILE, NICK HAD a problem on his hands. The press were legally allowed to enter the high school but had besieged administration by splitting into all directions to find students and teachers to interview as they exited rooms between classes. The principal had lost control. Nick called in for backup to corral the intruding journalists, but they refused to back down, stating their grounds as freedom of the press rights, compelling Nick to create a more organized means of information gathering. Meanwhile, scores of concerned parents began arriving after receiving texts from their kids that there was chaos erupting at the school. The parents wanted an explanation. And they wanted it now! Nick decided on the spot to hold a press conference, and instructed his police officers to direct parents and students to the auditorium, where he could address them about the matter at hand.

Once they were all settled, the principal introduced Nick. and he stepped forward to face a couple hundred probing stares.

"We appreciate your cooperation in gathering here and I'll do my best to apprise you of what's going on and answer any questions that I can. Currently, we are holding an investigation into the death of Julie Dobson, and we do believe that it was a homicide."

"Who do you think did it?" a parent piped up from the benches.

"We are currently interviewing a number of people who may have information. But I can't reveal the names of any suspects."

"What about that monster in that video?" shouted a father dressed in a business suit. "You need get your hands on him."

"You are right, sir—that's a very troubling video. And we are currently investigating its source."

A mother stood up and pointed at Nick. "I wanna know if my kids are safe. Do we have a serial killer on the loose here?"

"Oh no, no, ma'am. I wouldn't jump to that conclusion. This seems to be an isolated incident. However, I would always advise that you keep tabs on your kids and know where they are and who they are with. Let's continue to act with common sense and safety in our community. Let's watch out for one another like we always do. And if you hear of anything or see anything, please contact the sheriff's office."

The questions of unease and paranoia went on for another twenty minutes. Nick did his best to quell any rumors and conjectures before the principal dismissed the students and teachers back to class. As parents trickled out of the auditorium, Nick overheard the doubts of many of them. How could this have happened to one of their own? Was no place safe anymore? Maybe they needed a more competent police force? Was Larson really equipped for this kind of terror in the community? What if another dead body cropped up? What if the killer was another student? Was the video really real? Or just a publicity stunt the senator had arranged? Little arguments sprung up between exiting parents. Tensions were mounting before his eyes and would soon spread out into the community.

The only thing left for Nick to try was damage control via media. He led the journalists outside the school property to willingly answer a few more questions for them. He kept the sound bites neutral and diplomatic.

Yes, the Freeport Police were doing everything in their power to find Julie's killer.

Yes, he had employed the help of the state police who were sifting through the dozens of tips coming in each day.

Yes, each tip was being carefully recorded and explored.

No, he could not comment on whether or not the tips had revealed anything significant to find the suspect or suspects.

No, he could not say with certainty whether there was just one suspect or multiple suspects.

No, he was not aware that Julie was not cheating in the ring.

No, he was not aware that the senator was not buying off her competition wins.

No, he did not feel responsible for Gibbons moving the body from the scene.

No, he did not believe the scene had been compromised by Gibbons removing the body.

Yes, he had been properly trained in crime scene investigation.

Nick kept a straight face and even tone as he told them he was through taking questions. He politely excused himself and drew back into the school to find Emily. She was waiting on a threadbare tweed couch in the teacher's lounge with a strained look on her face. Sarah was gone.

"Her parents came to sneak her out of the building while you and the entire population of Freeport were in the auditorium."

"Did she tell you anything?" asked Nick, collapsing onto the couch next to her.

"Only that she was sorry," said Emily.

"What about her parents?"

"They were pretty hot about it when they came storming in here. Sarah told them she didn't want to go home with them. And then she bolted."

"Where?"

"She took off toward the parking lot. I don't think she got very far before the media surrounded her. I saw the security guard run over to help her into her parents' truck," said Emily. "Then they drove away. I swear, Freeport's gone crazy with this."

Nick shook his head, worried that if he didn't solve this thing soon, it would not only tear apart the Dobson family but the whole town.

TWENTY-ONE

AFTER THE ANXIOUS AFTERNOON, Emily returned to the hospital to visit her dad. Before stepping into his room, she found the cardiologist doing rounds and asked for a moment of his time to get her dad's medical diagnosis first hand.

"Three of the four vessels are completely clogged. And as you can see, the fourth is about half open," said the cardiologist. "He needs a quadruple bypass or he's not going to last more than a year."

"Can you do that here?" she asked.

"I prefer to do the procedure at the hospital in Rock River. They have better equipment and more experienced staff. I've worked with them before and never had a problem."

"When can you get him scheduled?"

"Immediately," he said. "But your father has refused the surgery."

"That doesn't make any sense. He knows what he's up against if he doesn't have the procedure, right?"

"He's quite aware. Which is exactly why he's concerned. It's a big surgery. Long recovery," the cardiologist said.

"How long for someone in his shape?" Emily asked.

"Three or four months until he can resume a semi-active lifestyle," said the doctor. "I'd say a good six months before he gets the all clear to return to work."

"And he knows that without it he's advised to be pretty much sedentary?"

"He knows. I'm just hoping you can convince him to pursue a better option for his life."

"I'm not sure I have much sway," said Emily. "Did you talk to Cathy?"

"Yes. And she feels like she's in the same boat as you are. Please try your best," said the cardiologist. "We'd hate to lose him so soon."

"I'll try. Thank you," she said, but she felt scant faith in her ability to do so.

Riding up the elevator to her father's room, Emily gazed at the images of her father's heart, wondering how on earth she was going to handle this. As she drew closer to her father's room, she could hear familiar laughter. Jo and Cathy were with him. That was a good sign. At least he'd be in a good mood. Emily entered to find Jo standing at the foot of his bed and Cathy sitting in a chair by his side. Jo was telling him some story about her children that he was thoroughly eating up. Emily paused for a minute as Jo finished her story. She started wondering what it might be like to be in Jo's place. Would it ever be like that between her father and her? Would she ever be joking with her dad about his grandchildren? Children. She and Brandon hadn't had a serious talk about children. She assumed he wanted them. She knew his mother sure did. Did she? Did she want to bring children into a city riddled with gang warfare, drugs, and murder? But then, here she was. Investigating a murder case in Freeport. No place was safe. How on earth would she ever feel she could be responsible for the life of a child? And what if that life were taken away unexpectedly? It was painful enough when her mother died. How could she ever bear the death of a child? What torment the Dobsons must be going through right now.

Then, Emily heard Nick's words in her head: *"Yeah, but it's the exception, not the rule."* She quickly shut down her negative train of thought. She was getting ahead of her skis, as Brandon liked to tell her. The truth of the matter was that murders were rare in Freeport County. It was a great place to raise a family and grow old. And she could not deny that she had loved the first fifteen years of her life here. The perfect memories of the people and places of Freeport were more than she could count. Being back here now felt like a parallax was at work, showing her the old, familiar things from a new perspective. She noticed this effect was triggered by little things, like the smell of the hospital hallway, a bite of Brown's bear claw, and Jo's laughter, which drew her back to reality. She slipped into her father's room.

"How's the patient today?" Emily said, trying to put on a cheery face.

"Emily. Hey. You look more rested. It's been so nice chatting with your dad," said Jo.

Cathy smiled from her chair, where she looked radiant and well put together as always.

"Jo, thanks so much for alerting us to that video," said Emily.

"It's strange knowing that guy is out there. Just walking around among us. Gives me the chills. You do think that guy in the video is the one who killed Julie, right?"

"Oh, well, we're not sure. It's a pretty big conclusion to draw at this time. But it gives Nick and his team a good place to start."

"Speaking of Julie Dobson, I have to meet with the

Dobsons in half an hour to make funeral arrangements, and in light of this news of her murder, it's going to be even harder than I originally thought," said Cathy, rising. "So, your arrival is perfect timing. You can keep your dad company while I'm gone."

"And I need to get back to work," Jo said.

Cathy bent over Robert's bed and kissed him on the lips. "I'll see you later." She turned and paused quickly at Emily's side. "See what you can do," she said under her breath.

Emily knew exactly what she meant. Cathy was beseeching her for collusion, and Emily would try. But it seemed an impossible task.

Jo also took her cue. "Dr. Hartford, I'll stop by again in a couple hours. If you need anything, just buzz."

She paused by Emily on her way out. "Hey, my kids are dying to meet Mommy's high school friend. The oldest two are showing their horses at Premiere on Saturday before the state competitions. Why don't you join us?"

"That's sweet. I'd like to meet them too," Emily said.

"Starts at nine."

"I'll do my best," said Emily, nodding, as Jo bobbed out. She closed the door, anticipating an argument. She told herself to stay firm. No mincing words. She placed the images of his heart on his lap.

"You've seen these, I'm told," she started.

"I have," said Robert.

"If you don't have this surgery, you're going to die. Soon."

"We're all going to die," Robert said.

"So you always say. But a bypass will get you a couple more decades," Emily said.

"The answer is no."

"Why are you being so ignorant? You know better."
Emily stared him down from the end of his bed.

Robert regarded his daughter with a slight grin.
"Your bedside manner could use a little finesse."

But Emily wouldn't have it. Despite their shaky relationship, she couldn't let her father throw his life away
like this.

"You realize what this means? You'll have to quit
practicing medicine. You'll have to give up the ME
office. And there's no way you can continue to live at
home. What if you pass out or have another heart attack
while you're doing something dangerous, like running
your electric saw, and Cathy's not there?"

"Okay, let's not get all dramatic."

"I'm not. I'm being a realist," she said. "If you won't
do this, then you need to think about a transitional care
facility."

"I won't be cast off to some godforsaken nursing
home," he protested.

"Then have the surgery," Emily insisted.

"Absolutely not."

"What does Cathy say?" asked Emily.

"She said she'd help me pick out a real nice casket.
She'll even give me a family and friends discount," her
father said, turning to her with a grin.

"Dad, not funny. Why aren't you thinking of her?"
Emily said.

"She respects the fact that I want to treat this in my
own way," he said.

"I don't believe that," said Emily. "You just got married. She wants you around for a while."

"I think the real question here is why do you care so much if I live or die?" he said, putting it back on her.

"Why can't I care?" she said. "You're my father."

"Why now? Why after all these years do you come running home when I'm at death's door? If you really cared, you'd pick up the phone now and then. What does it matter to you if I'm gone? One less phone call to ignore."

The response laid her bare. She knew she hadn't always been fair to him. "You didn't seem to care about me when you denied me what mattered most. Why was it so bad to care about wanting some closure to Mom's death?"

"What is it you want, Emily? After all these years, why didn't you just come to me?"

"I told you a million times. I want to see her autopsy report."

"You saw the police report. There's nothing else to know."

"Then why can I not see it?"

"Because I don't want you remembering your mother like that...a list of cold medical facts. Photographs of her dissected body." Robert shook his head. "No. She would never want that for you."

"Maybe not then. But it's different now. I can handle it, Dad."

He shook his head and Emily noticed his color turning gray. He was not getting enough oxygen through his body.

"You know you're breaking the law by not allowing me a copy of my own mother's public death record. And I never pressed it before...but I'm asking you now."

He didn't respond right away. Emily watched as he

sat there, his breathing becoming slightly more labored and shallow. She feared she was driving him right into another heart attack. She took a step closer to his heart monitor. It was low, but not dangerous.

"Should I call Jo? You don't look well."

He shook his head.

"Maybe I'm tired of living. Have you thought of that, Emily? Maybe I don't deserve a long life. Your mother sure didn't get one…and she, of all people, deserved…"

Her father looked worn beyond his years.

"Deserved what?" said Emily.

"The truth." Tears rimmed his eyes, and he tried to dab them away before Emily would notice.

"The truth about what?"

"Can you please tell Jo I need my heart meds?"

He had all but admitted it. There was more to her mother's accident. Emily padded out to the nurse's station. Whatever Dad had been keeping from her and from Mom, it was literally killing him. She had to keep her father alive.

TWENTY-TWO

AFTER VIEWING THE YouTube video, Nick immediately contacted the website provider and ordered them to take it down. He was praying to God that the original footage still existed, and he hoped it was in Sarah Dobson's possession.

He then proceeded to arrange yet a second visit of the day with the Dobson family, who were just returning from the funeral home. Sarah's parents had driven her straight home and demanded Sarah surrender the GoPro camera and memory card. Sarah admitted that she had found it in Julie's closet in a shoebox. Being a typical social-media-driven fifteen-year-old, Sarah's only thought had been to post the video in an effort to root out Julie's killer. Turning it over to the police had never occurred to her. Nick sent it down to the state crime lab digital forensics division to see of they could pull any more identifying information from it.

Then, Nick paid Gary Bodum a surprise visit. Due diligence required Nick to check on Gary's alibi during the events of Julie's death. When he couldn't find Gary in his office, Nick wandered through the stables until he saw him in a stall, hunched over a horse's leg as he trimmed the hoof with nippers. He didn't look up as Nick approached.

"Gary, good afternoon. I'm surprised to see you here working after such a traumatic event just occurred."

"Horses still need to be fed and tended," he said. "But that doesn't mean my mind isn't elsewhere. What can I do for you?" Gary looked up.

"Just have a couple questions for you," he started. "Where you were at the time of Julie Dobson's death," Nick stated.

"You mean murder? I've heard. Am I a suspect?" Gary said calmly.

"That depends. Can you prove your alibi?" said Nick.

"I can. I was home that morning."

"But who can verify that? You live alone," Nick said.

"So do you," said Gary. "Does someone know exactly where you are every single moment of the day?"

Nick understood his frustration. "Gary, if you can clear your whereabouts, that would help you tremendously," Nick said.

"I was home."

"But how can you confirm that? Did you use your cell phone? Computer? Did a neighbor see you walking your dog? Did the paper deliverer see you picking up the paper? Think. I'm struggling to give you the benefit of the doubt."

"I don't know. I..." Gary paused. "Yes. Someone saw me that morning. I was with a friend."

"At the time of Julie's death?" Nick asked.

"Yes. All morning until I left for the stables," Gary said.

"I'd like to confirm that with your friend," Nick replied. "What's your friend's name?"

"I don't want to get this person involved," Gary answered.

"I need a confirmation to clear you."

"I was with Mindy Wilkins," replied Gary.

"The cheerleading coach?"

"Yes. We've been dating for a couple of months."

"She spent the night?" Nick said.

"No. I was at her house. I meant to go home, but I fell asleep on her couch. Happy now?" Gary said.

"Folks in Freeport are gonna be tickled to hear you've still got a chance at a proper wedding," Nick said with a sly grin. "Come on, man, I'm just kidding. I'm happy for you."

"Discretion, please. For Mindy's sake. We haven't even told her parents yet," Gary said.

"I'm going to corroborate this with her, you know," Nick told him. Gary nodded.

"Is that all? I have a lot of work to do," he said.

"It's not all. Something more serious came to my attention." Nick showed him the GoPro video. "Have you seen this?"

"I've seen it. It's horrible."

"Are you the man in that video?" asked Nick.

"No. What? Are you kidding? I would never harm my horses."

"But you knew someone was harming Mercedes? Didn't you?" Nick said. "The proof is here. In your stable. You didn't notice anything wrong with Mercedes?"

"No. No. Look, I didn't know that was going on. See, the way it works is that a horse is sored, and then overnight the wounds start to heal. The next morning the horse is acting fine. But then right before the competition, the groom or the trainer inflicts an irritant that burns and stings on the open wounds, causing the horse to raise his legs higher, jump higher, perform better."

"So, the person who did this actually wanted him to

perform better?" Nick was confused. How was this a motive for murder?

"Or someone wanted Emily to get caught. When the judges perform an inspection before competition, the horse and rider can be instantly disqualified if they see soring wounds."

"That's a brutal practice, Gary," said Nick, his stomach turning.

"I agree. And I would never allow it. Knowingly."

"Some people seem to think you did know. Some are saying Julie came to you about this, and you did nothing."

"She did," said Gary, growing frustrated. "And there was no way I could prove it."

"Install cameras?"

"We're on a shoestring budget here. Besides, anyone can disarm a camera."

"Okay. Then who do you think might have done this, Gary? If you know, you need to tell me. Tell me now 'cause you know I'm gonna scratch like a rabid dog until I get answers. And I'm not gonna be happy if I have to come scratching back here."

"Julie was like a little daughter to me. I'm sick about that video. Even more sick to think it might be someone from my own stable. So, if I knew who it was, I would be the first person on your doorstep."

"Do you recognize the boots in this video?" He pulled up the video again, "Look again. Closely."

Gary studied the image on the screen one last time and shrugged.

"They're just your average work boots. Dime a dozen." Gary's face showed earnestness that Nick accepted for the moment. He was convinced there was something going on at Premiere, but as to whether Gary knew about it, he was unsure. In the meantime, with a few more careful inquiries, he was certain he could narrow in on a suspect list.

TWENTY-THREE

BISHOP & SCHULTZ FUNERAL HOME was just a few blocks east of downtown Freeport. Cathy Bishop had inherited the business from her father, Carl Bishop, who had inherited it from his father-in-law, Josiah Schultz. And so, like many mortuaries, the stately red-brick Victorian home had stayed in the family. The main funeral parlor encompassed most of the main floor, and in back was the prep area. Until she married Robert, Cathy had lived upstairs in a beautifully decorated upper level that boasted three bedrooms and three baths, a formal dining room, and a butler's kitchen. Now, she rented it out to a newly married couple who saw the value of the inexpensive rent and thought the macabre location was hip and unique.

Emily remembered eating dinner up there with Cathy, Hugh, and her sister, Anna, in the year after her mother had passed. There was also a cellar under the home, where Cathy kept her embalming supplies and extra caskets. A detached garage was set in the back of the property. Here Cathy housed the company hearse. Driving up to the house, Emily noticed that nothing had changed.

She parked and headed toward the back door, which led into the prep area where she knew Cathy would be working. Cathy answered, swinging the door open with her hips, gloved hands pointed up in front of her chest. She welcomed Emily with a warm smile.

"Come on in, sweetheart," Cathy sang as Emily entered. "Just finishing up on Julie. Dobsons want to hold the wake tomorrow night."

"That soon?"

"Yeah, they're holding it for three nights. We figure the crowds could get pretty big. And that leaves a few days for out-of-town family to arrive."

"How did it go with them?" Emily said as she followed Cathy to the table where Julie lay.

"Surprisingly well. And fast. They selected all the upgrades, so I'm not gonna complain," said Cathy who resorted to all-business when in the face of the darkest tragedy. "Gloria teared up a little, but not a single drop from the senator. Kinda strange, I thought."

"Same reaction when I told them the initial news," said Emily. "Politics."

"I guess. The memorial service is Saturday. They requested a private burial afterward. Immediate family only," Cathy explained as she cleaned up. "I can't even imagine what they must be going through."

"Me neither," Emily said as she took a closer look at Cathy's work. Julie was dressed in a classic red blouse, her riding pants, gold hoop earrings, and subtle makeup. Her chestnut hair flowed around her face. "You did a beautiful job on her."

"Thank you," Cathy replied. "But I'll admit, it's always a gut-wrenching job when it's young people."

"Any new leads on the video?" Cathy asked.

"Nick sent it to the state lab," Emily said. "I'll touch base with him later."

Cathy closed Julie's casket and pointed the gurney toward the swinging doors that led into the funeral parlor.

"I just hope Nick does a good job on this investigation. He missed a key piece of evidence at the scene," said Emily. "Not that he knew it at the time, but that's the point, right? You never know what you're going to find."

"You're a perfectionist, like your dad," Cathy said with a friendly glance. "And a bit of a skeptic."

Emily didn't take offense. It was the top personality trait of the best surgeons in the world. "You might call it an essential requirement of the job," she said.

"Or an occupational hazard," said Cathy. "Grab the other end of this casket?" Emily helped Cathy roll the casket through the swinging doors into the funeral parlor. They positioned it in the front of the parlor to face the guest area. Emily had been in this room dozens of times when she was working with her father, the last time at her mother's funeral. It hadn't changed much. A fresh coat of paint. New chairs and curtains. Same color scheme. Same feeling of serenity and sorrow. Only this time, she didn't feel as hopeless as she had before.

"Straighten out your end a little. Square it to the wall." Emily adjusted her side. She noticed along one wall of the parlor several dozen floral arrangements were already waiting to be placed around Julie. Their fragrant aroma sweetened the room.

"Well, now that we both know your father's diagnosis and the length of his stubbornness, how long do you think you'll stick around in Freeport?" Cathy asked.

"Actually, that's why I came over. I wanted to see if there's any way you can convince him to have the surgery," said Emily.

"It's his right to refuse," Cathy replied.

Cathy selected a gargantuan funeral spray and set it in front of Julie's casket. Emily took her cue and went to the wall to select the next biggest arrangement.

"And you stand by that? Even after losing Hugh to cancer?" Emily said. "I don't understand."

"I pushed Hugh into chemo, radiation, the whole gamut. And for what? He was miserable. I was miserable. And then he died in six months anyway. I'm not going to do that to your father," she said. "He gets to decide what kind of quality of life he wants."

"This is different. If Dad gets the surgery, he could live another ten or twenty years. Don't you want that?"

"Of course I do. But it's not up to me to decide." Emily brought her two more floral arrangements, and Cathy set them at the base of the casket. "I know you don't see it that way. You've lost a lot of years between you two, and it's natural to want to try to make up for some of that lost time," said Cathy.

"I don't know what to say. What else can I do?"

"Well, there is one thing I've been thinking about, and I wanted to run it by you," said Cathy. "This may come off as kind of harsh, but I don't think I can give your father the kind of care he needs, and I think it would be best if he went into a rehab facility. Maybe even a retirement home."

"I thought…he told me you were his therapy, and you would take care of him," Emily said.

"That was his hope. And as much as I love him, I'm worried I just don't have the bandwidth to do it. I'm not ready to retire. I would need to train a successor. That could take a couple years. And this community… well, they depend on the kind of care that I provide."

She continued to surround Julie's coffin with flowers and plants.

"Have you told him?" Emily asked.

"Not yet. I was kind of hoping for your help," she said. "I thought we could check out Birch Acres together. See if they have an opening. Maybe a one-bedroom overlooking the courtyard."

"He's gonna hate that," Emily said.

"I know and I'm sorry it has to come to this. I know it probably seems like a selfish decision. But I cared for Hugh for those six months before he died, *and* kept up with the funeral home. It nearly killed me," Cathy said. "I'm still gonna be there for your father. I'll see him every morning and come home to him every night. But I need some help because I'm not getting any younger either."

"What do you want me to do?" Emily asked.

"Help me convince him to do what's best," said Cathy.

"You can clearly see how well that's worked out," Emily said with sarcasm. "Look, I'm on board to try to help you. But how do you envision this playing out?" A text pinged on Emily's phone. Brandon.

"I've thought about it, and it's a little sneaky. We'll make the arrangements with Birch Acres first. Then I'll talk to him. And then maybe you can talk to him. If he hears it from both of us, he'll be more inclined to go peacefully. And who knows? Maybe this will prompt him to have that surgery. In that case, we can continue living at home," Cathy said optimistically.

"I see what you're doing," Emily grinned. "You're using reverse psychology to give him an ultimatum."

Cathy winked at her. "Call it what you like. I'm a

practical woman. Always have been. This is the most practical solution I can come up with."

"What about the house? Will you sell it?" Emily asked.

"We'll have to. I'll give you first right of refusal," she said.

"I don't know what I would do with the house. But if you need help downsizing, I can give you a hand," Emily offered.

"I would love it. And then, there's your father's medical practice to think about. We'll need to officially close it down. Go through the files. Notify the patients that he's retiring. Take care of outstanding bills. And there's the whole ME office to deal with. He keeps everything at home, so we need to get those ME records sorted and sent to the county so they can house them from here on out. I'm exhausted just listing all of this."

"That's going to be a big job. I can get some paid time off for a couple of weeks and then maybe manage a few weekends here and there," said Emily, checking her text from Brandon.

How are things? Are you coming home soon?

She knew she shouldn't read tone into a text, but she did. And she was annoyed. She had told Brandon she would be here through the weekend, and he had promised to come up. Why was he backpedaling?

Cathy opened a closet door and rolled out a long rack of folding chairs. Emily lilted a little as she read the text again, and knew she had to tell Brandon she would be here longer. A week or more. She glanced down at her diamond. This engagement was not off to a good start.

"Mind giving me a hand again with the chairs?" Cathy asked as she began unloading the chairs and stacking them in piles of five around the room. "I usually set up ten rows of ten. But this time I think we're gonna need all two hundred. So let's add another ten rows, five on either side, sort of angled off the middle two sections."

Emily was surprised by how quickly she was getting embedded in life here and how familiar and comfortable it felt. She climbed into her Leaf and texted Brandon.

Here for a while.

She drove a few miles and then pulled over when she heard the ping. Brandon: Not sure if I can make it up there. Work stuff. Call you later.

This was incredulous. Her father was in the hospital. Basically dying. Was work really more important? Was she glimpsing a sneak peek of their future? She immediately jumped into thoughts of the future... what if they had kids? Would she end up ditching her career to carry the bulk of the child care? No. That wasn't Brandon's style. He would never do that to her. No, instead they would employ a series of au pairs like the ones Brandon had as a child. This didn't sit well with Emily either. She knew the value of having a real mother around. And after losing her own, it would be hard to entrust the bulk of child care to someone else. But she didn't want to do it with an absentee father either. Anxiety stirred in Emily's gut again.

She took a deep breath. She wasn't ready to go visit her father again. She didn't want to go back to her hotel room and sit there. Alone with her troubled thoughts about Julie's unsolved murder. And there was no way she could fall asleep, although she needed it badly. Instead, she texted Nick: Any news?

He texted right back: Chasing a lead.

Emily thought for a second, then typed: Anything I can do?

Nick's response was immediate: Come to FHS.

TWENTY-FOUR

As EMILY TRAVELED up a set of steps that led into Freeport High School, it brought back a wave of memories. The last time Emily had been here, she was ditching school at the beginning of her junior year to catch a bus that would take her to Chicago. On that warm autumn day, as her tennis shoes hit the last step, she turned around and looked up to the second story, to the third set of windows to the left, where Nick was in trig class. He had been staring back at her, imploring her with a confused look. She gave him a little wave and a sad smile. And then disappeared. The only thing that assuaged her guilt about leaving so suddenly was the note she'd left in his locker. That, of course, he never got. Fate is tragically funny sometimes.

Emily entered the high school gymnasium, where Nick had said he would be, and saw him talking to Mindy Wilkins. Mindy had been a senior when Emily and Nick were freshmen. She and Nick were sitting in the bleachers while Mindy was overseeing cheerleading practice. Mindy held her attention on the floor for a moment as her girls performed a three-tiered mount, then dismounted perfectly. She held up her thumb in approval and then spun her index finger in a circle to indicate *"Again."*

Emily climbed the bleachers to meet them.

"Oh my gosh, Emily, how are you?" Mindy reached

TWENTY-FOUR

As EMILY TRAVELED up a set of steps that led into Free-port High School, it brought back a wave of memories. The last time Emily had been here, she was ditching school at the beginning of her junior year to catch a bus that would take her to Chicago. On that warm autumn day, as her tennis shoes hit the last step, she turned around and looked up to the second story, to the third set of windows to the left, where Nick was in trig class. He had been staring back at her, imploring her with a con-fused look. She gave him a little wave and a sad smile. And then disappeared. The only thing that assuaged her guilt about leaving so suddenly was the note she'd left in his locker. That, of course, he never got. Fate is tragically funny sometimes.

Emily entered the high school gymnasium, where Nick had said he would be, and saw him talking to Mindy Wilkins. Mindy had been a senior when Emily and Nick were freshmen. She and Nick were sitting in the bleachers while Mindy was overseeing cheerlead-ing practice. Mindy held her attention on the floor for a moment as her girls performed a three-tiered mount, then dismounted perfectly. She held up her thumb in approval and then spun her index finger in a circle to indicate *"Again."*

Emily climbed the bleachers to meet them.

"Oh my gosh, Emily, how are you?" Mindy reached

practical woman. Always have been. This is the most practical solution I can come up with."

"What about the house? Will you sell it?" Emily asked.

"We'll have to. I'll give you first right of refusal," she said.

"I don't know what I would do with the house. But if you need help downsizing, I can give you a hand," Emily offered.

"I would love it. And then, there's your father's medi-cal practice to think about. We'll need to officially close it down. Go through the files. Notify the patients that he's retiring. Take care of outstanding bills. And there's the whole ME office to deal with. He keeps everything at home, so we need to get those ME records sorted and sent to the county so they can house them from here on out. I'm exhausted just listing all of this."

"That's going to be a big job. I can get some paid time off for a couple of weeks and then maybe manage a few weekends here and there," said Emily, checking her text from Brandon.

How are things? Are you coming home soon?

She knew she shouldn't read tone into a text, but she did. And she was annoyed. She had told Brandon she would be here through the weekend, and he had prom-ised to come up. Why was he backpedaling?

Cathy opened a closet door and rolled out a long rack of folding chairs. Emily lilted a little as she read the text again, and knew she had to tell Brandon she would be here longer. A week or more. She glanced down at her diamond. This engagement was not off to a good start.

"Mind giving me a hand again with the chairs?" Cathy asked as she began unloading the chairs and stacking them in piles of five around the room. "I usually set up ten rows of ten. But this time I think we're gonna need all two hundred. So let's add another ten rows, five on either side, sort of angled off the middle two sections."

Emily was surprised by how quickly she was getting embedded in life here and how familiar and comfortable it felt. She climbed into her Leaf and texted Brandon.

Here for a while.

She drove a few miles and then pulled over when she heard the ping. Brandon: Not sure if I can make it up there. Work stuff. Call you later.

This was incredulous. Her father was in the hospital. Basically dying. Was work really more important? Was she glimpsing a sneak peek of their future? She immediately jumped into thoughts of the future... what if they had kids? Would she end up ditching her career to carry the bulk of the child care? No. That wasn't Brandon's style. He would never do that to her. No, instead they would employ a series of au pairs like the ones Brandon had as a child. This didn't sit well with Emily either. She knew the value of having a real mother around. And after losing her own, it would be hard to entrust the bulk of child care to someone else. But she didn't want to do it with an absentee father either. Anxiety stirred in Emily's gut again.

She took a deep breath. She wasn't ready to go visit her father again. She didn't want to go back to her hotel room and sit there. Alone with her troubled thoughts

about Julie's unsolved murder. And there was no way she could fall asleep, although she needed it badly. Instead, she texted Nick: Any news?

He texted right back: Chasing a lead.

Emily thought for a second, then typed: Anything I can do?

Nick's response was immediate: Come to FHS.

out for a hug, which confused Emily because she didn't remember a single time Mindy had ever spoken to her during her freshman year.

"I'm good. Nice to see you," Emily said, hugging her back.

"I heard you did Julie's autopsy on account of your dad and all. How is he? We're all really bummed about his heart attack," Mindy said. "The girls are putting together a bake sale to raise money for a memorial fund for Julie, did you know? Isn't that sweet of them? They make me proud."

"I didn't know Julie was a cheerleader," Emily said.

"Oh no, but her ex-boyfriend, David Sands, plays varsity basketball. So she kinda became a part of the basketball family," Mindy explained. "Came to almost all the games to see him play.

"Emily, you haven't changed a bit," Mindy said and lifted Emily's left hand to look at her ring. "That thing is huge. He's got some dough, huh?"

Emily squirmed inside, and thankfully Nick jumped in before she could think of an appropriate response. "Emily's helping me with Julie's case. Is it okay if we ask you a few questions?"

"Wait. You're here about Julie?" Mindy said, catching on. Emily had always remembered her as a little ditzy.

"Can we go somewhere private?" Nick asked.

"Sure." Mindy called to her girls to take a break. She led Emily and Nick outside the auditorium to a private spot in the hallway.

"I need to verify something, and I was told you could help me out," Nick said.

"I'll try. Of course. Anything to help," Mindy said

stopping them between the guys' and girls' locker rooms.

"I'm wondering, can you tell us where were you the morning of Julie's death?" Nick asked.

"I was at home," Mindy said simply.

"Your home?" Nick asked.

"Yeah, my house," said Mindy. "I'm confused. Am I under suspicion or something?"

"No, you're not under suspicion, Mindy," Nick said and then paused. "Was there anyone else in your home that morning?"

"Just me. I live alone. You know that, Nick," she said.

"Mindy, I want you to know that whatever you say here between us is confidential."

"Wait a sec, this is about…it's someone else you— hey, look. We haven't told anybody yet."

"Who are you referring to?" asked Nick. He couldn't lead the questioning.

"Well, Gary, of course. Is he a suspect?" she gasped. "'Cause, I mean Gary would never, ever, ever hurt so much as a kitten."

"Was Gary at your house that morning?"

"Yes, he was," she told Nick. "I made him breakfast, and then he left for work."

Nick nodded as he jotted it into his notepad. Emily noted how smoothly and graciously Nick conducted his questioning. People really responded to him. He was a natural. Firm, but friendly. Professional and candid. He cared about work, but he cared more about people.

"He's not in trouble, is he?" Mindy said. "Just be honest with me."

"Are you absolutely, one hundred percent sure about your answer?" Nick said.

"I'm being honest. Gary was at my house 'til about eight fifteen," Mindy explained, her voice steady and insistent. "Don't you believe me? Nick Larson, when have I ever lied to you?"

"You just did," said Nick with a grin. "Don't worry, I get it. And I believe you."

"Why would you think he did it?" Mindy asked.

"I can't talk about that, Mindy. You've been very helpful. Thank you."

"You're crazy to think Gary had anything to do with that girl's death. You stay out of our business. And you keep your mouth shut about Gary and me," Mindy said with an angry flush rising in her cheeks. "I've gotta get back to practice."

As Mindy turned and took off down the hall, Emily noticed a slight bump in her mid-section, tastefully hidden by her baby-doll top.

Once she was out of sight, Nick said, "Well, it didn't end as smoothly as I would have liked, but she confirmed Gary's alibi."

"And you believe her?"

"Why wouldn't I? What reason does she have to lie to me?"

"So, you didn't see it?" Emily asked.

"See what?"

"Her baby bump. Mindy's pregnant," said Emily.

"She is?"

"Guys are always so clueless to these things," Emily mused. "I'm a woman and I'm a doctor and I know a pregnant belly when I see one." She gave Nick a knowing smile, and he just shrugged. She knew he wasn't gonna fight this one.

Nick and Emily started to head back down the hall

and toward the school exit. They walked the halls in silence for a moment, confidently navigating the well-traveled landscape as they had done a hundred times when they were students here. Taking the stairs down toward the main entrance, they passed a memorial wall of former students, faculty, and staff who had passed away during their time at Freeport High. Emily couldn't bring herself to look at it. There was a secret luring there too—one she could find in her father's files. But that was a case for another time. Right now all that mattered was Julie Dobson.

"So, you confirmed Gary's alibi, and the crime lab has the video. What next?" said Emily.

"Gary provided me with a list of names of everyone with access to the stable," Nick said.

"How big is the list?"

"A couple dozen."

"It's gonna take a lot of time to investigate all those people," said Emily. "I hope you have some help. You look like you could use a break."

"I called in a few favors from the State Police Crime Team, and they're doing the rest of the interviews, but so far nothing's turning up," Nick said, trying to stifle a yawn. "Hey, Em, I want to thank you. It's been huge having you around the last few days."

"Not that I had much of a choice, right?" She cracked a smile, and their eyes met for a second. Nick held her gaze.

"How long are you staying in town?" said Nick. They were now on the sidewalk in front of the school. A cool autumn breeze rustled through the trees, sending a shower of leaves around them. Emily shuddered as goose bumps formed on her arms, another reminder that in her haste she hadn't packed enough cool-weather clothes.

"I'm not sure. Maybe a week or two."

"Life changes in an instant, doesn't it?"

"Yes, it does." *And oftentimes not for the better,* Emily wanted to add.

"Hey, how would you like to come over for dinner tomorrow night?"

Was he asking her on a date? He must have read her mind because he followed up with, "No, not like *that.* I've got some of the old gang coming over for a bar-beque," Nick said.

"Oh. Okay. Yeah, maybe."

"Six thirty. Four-seventy-five Spruce. Right on the lake down from the old Parker cottage."

"I know the place," Emily said, nodding. "You always said you loved that old heap."

"Still do. Even more now. You should come by and see what I've done with it."

"I'll see."

Emily split off toward her car in the parking lot as Nick walked to his cruiser along the sidewalk. After she had gone about twenty steps, Emily glanced back. As Nick was getting into his patrol car, his eyes met hers, and Emily could have sworn they held the same imploring look she'd left with twelve years ago.

TWENTY-FIVE

ONCE BACK INSIDE her hotel suite at the Pennington Inn, Emily took a few minutes to gather herself after her very full and emotionally draining day. She called Brandon and started to leave a voicemail. But what else could she say? She wasn't going to beg him to be somewhere he didn't want to be. She hung up, thinking about Mindy's comment, "Wow, that's huge!" But what good was a huge ring if he couldn't be by her side right now? When she really needed him?

She called her father at the hospital. Cathy answered the room phone. Her dad was doing fine and sleeping. Emily said she would be by later to check on him, but Cathy insisted she get some sleep.

Even though it was close to nine o'clock, Emily sucked down a mug of hotel coffee and flipped through all the TV and radio stations. Nothing satisfied. Finally, she tuned into a local classical station, hoping it would soothe her disquieted mind. She pulled up her emails on her iPad. Scanning down, she noticed one from the toxicology lab she had used for Julie's tissue and blood samples. She was surprised to see the results had come in so quickly. She clicked into the confidential link from the lab and swept through the analysis. Everything checked out normal except for one glaring result. Ketamine. A horse tranquilizer. The dose in Julie's system was not lethal, but was concentrated enough that it may have led to misjudgment and confusion. Questions bombarded Emily's mind. Why had Julie been taking ketamine? And where did she get it? Did the horse abuser from the video have anything to do with this? Had he found out about the GoPro and sought revenge? Maybe he'd drugged Julie, killed her, and then taken her out to the trail to make it look like she fell off her horse? Anything was possible. That had been cemented in her during her years of death investigation with her dad. She had to stop with the assumptions. Never jump to conclusions. Let the evidence guide you.

She immediately texted Nick and told him to call her. She expected an instant reply, but none came. He was probably at home, crashed out on his couch. Emily paced for forty minutes, listening to an entertaining podcast on small-town murders, did some sit-ups to get her blood flowing, and then dove into a medical-surgical textbook. She remembered that she had three surgeries scheduled for Monday, and she was sure that Dr. Claiborne had found a replacement surgeon, but she wanted to review the procedures to keep fresh. Just as she was diving into a chapter on appendectomies, there was a knock at her hotel suite door.

"Em? It's Jo!" came the familiar voice from the other side. Emily bounced off her bed and flung open the door.

"Are you busy?" Jo asked with a wink, holding up a bottle of red wine.

Emily ushered her in. "Jo, you have always known just what I needed. And when I needed it."

"I'm coming from my shift. Paul's at home, and the kids are down. I was too wired to go straight home, so I thought I'd see what you were up to."

"I'm so glad you did." Emily unwrapped the water cups from their sanitary plastic wrap. "This is the best I can do for now."

"I don't care if you pour it into a shoe. It'll taste good to me."

Emily found a package of crackers and a block of cheese in her mini fridge. With Jo's arrival, the stress of the past day just melted down her neck and shoulders.

"How's the case going?" Jo asked.

"No. No case talk. No hospital talk. No horse talk," Emily said as she handed Jo her glass. "Only girl talk."

"Agreed." Jo took her wine and flopped onto the double bed across from Emily.

"Let's talk about your life. Tell me more about your husband, your kids, your job."

"Oh, it's a real page-turner. Brace yourself. I met Paul in college. We got married. Moved back to Freeport. Popped out Jeremiah, Jessica, and Jaden. I work as an ER nurse. Paul works as a farming engineer. He travels some around the Midwest. And that's pretty much it."

"It sounds like a really full and happy life," said Emily. "Are you happy?"

"On most days, yes. Very happy. Of course, I daydream about an alternative life. One where I'm living in a little French village, riding my bike through the lavender fields in the countryside with my French lover and a picnic basket of baguettes," Jo said, laughing.

"I've had that same daydream, only mine takes place in Italy," Emily said, nodding with a grin. "Now I remember why we were friends."

"I wanna know what you're up to in Chicago. And

all about this wedding! That's way more exciting." Jo cut herself a slice of cheese and placed it atop a cracker.

"I'm in my third year of surgical residency. I live in the city. I love it. You should come visit sometime. Bring the family."

"And your fiancé?" Jo asked. "That rock is divine."

"Yes. Brandon. My fiancé. For exactly forty-eight hours now," Emily said.

"When's the date?"

"Didn't get that far. He proposed, and literally the next moment I got the news about my dad. Truthfully, it's all come a bit prematurely. I was hoping to be done with residency and settled into a job first."

"But that's like, what, a good two years away?"

Emily nodded. "Just feels like odd timing."

"You've got a lot on your plate right now. Give it a couple of weeks."

"I just thought he would make more of an effort to come up, you know?"

"Doctors, right? It was like this with your dad and mom too. Remember? He was always on call. He had to leave in the middle of your National Honor Society induction."

"And my piano recital. And my junior high graduation."

Emily appreciated Jo's candidness and perspective. It was refreshing. And so was her friendship.

"I can't remember the last time I sat down for a glass of wine with a good friend and had a talk like this," Emily said.

"Are you kidding? If you lived here, we would do this every week."

Over the years, Emily had tried to convince herself

that she hadn't missed out on friendships like Jo's as she sacrificed them to concentrate on school and career. But being here with Jo made her feel she may have been wrong. It was therapeutic. And made her feel connected.

A text from Brandon popped up.

Hey sweetie. Can u talk now?

"Sorry, it's Brandon. We've been phone-tagging all day."

"You should set a wedding date," challenged Jo lightly.

"What? No. When?" said Emily, texting him back her love.

"I'm telling you. Set a date. It makes things real."

Jo grabbed Emily's phone. "What are you doing?" Emily demanded.

"Playing wedding coordinator. Okay, what's your favorite time of year?" she asked.

"Jo, come on," Emily said.

"Summer?" asked Jo.

"Too hot and muggy," Emily replied.

"Spring?" Jo went on.

"Weather's too unpredictable," Emily said.

"Is it an outdoor wedding?"

"Not necessarily," said Emily.

"How about early fall? End of September? Still warm and with the leaves turning, it's just gorgeous. Like now," Jo said.

"Christmas," Emily finally said. "I've always wanted a Christmas wedding."

"Really? That would be amazing," said Jo. "Twinkling white lights. The smell of evergreen. White and red roses. A fresh snow blanketing the ground for your pictures. I love it!"

Jo started to type.

"What are you typing? Jo, come on!" Emily jumped over to her friend and leaned over to see the screen. Jo had typed out: What do you think about a Christmas wedding?

She held the phone out to Emily. "Okay, girl, get ready to rock his world. Press 'Send.'"

Emily looked at her friend and nodded confidently. She pressed "Send."

Within a few seconds his answer came back: That's less than three months.

"He's got a point."

"Tell him short engagements are healthy. I'll help you plan. You can imagine with three kids and a traveling husband how great I am at multitasking," said Jo.

"You're hired. But you may regret it," said Emily as she glanced over to the phone and paused for a moment.

"Text him, 'Found a wedding planner to make it happen.'"

They waited. No answer pinged back. Then Emily's phone rang. Jo passed it over to her.

"Brandon? Hey, how are you?" said Emily, putting it on speaker.

"So Christmas, huh?"

"Yeah. White lights. Snow falling. Horse-drawn carriage around Millennial Park. The city's so beautiful in December."

"Sure, I get it. And I like the idea, but my mom already called the country club and locked us into a date in mid-June."

"She what?"

"She even put down a deposit. I was waiting to tell you until you got back. You have so much on your plate right now, and she really wanted to do something to help."

"So you told her she could book our reception?"

"We can hold the ceremony there too. Down by the pond. They'll set up chairs and a trellis."

Emily rose from the bed, wine glass in hand, her jaw locked so tight no words could escape. Jo came to her side and encouraged her to take another sip of wine.

"Em? Are you there?"

"Mm-hmm." She swallowed her wine.

"Look, we can talk about this more when you get back on Sunday."

Emily nodded, but still no words would form.

"Em? Hello? You are coming home on Sunday, right?"

Emily finally found her voice. "What's so important that you can't break away to come up here?"

"When you said your dad was no longer in critical condition, I told Dr. Claiborne he could have me all weekend to work on research for the article."

"I thought you wanted to meet my dad."

"We'll make that happen another weekend. Besides, he'd probably rather meet me when he's feeling better." Brandon had it all planned out. Simple and practical.

"You're not taking me into consideration here."

"I could say the same."

She wasn't expecting this backlash. "What do you mean, Brandon?"

"Let's be honest, Em. How much time are you really spending with your dad?"

She didn't know where this was going.

"You're up there working a death investigation case. Right after we just got engaged. So I could make the argument that you aren't taking me into consideration."

"You're mad because I'm helping my dad out with his work?"

"You completed the autopsy the first night. What else is there to do? Then I hear you're gallivanting around the county, playing detective. With a guy who was your high school sweetheart."

"How did you even—?"

"I'm not dumb."

"You're jealous."

"Of a two-bit town sheriff? Come on, Em. All I've ever wanted is for you to let me in. And I'm really tired of begging."

"I want you here. But I'm not going to beg either."

They said little more and hung up. Emily turned to Jo.

"So…'no' on the winter wedding?" asked Jo, pouring more wine into Emily's glass.

TWENTY-SIX

EMILY AWOKE AROUND seven the next morning to her phone buzzing. There were at least twenty texts pointing her to a news story that had broken, via a local blogger, about Julie having ketamine in her system.

What in the world? How did this get leaked? She bolted straight up in bed and clicked onto the story. The facts were right. She had to call Nick! But he was already ahead of her by three voicemails she'd obviously slept through. She dialed him without listening to the messages.

"What's happening?" Her voice sounded a little gravelly.

"More damage control."

"I just got the results last night. How did this get leaked?"

"I should have called you back right away last night. But when I got home about seven, I crashed on the couch. Ten minutes later I got a call from a local blogger who was about to release Julie's tox reports unless I told him the names of the suspects. Found out he got chummy with the lab technician down at the university who ran Julie's blood work."

"He paid him off?"

"Naturally. I was up all night booking them for interference and disclosure of key evidence in a homicide case."

"Have you heard from the senator?"

"That shoe should drop any minute."

"Any idea where Julie got the drug?"

"Well, it's a commonly prescribed horse tranquilizer. And Julie was around horses. So, my first inquiry will be to Dr. Lillen."

Emily got out of bed and stretched out her stiff limbs.

"Is there any chance I could get you to head over to Dr. Lillen's practice and look into this ketamine thing?"

"Me? Why?"

"It's toxicology related. You and Dr. Lillen speak the same language."

"She's a horse doctor. I'm a people doctor."

"Please. I'm swamped today with all this backlash."

"Isn't there someone else in your office who can do it?"

"I can't pull my street cops off duty for this. Especially when the media is telling everyone Freeport County is on a witch hunt for a killer ketamine dealer."

"Fine. Fine." Emily gathered up a bath towel and her clothes. "Any news on Julie's bracelet?"

"I got nothing. But don't worry—I haven't forgotten about it."

"Keep me posted."

"Touch base with me after you see Dr. Lillen. Oh, and don't forget about the barbeque tonight."

"You're still doing that?"

"I've got a keg, a roast pig, and fifty dinner guests coming. No killer is keeping this town from the annual Nick Larson early autumn barbeque."

"You mean there's a late autumn one too?" Emily was grinning.

"Yeah, it's basically my version of Thanksgiving

dinner. And then a month later is the New Year's open house outdoor grilling challenge."

"In the snow?"

"Snow. Sleet. Blizzard. You name it. That's what gives it the challenge part."

Emily laughed. "Do you ever take a break?"

"Only during ice fishing season." She laughed again. "But I start right back up again for the basketball tournament buffet open house."

When she hung up, she felt light. And then she saw she had missed several texts from Brandon, telling her he couldn't wait to spend the rest of his life with her. Pictures of the country club. The pond. A blissful couple posing under the trellis arch with a soft sunset behind them. It was so manicured. So Brandon's family. And so not her.

She sighed. All she could think to respond was *What? No doves?*

She needed a shower to clear her mind and prep for her visit to Dr. Lillen. Within a half hour, Emily had was ready and grabbed a stale pastry breakfast in the lobby. She took one bite and threw the rest away. *Note to self: Brown's Bakery tomorrow.*

She was on her way to the hospital when Cathy phoned to warn her that she had "had the talk" with Robert about entering Birch Acres retirement facility, and it had gone as expected. Robert had been plaintive about it to her face, but aggravation and stubbornness were simmering below his surface. Regardless, Cathy had told him that she had spoken to the residence director late yesterday afternoon and put a one-month hold on a one-bedroom until he came around to his senses and could see that he was unfit to be home alone.

"Are you going to see him this morning?" Cathy said.

"Yeah, I'm heading over now." Emily pulled into the hospital parking lot. She noticed there was a news van trailing her. Relentless. She knew they were just doing their job, but there was nothing more she could give them. Why couldn't they leave her alone?

"You're on my side about this, am I right? You'll talk to him?"

Emily didn't argue. They had to work this out as a couple. There was little she could do about the residence situation. She needed to focus on pressing him to get that surgery or to tell her his secret. Both would be ideal, but at this point she could only hope for one.

Without even thinking, Emily steered her car around toward the back of the hospital to the first spot next to the back door. A sign above the spot read "Dr. Robert Hartford." It had been his reserved spot since she could remember, because it led directly into the morgue. Patients and guests weren't allowed back here, and hardly any of the other employees ever used this entrance. She jumped out of her car and dashed for the back door, then was immediately confronted by the coded entry panel. *Darn it!* She'd forgotten it would be locked. The reporter and cameraman were rushing toward her and were within ten yards.

"Dr. Hartford? Excuse me, Emily Hartford? Can you comment on the toxicology reports for Julie Dobson?"

Out of instinct, Emily pressed four numbers on the coded entry panel. Zero-nine-one-nine. The first digits of her birthday. The red light blinked green. It worked!

"Why was there ketamine in Julie's system? Do you know how it got there? Is that what killed her?"

Emily slipped inside, cutting the reporter off.

Twelve years and her father had never changed the code. Amazing.

TWENTY-SEVEN

WHEN EMILY ENTERED her father's room, she noticed his color looked better, and the I V was no longer hooked up. He held a mug of hot tea on his lap and was no longer wearing pajama pants, but a pair of sweatpants and a wool sweater. His pensive face was fixated on CNN. A good sign.

"Cathy wants to get rid of me already," Robert said, looking up at his daughter.

"That's ridiculous. She loves you."

"She told you about her plan?" Robert said.

"She did. She thought it would be best for you to have more consistent care than she can provide right now."

"She's casting me off to an old people's home. I might as well be one of those drooling, urine-soaked, wheelchair invalids," he growled.

"It's not that kind of place. It's fifty-five plus. An active community."

"I can be active and healthy in my own home and my own property," he said.

"It doesn't have to be this way, you know. If you get the bypass and work hard at rehab, then you can live at home eventually."

"You two conspired together on this, didn't you?" Robert said.

"It's not a conspiracy against you."

"I'm just a burden to her now," Robert said.

"No. You're not. But you can't expect Cathy to just up and leave her business," Emily insisted.

"I'm not asking her to give up the funeral home," he said.

"You need to be in a place where she knows you'll be safe and taken care of when she's not there," Emily said.

"It's adult day care. Not how I envisioned us growing old together."

"You gave her practically no choice by refusing to have a surgery you desperately need," said Emily starkly.

Robert held a stare on Emily. A flicker of concern crossed his face.

"Why am I surprised? You were always an insistent and strong-willed child."

"Got it from you," Emily said.

"Well, your mother had a strong streak too. So I suppose we're both to blame."

"Or thank. I think both have served me pretty well." Emily tried to soften the moment.

"Sometimes I feel I didn't do the best I could with you after she died."

You let our family dissolve to nothing, Emily wanted to shout as her frustration mounted. But then, she asked, "What did you mean the other day about Mom deserving the truth?"

His gaze moved once again to the TV screen, and he and Emily remained quiet for a moment.

"How long are you staying in town?"

"Long enough to help you and Cathy get the house and practice in order," Emily stated.

"In order for what?"

"Dad, please. You can't hang on to them anymore.

It's time to start thinking about what you'd like to keep, sell, or give away."

"Emily, you should know that I didn't agree to go to Birch Acres. I will not live in that place."

"I realize it's a big shift in your plans right now. So, let's just do this one step at time," she said. "We should start with the barn and the yard. Get them cleaned up and cleared out. All those tools and machines are strictly off limits to you. And you'll need a lawn service."

"I'll agree to that. Call Mike Sneller. He and his boys do yards," said Robert. As he said it, Emily remembered when she and Anna spent Saturdays in the fall raking and bagging for a few bucks of allowance money. "And he plows the driveway in the winter. His number's in the book." Oh, yes, the yellow pages phone book. No need for Yelp in Freeport.

"Do you know what he charges?" Emily asked.

"I have the money. It won't be a burden on you or Cathy," he said and drew quiet.

"Dad, stop feeling sorry for yourself."

"I think I need a little rest, if you don't mind." She knew it was his way of getting her to leave.

"Fine. I'll check in later," said Emily. There was no use arguing anymore. She had made a little headway. And it looked like she would be sticking around for longer than the weekend.

Emily exited the hospital the way she came in, making sure there were no lingering reporters. As she pulled onto the city street, her mind began compiling a list of things she would have to do to transition her father from work life to residential life. Would Dad want to sell his home or rent it out? She would need a realtor. Maybe a property manager. Would the place need remodeling to fetch a better price? It was tidy and in good repair, but nothing had been updated in twenty years. Maybe they should hire movers to remove everything to a storage unit until they could make a better decision about the next steps. A housekeeping team could provide a thorough cleaning of the home. Carpet cleaners could sanitize the rugs. And the place probably needed a fresh coat of paint.

Emily sighed audibly and rubbed her hand across her brow as if to prime her brain. And how in the world did one shut down a medical office? There were hundreds of patients to contact. Equipment to sell. Outstanding bills to pay and bank accounts to close. Dad could sell the practice to a newly minted doctor—but how to go about finding that person? It would require hiring a recruiter and an attorney. The list blew her mind.

As she got into her car, she drew in a few deep breaths. Pressing her eyes closed, she took a moment to visually prioritize the massive load of tasks, but she found that she had a hard time processing the list. And then, there was a wedding to plan. Or was there? If she didn't step in soon, Brandon's mom would have it taken care of, down to matching strings of pearls for her bridesmaids and those miserable candy-coated almond table favors. Emily wagged her head and released the tension from her shoulders down to her wrists. She shook it off and tried to gain a proper perspective on her wedding problems. These were nothing compared to what the Dobsons were suffering. A daughter's life cut short—and seemingly without motive.

TWENTY-EIGHT

EMILY FOUND HER way into Dr. Lillen's horse barn turned veterinarian clinic and trekked into the wide-open barn doors.

"Hello? Dr. Lillen?" Emily called out. "I'm Dr. Emily Hartford."

"Come on down." Dr. Lillen waved her over, and Emily saw that she was tending to a large black and tan horse, who shook his mane playfully when Emily approached. He didn't seem at all alarmed by the new visitor and moved his head over so Emily could stroke him.

"This is Mercedes. Go ahead—you can give him a pat," Dr. Lillen encouraged.

"He's so gentle and beautiful," Emily said, rubbing Mercedes's slender snout. She looked down and saw a sling holding up his front right leg.

"Is that from the…ah…incident?" asked Emily, reaching for the right word.

"It's an elevation device I use to keep the pressure off the leg, and it helps with circulation. I'd give him another month of rehab, and he'll be almost good as new."

"Is he in much pain?"

"Yes. I'm controlling it with painkillers. I'll start weaning him off next week and up the physical therapy. He's making great progress. I don't think he'll ever be a show horse again, but he'll be a great companion," said Dr. Lillen. Emily was relieved to know the horse would be kept alive.

"What do you think was the cause of his injury?"

"My guess is that he was spooked and then fell. Might have landed in those rocks along the creek."

Emily nodded. "Did you take X-rays?"

"Of course. Would you like to see them?"

"I would."

Dr. Lillen led Emily to her animal examining area, which was a large medical room built into one end of the barn. She flipped on her light box and leafed through a box of charts until she found Mercedes's X-rays. Dr. Lillen slipped a couple of X-ray scans into place and illuminated the image of the horse's cannon bone.

Emily couldn't believe the damage to the bone she was seeing. "That's quite a fracture."

"Horrifying, isn't it?" said Dr. Lillen. "I'm amazed he's doing so well."

"I'm glad the Dobsons didn't put him down."

"Most owners would have." Dr. Lillen turned off the light box and led Emily out of the office. "But I'm guessing that's not what you came here to discuss today."

"Toxicology found ketamine in Julie Dobson's system. I understand it's a horse tranquilizer that only vets can prescribe."

If Dr. Lillen was surprised by the news, she hid it under her professional demeanor. "That's right. But I never prescribed it for Mercedes." Dr. Lillen and Emily returned to Mercedes's stall, and she started brushing Mercedes down.

"Do you supply it to Premiere?"

"Of course. It's a common drug used for minor procedures. Mr. Bodum keeps some in his office in case there is an emergency."

Emily nodded. So that meant Julie would have had easy access. Or anyone else working at the stable, for that matter.

"You don't seem surprised about the ketamine in Julie's system," said Emily, fishing.

"I am actually," said Dr. Lillen carefully. "Unfortunately, I've seen this a lot around stables. It's a cheap drug and easy to access."

"What do you think about the possibility that she was drugged unknowingly or unwillingly?" asked Emily.

"I can't really make any speculations about that. I mean, it's possible. Disturbing as it may seem. But Julie was kind and gracious to everyone. I just don't know who would want her dead. The equestrian folk are like a large family. Close-knit bunch."

It's usually the ones closest to one another who commit the most crimes against one another, Emily thought. Spousal abuse. Domestic violence. Want to find your suspect? Start with your kin. By blood or marriage. There was nothing pointing a finger to anyone in Julie's immediate family as a suspect. It was incredulous to even think it. But what about Gary Bodum? Yes, Nick had already questioned him. But he could be lying. He was like family to the Dobsons, and he'd had a lot invested in Julie's success. He might have played a part in soring Mercedes for the win. Julie would be graduating soon. His prize student. His most profitable one too. With her gone, the stable would suffer. If he could guarantee Julie's win, it would mean instant fame for Premiere. It would mean more equestrians training. More horses being stabled. And a lot more revenue streaming in.

Dr. Lillen interrupted her train of thought. "Dr. Hartford, how well do you know the competitive equestrian world?"

"I don't know it at all, really," said Emily.

"Julie was on a fast loop for a professional equestrian career. All she needed to complete that loop was entrance into a collegiate equestrian program. There are only ten that award scholarships. Typically, less than half of those are awarded to females."

Dr. Lillen started to saddle Mercedes as she spoke.

"That seems discriminatory," said Emily.

"It is. Here we are fifty years after the biggest feminist movement in history, and it's still a man's world."

"What were Julie's chances in all of this?"

"When Julie was nine, she wanted her own horse. The Dobsons came to me to ask about breeds. I pressed the senator and his wife with the same question. I take horse handling and ownership very seriously. They told me Julie had been obsessed with horses since she was three."

"But lots of kids like horses."

"I said the same thing. They told me Julie had been saving every penny of her allowance since she was seven to buy a horse. She had saved one hundred fifty-six dollars and thirty-nine cents." Dr. Lillen smiled as she recited the exact amount.

"I guess that's pretty serious for a kid," Emily said.

"It was very impressive. I told them to bring Julie here, and I did a little riding test so I could determine what kind of rider she was and what kind of horse might be best for her. Then I did a little digging and found a breeder with exactly the right fit. Mercedes was just under a year when he came to live in Freeport."

"But what made her want to compete?" asked Emily.

"It was in her. Julie was highly competitive and a very skilled rider. She competed locally, regionally, and then nationally, and never took home less than third place. Ever."

"Sounds like she was born for this."

"She was. And she died doing what she loved." Dr. Lillen's eyes turned red and watery. She paused to swallow the lump in her throat. Emily could see that to Dr. Lillen, Julie was more than a rider, and Mercedes was more than a patient. They were family. "Julie had such a clear sense of her calling as an equestrian…such a great love and respect for the horses. They responded to her as if she were an extension of themselves. I've never seen anything like it."

Emily noted the wistfulness in Dr. Lillen's voice as she spoke.

"That's beautiful. And it sounds like her chances for that college scholarship were pretty favorable?"

"She had it locked in. Despite the uphill climb. Julie applied to ten universities that offer equestrian degrees. A couple weeks ago, she found out she was accepted to three of those universities. But only one was awarding equestrian scholarships. Texas A&M. They planned on sending a scout up."

A lot was riding on this Saturday's competition, thought Emily, weighing the information. "Was Julie nervous about winning?"

"Julie knew she could capture the victory, but her dad groomed her to be a perfectionist. He was hard on her.

Demanded a lot. Put a lot into her training. He liked to remind her of that."

"A little ketamine might have relieved some of the pressure Julie was feeling."

"Makes sense to me. More sense than someone drugging her," said Dr. Lillen. "Is this what she died from?"

"No. It wasn't a lethal dose. Just enough to, like you say, take the edge off," said Emily.

"You can get this drug a lot of places. It's become a common street drug," said Dr. Lillen.

"I know. But it doesn't sound like Julie had a lot of free time to be on the streets hunting drugs," said Emily as she stroked Mercedes's thick mane and spoke to him in a gentle manner. "You saw it all, didn't you? I wish you could tell us what you saw that morning."

Emily thanked Dr. Lillen and headed out of the barn. As she looked down the pathway between the stalls, she began to notice all the equine tools and pieces of equipment that lined the walls above the stalls. Bits and bridles hung on pegs. Boots and riding gear leaning against walls. Saddles slung over wooden partitions. What an investment. This was not a cheap hobby like ballet or Little League.

Emily thought about the hundreds and hundreds of hours these kids put into practice and care of their animals. Parents were sure to dump thousands of dollars in fees, food, uniforms, equipment, transportation, and competition expenses. The stakes seemed high to perform well, to make good on the investment. She turned around and walked back to where Dr. Lillen was buffing out a saddle.

"Will you please keep me posted? I'm horrified something like this could happen here, in Freeport," said Dr. Lillen, her voice cracking again. "And I'm going to miss her very much."

Emily nodded and paced out of the barn to her car in the driveway. She felt an odd closeness to Julie. She had only been a part of her world for a couple of days now, but it was as if Julie was the next-door neighbor kid she had known for years.

The visit had raised suspicions about what was really going on at Premiere. It made sense that Gary would be a part of this scheme. Or perhaps hired someone at the stables to carry out his plan. She felt only slightly closer to any answers about Julie's killer. Hopefully, Nick was getting somewhere with that list from the stable. Everyone on that list had access to Julie. And although motive was still unclear, one of them had to be the tormentor who'd killed Julie. It was an awful way to go. Blunt force trauma. Emily had always hated the ugliness of those words. And the violence of the act. She could feel her chest tensing. Anger and justice warred inside her. Even if her father and Cathy didn't need her, Emily wasn't sure she could leave Freeport until she and Nick had found Julie Dobson's killer.

TWENTY-NINE

EMILY CHECKED HER phone when she got to her car. There were two messages. One was from Brandon, asking if she knew how many guests she would be inviting from her side of the family. This was definitely something his mother had put him up to. And it was not something she could think about just now. How could the family be so insensitive to her needs at this moment? They weren't unkind people, but they sure seemed to be disconnected to any life she had apart from Brandon's.

There was also a message from Jo, reminding her about the equestrian show on Saturday and inviting her to their house for dinner afterward. That sounded like a nice break from everything she had been dealing with. She was hoping Nick would have called with an update. She phoned him and he answered right away.

"Great timing. I'm between interviews. What's up?"

"Dr. Lillen thought Julie might have been using ketamine to wind down. I think you should have another chat with David Sands about it. He would know."

"I'm double-booked over here. Can you take this one?"

"Nick, I'm not qualified for this."

"You did the autopsy on his girlfriend. You have the authority."

"Won't he think it's weird?"

"I guarantee you no one else is giving him the answers about Julie's death that he really needs."

EMILY WAITED IN the auditorium of Freeport High School for David to arrive for basketball practice. When he came dribbling onto the courts in practice clothes, Emily called him aside and drew him into the hallway.

"Do you know who I am, David?" she started. He shook his head. "I'm Dr. Emily Hartford. I did the autopsy on Julie Dobson. I wondered if I could ask you a few things."

"Have you figured out who killed her yet?" He continued dribbling his ball, switching off hands—left, right, left, right—while Emily searched for the right words. "I heard a rumor she was hit in the head," said David.

"David, Julie had ketamine in her system. Do you know what that is?" Emily asked.

"Horse sedative," he replied.

"That's right. Do you know if Julie was taking it?"

"I think your lab made a mistake," David said, bouncing the ball off the brick hallway wall.

"There is no mistake," Emily pressed. "Help me figure out what happened to Julie."

"Did you tell her folks?" David dropped the ball and dribbled nervously and scrambled after it as it rolled a few feet down the hall.

"I wanted to talk to you first," Emily said with a probing look. "Was Julie taking ketamine?"

"We both took it. Just a little," David said.

"I see."

"We just wanted to feel better."

"Feel better about what?"

"Life."

"Can you be a little more specific?"

"I don't see what the big deal is."

"I'm not going to rat on you. I'm just trying to figure some things out to help find the person who killed her."

"See them?" David nodded to the center quad, where teens were milling about after school. "That Asian girl twirling her hair has anxiety issues. Pops antidepressants like chewing gum."

His gaze shifted to a hipster couple sharing ear buds. "That guy has a bad back. Uses his mom's medical marijuana card."

Emily glanced around the room at the seemingly normal clusters of teens, heads bent over their phones.

"That girl in the black frames is ranked number three in our class. Takes Vicodin for migraines. Can't hold her GPA without them."

Emily tried to remain calm, but she wanted to wring him out. She knew he hadn't dealt with half the things she'd had to contend with when she was his age. "But why Julie? Why you?"

"Stress, dude. Parents. Grades. SATs. College. Basketball scholarships. Julie's riding competitions."

"These seem like normal things every teen has to cope with." Emily wasn't sure where to go with this conversation. Nick was so much better at this.

"Have you ever met Senator and Gloria Dobson? Stress balls." David pounded his basketball in an aggressive dribble back and forth between his palms.

"They are only the first of many stressful people and stressful situations you're going to encounter from here to eternity."

David didn't respond. But Emily wasn't surprised by

this reaction. David's attitude was nothing new to her. She saw it all the time in Chicago too. Kids were growing up ill-equipped for the challenges of life because of helicopter parents who didn't want them to land too hard on the ground.

"Julie's parents hated me," said David. "And they're gonna blame this on me."

"David, did you and Julie get the ketamine from Gary Bodum's office?" she asked.

David dribbled nervously.

"No way. He kept that thing locked tight," said David.

"Where then?"

"Why should I tell you?" said David. "What does it get me?"

"You get a clear conscience. And a chance to help the girl you loved," Emily said. David stopped dribbling and tucked the basketball under his arm. He glanced from the floor to Emily.

Emily softened her tone. "This is the girl you wanted to spend your life with, right?"

"Yes."

"You won't go to jail for telling me," she said.

"It's not jail I'm worried about," he said. "It's him."

"Him? Who? If you tell me, I'll be sure to keep your name confidential," Emily reassured him.

"What guarantee do I have?"

Emily paused. "I'll do my best to protect you. But I'll be honest: I don't know what the future holds for this case."

David started to dribble back to the gym.

"But I can tell you that if you don't help me now, there's a good chance you'll be in deeper trouble later, and…Julie's killer may never be found."

David turned around and looked her directly in the eyes.

"You know how she really died."

"Yes." Emily paused. "Was it Gary Bodum?"

David paced back to where Emily was standing. He held the ball close to his chest, as if he were protecting his heart.

"Did she suffer?"

It was the one question a victim's family and friends always asked.

"If I tell you, will you tell me what I want to know?" Emily bargained. She hated using this as leverage. It felt coercive. David nodded.

"She was struck in the head and suffered a brain hemorrhage," Emily told him gently.

"Was it...quick?" David asked with a quiver in his voice.

She wanted to tell him that Julie had been knocked unconscious and slipped into her death peacefully and painlessly. She wanted to protect him from the truth. But her father hadn't trained her to lie about the manner of death. He never sugarcoated the truth. He was gentle and respectful. Yes. But he had taught her that, number one, the truth always comes out. And number two, it is always easier to heal from the truth than a lie.

Emily looked David in the eyes levelly, in a way she felt was more warranted than it had been with Sarah. "She probably felt immense pain after impact. Like a really bad, bad headache. And most likely she felt her skull crack. She would have been conscious for about a minute. Maybe less. And then it was over."

David looked away, digesting the raw information. Emily knew he was experiencing surging emotions as he grappled with it. She wished no one ever had to hear what she'd just told him. This was a turning point for David. He hung his head and dribbled the ball a few feet down the hall. He couldn't face her.

"David? Are you okay?" Emily asked. David moved the ball back toward Emily, slowly palming it across his chest again. "Was it Gary? Just nod or shake your head."

"No. It was Tim Hart. He works at the stables," said David. "He's a groom."

"He had access to the ketamine?"

"Yeah. He had the key to Gary's cabinet. He had other stuff too."

"Other drugs?"

"That's what he told us. But Julie and I only did ketamine," said David.

"Do you think he killed Julie?"

"We had a falling out with him."

"Explain." Emily didn't like the sound of this.

"We owed him money."

"How much money?"

"Couple hundred."

"Couple hundred like two? Or couple hundred like five?"

"Eight-fifty."

"How did he let you rack up such a high debt?"

"I guess he knew we were good for it. At least Julie. With her dad's money," he said.

"Didn't Gary know someone was stealing his ketamine supply?"

"Tim would sell it off and then invoice the vet for more to replace it," David explained.

"But, again, didn't Gary notice that in his books?"

"Are you kidding? It all balanced out. And it's such a

little amount compared to what he spends in his whole budget. It's an easy score."

"You seem to know a lot about how Premiere operates," Emily said.

"Julie used to help Gary sometimes in the office," David explained.

"So this debt you had, how were you planning to pay it?"

"I had a little in savings. And Julie was gonna get the rest from her dad. Tell him she needed it for horse supplies. He was putting so much money into her training, what was another couple five hundred?"

"Did that work?"

"It would have. But then he asked for invoices from the stables. We were trying to forge something, but Tim was getting impatient. Said he was gonna make things really rough for Julie if we didn't pay right then."

"What did he mean by that?" Emily asked.

"This one kid from school owed him, like, two hundred dollars. He raised hogs, you know, for show—the fair. And Tim went to his house one night and led one of his hogs into the back seat of this guy's car that was parked near their barn. Then he killed the pig in the car and left it there."

Emily's stomach rolled over. A hog-killing drug dealer. Revolting.

"We just didn't think he'd do anything like that to Julie because, you know, with her dad being a senator and stuff."

"You thought you were untouchable," Emily said. "But you set up the GoPro just in case."

David nodded. "Julie wanted it for blackmail."

"But when you caught Tim, you couldn't tell anyone because then she wouldn't be able to compete?"

"Right."

"How did you hide Mercedes's wounds?"

"We cleaned the sores and applied an antibiotic and a numbing agent so that Mercedes wouldn't feel the pain. The judges don't test every horse, and thankfully Mercedes wasn't called in that day."

"So no one suspected a thing, and Mercedes was able to perform," said Emily, piecing it together.

"They won the competition."

David's breathing had increased, and Emily noticed his forehead and arms were sweating. A good sign. He was telling the truth. She wished he had come clean for Nick. And whether or not Tim was involved in Julie's death, he seemed strongly connected to this misdeed. Ire and sadness intertwined in Emily as she thought about the deadly consequences of Julie and David's actions. No one was left untouched by their string of poor teenage choices. Even the innocent Mercedes.

THIRTY

EMILY ZIPPED ACROSS the street to the Freeport Public Library. She wanted to find out more about Tim Hart so she could tell Nick. Emily also knew that now that the toxicology report was released, there would be even more finger-pointing. The Dobsons would blame David for leading Julie into a life of drug abuse and criminal activity that eventually led to her murder. They would demand to put him under the microscope. This was exactly the kind of juicy tale that could garner all sorts of media attention and sway community and jury members. If Emily could come up with solid evidence that pointed this investigation in the right direction and potentially even result in an arrest before the news broke, Nick and his team could sweep in and make Tim's arrest. David could be saved from public harm.

Emily selected a computer and tried to log in. She quickly realized she needed an account. Of course. She found the only librarian on duty, stacking books in the shelves.

"Oh, you're a familiar face, Emmie Hartford. Remember I used to call you that?"

"Miss Sally Overzet?" Emily exclaimed, recognizing the woman. She had let her hair go gray and had put on a few pounds under an oversized sweater and elastic-waisted polyester pants. She had the same warm smile and calming personality.

"I suppose you're back in town for your dad? How's he doing?"

"A little better. Thank you for asking." Emily didn't want to get into it with her. "I need to use the computer, and it's asking for my log-in. Can you help me set up an account?"

"Of course. Have you tried your old log-in?"

"Well, no, I didn't think it would still be active."

Sally walked with Emily to the computer station. "Try it. Let's see. If not, we'll get you set up with a new one."

Emily typed in first initial and last name.

"Do you remember your password?" said Sally.

Emily thought for a second. She had started her own account shortly after her mother passed away. So...what would have been important enough for her to set as a password when she was fifteen? Then, in a flash, it came to her. She entered "NICK4EVER." The log-in screen disappeared, and she was in the system. Emily laughed out loud.

"What's so funny, dear?"

"Oh...oh...just... I can't believe it...after all this time."

"I'll let you get to work. If you need anything, I'm just right over there in the steamy romance section," Sally said with a wink.

Once in the local periodicals system, Emily did a quick search for Tim Hart. From what she found, she learned that Tim would have been a freshman at Freeport High School when she had been a senior. But he didn't look familiar to her, and she wondered why she had never heard of him. His address popped up. She jotted it down and then scrolled down a few pages to see if she could find out anything more about him.

The Freeport County Examiner had featured him in

a few hunting photos when he was a teenager. There was a graduation picture from seven years ago. She kept scrolling until a link titled "Hart Arrested for Assault" caught her eye, and she clicked onto the link.

Timothy Hart, age 23, was arrested Saturday night for assault on his girlfriend, a Freeport resident. Hart and his girlfriend were leaving Bart's Bar a little after 1 AM, when a witness reported Hart threw his girlfriend to the ground and kicked her. Police took Hart to the Freeport County Jail, where he was placed in jail with a $500,000 bond. Trial date to be set Tuesday.

Nice guy, Emily thought smugly. She clicked onto another link. Hart had been sentenced to eight months in jail two years ago. Another link informed her that he had been released from jail on good behavior after five months.

Emily clicked on a third page of links and found a source stating that Tim had been arrested as a minor for robbing a gas station and for truancy. He had been sent to juvenile detention. Between his truancy and juvenile detention, Tim had virtually been absent his freshman year. No wonder she didn't know who he was. And now he was dealing to the high school population of Freeport and quite possibly Julie's killer.

Emily got back into her car and pressed Nick's number. It went right to voicemail. He was probably tied up in interviews. She wasn't sure what to do. A text pinged from Nick: In interview. Urgent?

She quickly texted back: Tim Hart is go-pro guy. Dealing drugs to Julie & David.

Nick came right back with Nice work.

She waited for more. Nice work? That was it?

Are you gonna arrest him? she texted.

Based on what cause? came the answer after a few minutes.

Based on wht Davd said, Emily typed quickly, misspelling half the words.

Doesn't work that way. Gotta go.

Emily was quaking inside. Why wasn't Nick dropping everything? Certainly none of these other interviews held this much weight! She had practically handed him his killer.

Emily stewed for a minute about her next course of action. She had to get in front of this story before the news cycle did. Once Tim got wind of Julie's tox results, there was no doubt in her mind that he would go on the run. He might even head out of the country. The Canadian border was only five hours away. David was counting on her.

Then she remembered one very important detail about the position of medical examiner. The medical examiner outranked the sheriff when it came to matters involving death investigation. And if public safety was at stake—and she believed it was—Tim Hart was dealing drugs to minors. Worse, if Tim even got a tiny whiff that he was being considered as a suspect in Julie's murder, she knew he would ditch Freeport. This had to be handled carefully. And even though Emily had the right to demand the sheriff's department to take immediate action to secure public welfare, she thought she would do a little more reconnaissance first. The more puzzle pieces she could put together for Nick, the better equipped he would be to make a clean arrest.

THIRTY-ONE

THE LATE AFTERNOON October sun spread a glow across the sky as Emily coasted her Nissan Leaf a quarter mile from the trailer park and pulled into a turnout alongside the road. She parked and hoofed her way toward the entrance to the trailer park where Tim Hart lived.

The trailer park only boasted a hundred or so trailers, each with an ample half-acre yard that allowed a certain amount of privacy Emily hadn't expected from such a place. Within a few minutes, Emily had located Tim's address, spray-painted in hunter orange on a rusted mailbox. The yard was overgrown in thigh-high weeds. Fifty-five-gallon barrels and an old wooden rowboat sat like misplaced chess pieces along the front and side of the trailer. Tim's pickup truck was parked cock-eyed in the gravel driveway. Inside she could hear a TV blasting.

She snuck up on Tim's trailer from behind and then realized she hadn't exactly formulated a foolproof plan. She paused to think carefully about how to execute her next steps.

First, she needed to get a lay of the area. A game show blaring from a television inside hid the sound of her footsteps as she crept up to the bottom corner of a curtainless window that looked into the living room.

Peering in, she was surprised at what she saw. Tim's place was tidy, a throwback to the 1970s. His walls were plastered in silver-framed rock posters, floor to ceiling. The vintage olive shag carpet matched the black vinyl furniture and orange lamps. A lava lamp gurgled on an end table. Tim had actually taken a great deal of pride in his interior decorating. It was an eye-catching, eclectic combo of early attic vintage, which, if featured on Pinterest, would receive thousands of re-posts, she was certain. Was this the home of a drug dealer?

From her purview she could see that Tim was not in the living room. Nor in the kitchen just a few feet away. And that was all the view she had of the inside. Emily watched and listened for a few minutes. Then she moved to the other half of the trailer, where the bedrooms were situated. She jacked herself up on the ledge of the home to look into the smaller bedroom, which she found dark and empty. She slipped over to the master bedroom window and again propped herself up to see in the window. The blinds were closed, so Emily did her best to squint through the bent metal slats. There was a small light on in the bedroom, but from what she could scan, it also appeared to be empty.

Strange. Tim's truck was here. The TV and lights were on. Where was Tim? Maybe he had stepped out to run down to the gas station for cigarettes or a snack? Maybe visiting a neighbor? Maybe he was watching her right now from another trailer? She had to act quickly.

Pacing toward the front of the trailer, Emily headed for the front door. She noticed it was cracked open and stepped inside, shutting the door behind her gently, but not latching it. Her eyes were drawn to horse and rider magazines fanned out neatly on the coffee table. She immediately started to search for evidence of drugs. She looked under couch cushions and in the bookcase.

She lifted the top of an ottoman, which only yielded a folded pile of hand-crocheted afghans, also vintage treasures. This guy was impeccable. Sure wouldn't have guessed it from the weed-thickened yard. But still no drug evidence.

She scanned the kitchen. Two brown leather objects shoved under the table grabbed her attention. She moved closer. It was then Emily recognized she was looking at a pair of boots. The exact pair from Julie Dobson's GoPro video. The attacker's boots. Emily drew in a sharp breath. She whipped out her camera and snapped several shots of the evidence until she heard a thud from the back of the trailer.

Emily froze. Should she run? Hide? What if he came out and attacked her? What if he held her hostage? She instinctively pressed 911. And then immediately regretted it. She ended the call. How on earth was she going to explain why she had trespassed on Tim's property? If he found her now, he could legally attack her, claim self-defense, and she would find herself going to jail. But what if he did attack her and she couldn't hold him back? Wasn't a trespassing charge worth her safety and maybe her life? Pride got the better of her, and she resolved to choose a different option.

Emily's eyes darted across the kitchen countertop, her sights finding a large butcher knife. She paused for a moment. She should go. Leave right now. She had ample evidence to match her pics of his boots with Julie's video. Certainly that would establish probable cause. Nick could take it from there. She turned to head out, when a noise from the rear of the trailer stopped her. A moan. A gasp. A gurgle. Emily was familiar with this sound. It was common in patients who were about to die.

Emily summoned her courage, grabbed the butcher knife, clutched it at her shoulder, and inched toward the first bedroom. The door was wide open, and the room was dark, but empty. She nudged her way to the next door. Nothing in the house stirred except for the tinny sound of a cheesy local car commercial. She drew in a breath and dared to glance into the next doorway, the bathroom. With a quick bob of her head around the doorframe, she got a blurred view of Tim's form slumped onto the floor in front of the toilet. Her heart thumped wildly through her rib cage. She waited a few minutes, listening intently. Tim wasn't stirring.

She bobbed her head back in, this time taking a slightly longer look, enough to see that Tim was lying on his side, motionless, foaming at the mouth. She felt awkward and frightened at the same time. She pulled her head back into the hall.

"Tim?" she called out. No answer.

"Tim!" Still nothing. She poked her head back in. Tim had not moved. His eyes were open, glassy and unresponsive.

"Tim? Can you hear me?" No response.

Emily's doctor instincts kicked in. Tim wasn't a threat. He was dying.

Emily crawled into the bathroom and pressed her first two fingers to his wrist to find a pulse. Just to be on the safe side, she held the knife ready with her other hand. A weak pulse palpitated below the skin's surface. Tim's shallow breath told Emily he was hanging on. Emily dropped the knife, grabbed him by the shoulders, and rolled him onto his back to open his windpipe. As she did this, a small plastic bag fell from his left hand and clued her in to his condition. She found a syringe tucked under his right thigh. He had overdosed.

Emily pulled out her phone and dialed 911. When dispatch answered, she gave them the address, Tim's condition, and her full name. There was no way around it. As a physician, she couldn't abandon her patient. As acting medical examiner, she couldn't risk damaging Julie's investigation. And as a human being, she couldn't ignore the dignity of another life, even if that life belonged to a murderer.

THIRTY-TWO

EMILY STABILIZED TIM and waited for the ambulance. It arrived and the paramedics took over. The police appeared right on their heels and wanted to question Emily, who was standing in the yard, watching Tim being lifted into the ambulance.

"No questions right now," she told them. "I'll answer them at the station. In the meantime, you need to search Tim's trailer for ketamine from Premiere."

Seconds later, Nick's pickup barreled up. He got out and stormed over to Emily with a surly look. He and Emily drew away from the officers so they could speak privately.

"What are you doing?" Nick could hardly believe what he was seeing.

"I know. I know it looks bad," she started. "But this was a matter of public safety."

"How do you figure?" Nick asked.

"Can we discuss this later?"

"No, I think we better tackle that now. I'm actually dying to know how you made Tim's acquaintance," said Nick with a smidge of sarcasm.

"Medical examiner outranks sheriff in these kinds of matters," Emily said.

"What kind of matters?"

"Public safety. Tim is a dangerous drug dealer and—"

"Are you crazy? You could've been killed!"

Emily pulled up the photos from her phone. "It was worth it. Look. I found these in Tim's kitchen."

Nick studied them, "The boots from the video. Are you sure they're the same ones?"

"They're right inside. Go take a look for yourself," she said.

"This is exigent circumstance enough for me," said Nick. "We're going in there." He motioned to the other officers.

"Can I go in?" Emily asked.

"Are you kidding me? You stay right out here and don't move."

"Don't I get so much as a thank-you?" she said with an impish grin that deflected Nick's frustrated look. Emily's curiosity and stubbornness carved a path around almost anything that was in her way.

"I think I'll hold off on the praise and gratitude until this all pans out," he said as he headed into Tim's trailer.

"Oh, it will," said Emily, smiling as she crossed her arms and rested up against Nick's truck.

INSIDE TIM'S TRAILER, one officer recovered the boots from the kitchen while another searched the living room, small bedroom, and bath. Nick took Tim's bedroom. It didn't take long before he uncovered bags of pills neatly lining the dresser drawers under the folded clothes. He collected and recorded them, sealing them into several evidence bags. He continued his search of the closet, the mattress, under the bed, and behind furniture. Nick even checked underneath the carpet, which was fraying away from the walls. Nothing.

The last place Nick searched was Tim's nightstand. On it was a nasal spray bottle, whose labeling had long worn off. From the wear, Nick could tell the bottle had been repurposed several times. He knew it was a popular trick to fill spray bottles with a liquid ketamine mixture. Effortless to inhale. Quick to penetrate the system. Easy to hide. Nick suspected this was what Tim had sold Julie and David. And he had a good hunch that this was the bottle from the stable.

He added the spray to his evidence bag and then began looking through the single drawer on the nightstand. He lifted out a few porn magazines, pens, old tissues, and a pocketknife. He thought he had emptied the drawer, when an object from the back glimmered as it caught the light. Nick pulled the drawer out to the end of its rail. A piece of silver jewelry was coiled up in the shadowed corner. Nick immediately recognized three charms: a horseshoe, a horse, and a heart.

THIRTY-THREE

COMING OUT OF Tim's trailer post-investigation, Nick politely thanked Emily and reassured her he could take things from there. Emily felt a bit snubbed but remained justified in her actions. Nick told her in a stern voice they would talk about this "little incident" later. Emily brushed him off. She didn't regret what she had done. If she hadn't arrived when she had, Tim would have been dead. And now Nick had his prime suspect.

When Emily arrived at the Pennington Inn, she was too tired for dinner. She slid into her sweats and a T-shirt, feeling assured Julie's killer was behind bars.

She texted Nick two words: You're welcome.

She fell asleep waiting for his response. It was the soundest sleep she had gotten since she had arrived in Freeport.

The next morning, Emily awoke, freshened, to a voicemail from her father. He was being released at 9:00 am. She dressed and was out the door by eight so she could stop at Brown's for a fresh cinnamon roll.

"You look rested," Delia said, handing over the warm pastry.

"I am. I slept great. I feel great. And we found Julie's killer," she said, grinning as Delia steamed a small pitcher of milk and added it to a double shot of espresso for Emily's latte.

"Yes, I heard."

"You did?" Emily took a sip of her drink and burnt her tongue.

"Everyone heard."

"How?"

"Doll, I was at the barbeque last night. Where were you?"

Emily's mouth dropped open and her stomach sank. "Oh my gosh. I completely forgot."

"Well, there's always the next one. But I suppose you'll be back in Chicago by then."

Emily slumped into a seat at one of the café tables. "I'm so bummed. He's going to think I purposefully ditched him."

"Maybe it's better you didn't show. He was pretty mad about what you did."

"He was? Is that all over Freeport too?"

"No. He pulled me aside and told me."

"Oh. And? What did you say?"

"I listened." Delia wiped off the steamer nozzle and polished it until it gleamed.

"Delia, I was within my rights as acting medical examiner to—"

"I know, doll. That's not why he was mad."

Emily was puzzled. "He thinks I went over his head on this."

"No. You don't understand. You put yourself in grave danger."

"But it all worked out. I'm fine. And Nick got his suspect."

"You're missing the point, Em." Delia looked up as the front door chimes rang and the door opened, bringing in her next set of customers. "Good morning. What can I get for you?"

Emily suddenly lost her appetite. She rose from the table, leaving her pastry untouched. She took her coffee cup and waved a quick goodbye to Delia.

"I've gotta go. My dad's being released this morning."

"Glad to hear it," said Delia, tossing Emily a concerned glance as she headed toward the door. "And think about what I said."

THIRTY-FOUR

WHEN EMILY PULLED up to the hospital entrance, she was surprised to find a nurse wheeling her father through the front doors to the pickup curb at eight thirty. Her father sprang from the wheelchair as soon as Emily idled to a stop. His hand was on the door handle as Emily put the car in park. She didn't even have a chance to get out of the car to help him in before he was angling his body into the front passenger seat. Thankfully, the nurse was close behind, spotting him. She handed Robert the discharge paperwork and shut the door as he grunted a thank-you.

"Good morning, Dad," Emily started as she pulled away. "How'd you sleep?"

"Horribly. I'm glad to be out of there," he said. "I heard you had a busy night. Saved a life. Caught a criminal."

"Something like that."

"Nick came in here raving mad and told me the whole thing. Thought maybe I could talk some sense into you."

"And you said…?"

"That it would be a waste of time. You were well within your right to do what you did."

"Thank you." Emily felt vindicated in her decision.

"So, how does it feel being back in coroner shoes?" Robert said with a pleased tone.

"Better than I thought it would," Emily answered. "I've guess I've kind of enjoyed the challenge. And I'm a little surprised at how quickly it's all coming back to me."

"You ever wonder what your life might have looked like if you had stuck around here?" asked her father.

"I never really thought about it."

"You always talked about wanting to go to U of M for med school. Then returning to help me run the practice and ME office."

"Those were the ideals of a fifteen-year-old," Emily said.

"I suppose so," said Robert with a long sigh that she recognized as an expression of her father's disappointment. Her cheeks flushed in aggravation.

"Have you thought about who you want to ask to replace you?"

"A little. I have one young man in mind. He's starting a practice up north of the county. He's not as bright as you, but I think he'd be a good fit for the community if he's up for it."

"Do I know this guy?"

"I don't think you ever met," said her father. "His family moved up here after you left."

Dad measured everything by the time frame defined by before she'd left and after she'd left. As if he was some inculpable innocent bystander. Emily repressed her desire to discuss anything further with him as she drove the rest of the way. When they reached Robert's home, Emily pulled her car into the driveway and parked as close to the front door as she could. She circled around to the passenger door to help her father out of the car, but he brushed her away. "I'm not an invalid."

Emily relented and stepped away, gathering his things from the back seat. She glanced across the expanse of his yard. The grass needed mowing, and the bushes and trees were starting to glow with the tinge of fall hues. Leaves blanketed the lawn.

"I called Mike about the yard work. He's going to work it into his schedule," said Emily. "He wants to wait a few weeks to make sure all the leaves have fallen."

"What about the grass in the meantime?" Robert steadied himself and started walking toward the house.

"I wouldn't worry about it." Emily traipsed behind him, letting him take the lead. "And don't get any bright ideas about mowing it yourself."

Robert found the door unlocked. "Cathy must have left it that way when she went to work. She's prepping for the Dobson funeral this weekend."

"Yes, it'll be a big one. She's got her hands full for sure," said Emily.

Robert shuffled in to find a fresh apple pie sitting on the kitchen table.

"Will you look at that? Apples are fresh from our trees. Can't wait to slather a scoop of ice cream on a piece of that pie," he said and then wistfully added, "Your mother…boy, she could bake a divine pie. Remember?"

"Mm-hmm, my favorite was her peach-blueberry," said Emily, settling her father into his recliner in the living room. "Want me to bring you a slice?" she asked.

"Yes. Exactly what the mortician ordered," he said with a wry smile.

Emily sliced up two pieces. She was pretty hungry herself and couldn't remember the last time she'd had a homemade piece of pie. She hadn't picked up her mother's baking finesse, and Brandon's mother wasn't exactly the Martha Stewart type. Thank goodness Brandon was good in the kitchen.

They sat together in the living room, enjoying Cathy's apple pie. After a few bites, Robert reached into his shirt pocket and pulled out a piece of paper.

"Here. This is for you. Cathy wanted me to give it to you. She helped me make it last night." It was a list in Cathy's handwriting. Emily read down the paper:

"Wait, 'Stage the house, find a realtor, put house on market.' Does that mean you and Cathy are selling this place?" Emily asked.

"You can scratch those off the list. We're not selling this house." Robert leaned forward in his recliner and rocked himself to a standing position. "I think I'll take a walk around the property. Work off this pie."

"Is that a good idea?" Emily asked. "You shouldn't be straining yourself."

Robert was already headed for the sliding glass door that led from the living room to the backyard. She watched him cross the lawn and disappear behind the barn. On the other side of the barn was Robert's small orchard and vegetable garden. Emily went to the kitchen for a roll of aluminum wrap. She wrapped the pie in foil and placed it into the fridge to keep it fresh.

Her eyes strained as she read down the "To Do" list again and she contemplated how much work all of this was going to be. This was more than a couple weeks' work. She wondered if she might have to take a leave of residency. Was that even possible? She'd have to make a call to Dr. Claiborne. Emily paced the house for a few minutes, looking at all the furniture that would have to be moved, stored, or sold, before her worry about her father sent her out the door after him. Robert was whittling slices off a freshly picked apple with his pocketknife when he noticed Emily's presence in the orchard.

"Just picked it from the Macintosh," Robert said. "Want one?"

"No thanks. Still full from the pie."

"That tree is overloaded. The lower branches are almost touching the ground. You can see where the deer grabbed a few snacks. But the rest are ripe and ready. We should call the food bank to come over and harvest it. Shame it should go to waste this year," he said.

"I'll put it on the list."

"I worked like a fiend to keep those tent worms off the trees."

"Seems to have done the trick," she said. "You know, Dad, despite the way things turned out, I have some really great memories of this place."

Robert nodded and surveyed his beautiful little country kingdom. A satisfied look settled over him. He turned slightly to Emily and drew out his words slowly.

"When I die, whether it's next week or ten years from now, it's going to be here. At this home. On this land."

Emily was about to open her mouth.

"Emily. Stop. This is how it is," he said with a calm tone.

"Speaking as a doctor, not your daughter, you're making really bad choices for yourself."

"Well, they're mine to make," he told her. "And I need you to know that it meant the world to me that you came up here to see me."

"I'm not sure it made any difference," she replied.

"Not if you're measuring it by how much you can manipulate me," her father teased.

They stood there for a moment in the stillness of the orchard grove. Emily wished he would say more. Say he was sorry. Tell her he loved her and was proud of her. Explain what truth she deserved to know. All of the things that would have stopped her from running from this place. But her father remained quiet. Emily's gut churned, and she left her dad to his Macintosh tree.

THIRTY-FIVE

NICK HAD LET Tim hang out in jail for the night, before he interrogated him. And then took his time the next morning going through paperwork and emails and prepping his questions. He wanted Tim to sweat it out a little. When he entered the interrogation room at the police station, Nick found a jittery Tim cuffed to a table. The clerk on the other side of the room started recording the conversation through a sound system wired into a locked room next door.

"Tim Hart, tell me about your job at the stable," Nick said.

"I dunno. Not much to tell. Hey, so why am I in here?"

"When did you start working at Premiere?" Nick went on, ignoring Tim's question.

"Gary gave me a job when I got outta jail," said Tim.

"So, that was about two years ago?"

"I guess so," said Tim. "Don't I get an attorney?"

"We can stop right now and get you an attorney, but it may take a day or two, and you'll just have to sit in jail while we run the process. Is that what you want?"

Tim shrugged. "What was the question?"

"What do you do at Premiere?"

"I'm a groom. I take care of the horses. Feed 'em. Water 'em. Clean up after 'em," answered Tim. "I like horses."

"You ride?" Nick asked.

"Yeah. That's one of the perks of the job. I get to exercise the boarder horses," said Tim.

"Sounds like a good gig," Nick said. "You have a favorite horse?"

"They each have their charms," Tim answered. "Hey, are you keeping me overnight again? Bodum's expecting me to be at the stables to feed 'em tomorrow morning."

"He's been notified," Nick said. "Did you have any favorite owners?"

"That's an odd question."

"Were you keen on any of the owners? Take a liking to any of them?"

"No. They were all fine, I guess. No one really gives you trouble if you do your job," said Tim.

"What kind of trouble did Julie Dobson give you?"

"Huh? I don't know what you're talking about," said Tim.

"You did know Julie Dobson, didn't you?" Nick led in.

Tim looked at Nick and sat up a little.

"Why do you wanna know about her?"

"I just wanna know if you knew her. Did you talk to her? See her? Did she talk to you?" said Nick.

"Well, yeah. She was there every day training," said Tim.

"What kind of relationship would you say you and Julie Dobson had?"

"I don't get it. Relationship? Why are you asking me this stuff?"

"Did you harm her horse, Mercedes?"

"I feel like I should have that lawyer here," said Tim.

"Are you requesting a lawyer be present before we continue?"

"Maybe. I dunno. Should I?"

"I dunno. Should you?"

"I ain't gonna tell that lawyer anything different than I'm gonna tell you."

"Then let's proceed. There's something I want you to watch," said Nick, cueing up the GoPro video on his phone. Tim watched it. When it was over, Tim looked away.

"So, is that you?" said Nick.

Tim didn't answer. Nick raised his voice in a slow, steady manner.

"Is that you in that video?"

Tim shrugged and looked past Nick as if he was seeing something on the other side of the brick wall.

"We found a pair of boots in your trailer that look an awful lot like these ones. Sent them down to the crime lab to get a soil composition comparison." Nick lowered his voice. "Did you know they can match the exact composition of horse manure to the exact horse that shat it out?"

Tim stared at him.

"Is that you in the GoPro video?"

Tim nodded slightly.

"Say it, Mr. Hart. I need you to say it out loud."

"Yeah, that's me," he said.

"Explain this to me. 'Cause it looks really bad."

"It was a warning," said Tim.

"Looks like abuse to me."

"It was the only way I could get through to Julie and her stupid boyfriend."

"Why did you need to get through to them? What for?"

"'Cause she had missed a few payments."

"Payments for what?"

Tim shook his head, "She owed me some money."

"I need you to say what for," Nick said.

"Some medication," Tim said.

"What's the name of the medication?"

"Ketamine," Tim replied.

"It's a horse med, right?"

"Yeah."

"Where'd you get it?"

"From Bodum's supply."

"And to your knowledge, was Julie taking ketamine?"

"Yeah."

"So you were dealing to a minor?"

"She begged me for it. She was breaking under the pressure."

"Why would you risk your job for her?"

Inside, Nick boiled, but he kept his cool and pressed on with the interview. Tim waffled, his eyes darting away from Nick and scanning the ceiling to the floor. Nick recognized this behavior. Tim was searching for a lie.

"She was nice to me. I liked her."

"A lot of people are nice. Why would you risk that?" Nick pressed.

"She came from money," he said. "I thought it would be an easy sale. But then she got behind. Hurting Mercedes was the only way I could get through to Julie. I don't run no charity."

"How far behind was she exactly?"

"Eight. Eight hundred."

Nick gave a low whistle. "That's seems like a lot, Tim. Were you ever worried she wouldn't pay you back?"

"Not at first. But then a couple weeks went by, and I started to wonder. She told me she had a plan and not to worry, and I'd have the money by that Thursday."

"And did she?" said Nick.

"No, she didn't show up to the stables on Thursday," said Tim.

"And that's when you attacked her horse?"

Tim nodded.

"Say it," Nick demanded.

"Yes. That day. I didn't know she had a GoPro in the stable," said Tim.

"Obviously not," said Nick. Criminals were not usually the sharpest tools in the shed.

"And there were other attacks on Mercedes too. Weren't there?"

"I don't get where you're going, buddy." Tim's gaze shifted again to the wall.

"Tying his head up. Rollkur? Sound familiar? Who did that?"

"That's different." Tim's voice was agitated.

"How?"

"That wasn't about the payments."

"What was it about?"

"The senator. He paid me to do those things to Mercedes so he would perform better," Tim blurted out. "Had nothing to do with the money Julie owed me."

Nick couldn't believe what he was hearing.

"You're telling me Senator Dobson, Julie's father, hired you to harm Mercedes?"

"Happens a lot. It's a cheat tactic."

"How?"

"It helps stretch their heads so they can achieve hyperflexation in dressage."

Julie was a great equestrian. Why would he need her and Mercedes to cheat? Nick was scrambling to make some sense of this.

"He threatened to send me back to jail if I said anything," said Tim. "I hated doing it. Mercedes is a good animal. Once Julie discovered Mercedes was being tortured, she was hell bent on finding out who done it."

Nick was sickened by what he was hearing. *What kind of parent would do this to their child?*

"What about the morning of Julie's death. Did you see her then?"

"Wait a minute, man. I know what you're doing here, and I didn't kill Julie Dobson," Tim said with flaring anger. "Don't pin this on me."

"We found her bracelet in your dresser drawer." Nick laid the bracelet on the table between them. "I did a little research, and judging by the quality of the metal and the number of charms, it's worth almost a thousand dollars. So, how did this get into your possession?"

Tim looked down at the table, his eyes tracing a pattern in the wood grain. He blinked a few times and fixed a steady gaze on Nick.

"I didn't kill Julie Dobson," he insisted.

"This looks bad for you, Tim. Real bad. Especially since we know Julie was wearing it when she was found."

Nick could tell Tim's fear was growing by the way he started bouncing his knee under the table. "Look, don't make this harder for yourself. Just tell me what happened that morning."

"I was at home working on my truck with a friend," Tim told him.

"What's your friend's name?" Nick asked.

"Jason Settman. He lives next door. I got to work late that day because my truck wouldn't start, and Jason and I had to replace the battery. He'll tell ya," Tim said. Nick recalled what Gary Bodum had said about Tim being late and claiming vehicle troubles as the excuse.

"Okay. But that still doesn't explain why you had Julie's bracelet," said Nick. "Did you have someone else kill Julie?"

"Of course not."

"But it seems like you're capable. I mean, you abuse horses," Nick said.

Tim wouldn't answer.

Nick pounded his fist on the table next to the bracelet. "How did you get this? Get your story straight now! Save yourself a lot of trouble and jail time down the road."

"When I got to the stables, Farmer Gibbons had already discovered Julie's body. He and Gary were calling the cops about it, and I went outside to get a look at her. I couldn't believe it. I saw Julie lying there, and my first thought was that I'd never get that eight hundred back."

Tim paused. Nick knew he was close and kept silent. "I know that's a crappy thing to think about someone who's dead. But there it is, ya know? She owed me."

Nick nodded and kept his attention lasered on Tim. He kept silent, hoping Tim would offer more to his confession.

"I knew that bracelet was worth a couple hundred."

"And then what?" Nick asked.

"I swiped it off her wrist. I was gonna wait 'til the dust settled and then pawn it," Tim said.

Scumbag. How did those cops in the big cities deal

with people like Tim day in and day out? Never a break from the ugliness of human depravity.

"Okay. We're done here," said Nick.

"You're releasing me?"

"No, now you go back to jail. You're not off the hook for selling drugs and stealing personal property." Nick got up and left the room. Another officer came in and took Tim back to his holding cell. Nick gathered a few things from his office. He wasn't inclined to believe a word of Tim's story until he could cross-check his alibi with Jason Settman. And now he also had a bone to pick with Senator Dobson.

THIRTY-SIX

WHEN EMILY LEFT her father in his orchard, she went straight to the attached garage off the east side of her family home. This was where her father had built his practice some twenty-five years prior. She entered via the patient entrance, which opened into the front room of the three-room structure. It was a tidy waiting area with seating for about six persons, end tables, magazines, and a toy box. Beyond that was the administrative area, where Dad kept the files, computer, and copy machine. A part-time receptionist/nurse/office manager staffed the small desk and kept the business running smoothly so Robert could focus on patient needs. The largest room was in back, the examination area where Robert saw patients and performed very minor surgical procedures when needed. It was organized and sterile in accordance with health codes. Emily felt a sadness as she realized that soon this space would be emptied, and its items would belong to a new doctor. What seemed even worse was that he and his family would be moving into her childhood home. Despite her mixed feelings about this place, it hurt to think she would never be able to be in the same rooms where she had once lived with her mother and father.

Emily decided to start by inventorying the file room. It would take the longest and require the most energy. The biggest task in the office was the thirty-five years of patient and medical examiner files stacked in boxes that lined floor-to-ceiling bookcases. Before she could properly store each box, the files needed to be scanned and saved electronically, then the originals sealed in an envelope and mailed to each patient.

Emily groaned as she looked around the room. Quick calculations told her there had to be several thousand files. She set a goal of three boxes for the day and decided to start at the top and work her way down. She had to use a ladder to get the top shelf of boxes down. She opened the first box and started scanning the contents. After several hours, Emily had completed only one box. She felt the job would be insurmountable for her to complete on her own. She would let her dad know that he needed to hire out some help, or perhaps this was a light enough task that he could continue it on his own after she left. At least it would give him something to do.

She decided to put the finished box in the back storeroom. She unlocked the door, turned on the single lightbulb hanging from the ceiling, and started to move things around to make room for the new box. On the top of a shelf, there was one long white box that drew her curiosity. She reached for it, expecting it to be heavy. The box turned out to be light and slid into her arms. She lifted it down, gasping at what she saw. Through the thick, clear plastic on top of the box, she could see her mother's wedding dress, perfectly preserved.

She didn't dare unseal it. Emily stood there under the bright beam of the bulb, staring at the beading on the bodice of the puffy-sleeved gown, a classic mid-80s style with a V-shaped waist. She knew from the photographs that the full skirt billowed atop a hoop slip.

The size tag read four. Emily was taller and broader than her mother had been. At a size eight, she wouldn't be able to wear the dress, but wondered if she could borrow from it if she could find a seamstress to create something unique and meaningful for her. Brandon's mom might throw a fit that she wasn't going the designer route. How would his mother be able to brag to her friends about the dress? And Jo might be disappointed at first that they couldn't do the whole wedding dress shopping bit. But Emily didn't care. On her wedding day, she would be wrapped in her mother's presence and love.

Needing a break, Emily set the dress aside and went into the house for a cup of tea. She found her father napping in his recliner. In the sink were a dozen apples he had picked. Emily quietly prepared her tea, washed an apple, and headed back to the office.

Emily sunk her teeth into the fresh fruit. It was delicious. Sweet, crisp. And full of way more flavor than those tasteless organic apples she overpaid for from the health food store in the city. Emily opened the second box of files. Instead of finding a row of manila patient files, the box was half empty. In several envelopes she found county contracts for each year of her father's medical examiner work. Several handwritten ledgers tracked the bookkeeping of the ME business. And there was a large black, hard-cover journal she had never seen before.

Emily took a seat in the office chair and sipped her tea as she cracked open the journal. Her father had written in the front: "Record of Freeport County Medical Examiner Dr. Robert Hartford, M.D., M.E." Paging through, she saw that the journal was a personal record of every death her father had investigated. Each was dated and given a paragraph that outlined the brief details of the case, what Robert had discovered about it, if there were any notable events from the death, and how or why the death had been caused. Homicide cases were also assigned trial notes and outcomes, names of the accused, and sentencing details.

Emily leafed through slowly, recounting Robert's lifetime of death investigation. When she reached the end of the journal, there was a special tabbed section devoted to cold cases. There were only a few, and she chose not to look. One of them still gravely haunted her.

Emily closed the journal and put it back into the box. A lifetime of work. So many families helped. So many big and little mysteries solved. Would the next ME be as thorough? As caring? Would he go the extra steps as her father always did? Emily doubted anyone would live up to the legacy her father had created. But she had to let that go.

THIRTY-SEVEN

IT WAS LATE AFTERNOON when Nick returned to his office from questioning Jason Settman. Tim's alibi had checked out on three levels. First, Jason was with Tim at Tim's house the morning of Julie's death. Tim's truck battery had died, so he'd gone next door to Jason's trailer to get a jump. The jump didn't work. The battery was a goner. So, Jason drove Tim into town to the Napa store, where they bought a new battery.

The alibi was confirmed a second time by Jason's wife, Ashley, who was also home at the time and made coffee for Tim, and stated that he didn't leave their house until well after 8:00 am.

A third person corroborated Tim's alibi when Nick checked into the Napa battery purchase with the store owner. Tim had made a purchase at Napa that coordinated with the approximate time of the murder. The store owner recalled the event and a description of Tim. He also provided a sales record with Tim's credit card receipt. It all stacked up in a provable manner just as Tim and Jason had said.

Now what?

Nick wasn't exactly sure "now what." With the autopsy completed, the toxicology reports back, the bracelet found, and the GoPro video explained, there was no more physical evidence to draw from. Had he reached a dead end? Would Julie end up a Freeport cold case?

Nick retired to his office to think, and instructed his team to do the same. He paced restlessly, squeezing a tennis ball between his palms. He was hungry and ornery. All his hard work on this case had amounted to very little progress. What and who were they missing?

On top of this, Nick knew he had to follow up with the senator about Mercedes's abuse. His stomach sank at the thought. Other than Tim's accusation, he had no physical proof that the senator had paid Tim to perform the incidents. He would be hard-pressed to make an arrest, and doubted the senator would make a confession. Perhaps he should talk to Gary Bodum about it first. Gary should know.

Finally emerging from his office, Nick set some paperwork on his secretary's desk so she could file it in the morning. It was then that he remembered his secretary had left early to take care of a sick child. It would be another hour before the night secretary started her shift, and the other cops on duty were off on street patrol. Being the only one at the police station, Nick needed to stick around until the secretary arrived. He was heading back to his office to return some emails when he heard the door open from the outside and footsteps clomp toward the reception area. He turned and saw the figure of Senator Dobson through the sliding glass reception window that overlooked the police pen.

"Hello! Hey! Larson! Larson!" yelled the senator. Nick was already walking toward the reception desk. "Why wasn't I informed about my daughter's toxicology results?" the senator demanded through the glass separation window. "Sheriff, you better have some answers for me!"

"Senator Dobson, calm down," Nick said through the glass.

"My daughter's report? Where is it? And why didn't someone contact us?"

"Senator. Please. Calm down."

"I will not! I'm at my own daughter's wake, and I hear she had drugs in her system! You'd better produce that report. Now!" His anger and pain permeated through the glass, which Nick refused to unlock.

"I'm sorry you had to find out the way you did. I can assure you, it wasn't our agency that released the official toxicology report."

The ruffled senator collected himself, straightened his jacket, and snugged up his tie. He nodded at Nick. "Open this window."

Nick shook his head. The senator pounded his fist on the window. "Open it! You son of a bitch!"

Definitely not, thought Nick, taking a careful step back. He folded his arms across his chest and waited for the senator to calm down.

"I'm in a public position, and this is making me look very vulnerable right now. Reporters are outside my house asking me about Julie's drug habit. What drug habit?"

"I can't speak to Julie having a drug habit," said Nick diplomatically.

"Those reporters say you've got Tim Hart arrested up here on selling drugs to a minor. *My* minor."

"Tim was selling drugs to a good number of young people in this community."

"I can't have these rumors circulating about *my* daughter. I need you to make this go away."

Nick did not appreciate being ordered around. "Was Julie taking drugs?"

"No," Senator Dobson said firmly.

"You're sure?" Nick asked him.

"Yes, I'm sure."

Why is it that parents are often the last to know? Nick let a few moments of silence build up between them. The senator loosened his tie and started pacing in front of the window. After a moment, he stopped and sat in one of the orange vinyl waiting room chairs that should have been replaced three decades ago. Nick moved toward the window but did not open it.

"Toxicology lab found ketamine in her system. Tim Hart confessed to selling it to Julie from Bodum's stable stash," Nick told the senator. "Tim was the man in the viral video, and he says you hired him to score Mercedes's legs. How do you plead to that?"

The senator sat there as the information sank in. After a moment he responded with a tormented look, his voice cracking, "He killed her, didn't he? That groom killed my little girl."

"No, he didn't. His alibi checks out," said Nick. "But maybe I should be investigating you."

The senator sent a seething look to Nick. "What are you implying, Sheriff?"

"That you lawyer up."

"What exactly are you accusing me of?"

"Equine abuse. To start."

"With what proof?" His chin tipped up in a defensive manner.

"Tim's statement is rather damaging." Nick wasn't about to give him specifics. But he did want to make the senator squirm.

"I wanted only the best for my daughter... I invested everything for her future...how dare you—" He pinched off his words and straightened his shoulders. Nick knew he was smart enough to guard his statements.

"What were you hoping to accomplish when you paid Tim to torment an innocent creature?" Nick pressed.

The senator's stare never left Nick as an angry resolve filled his eyes. "What happens to our property and our family is none of your concern."

"Actually, it is. Your daughter's death is being investigated as a homicide. Your life should be a wide-open book to me."

Nick had known many parents who would go pretty far to protect their children's best interests, but the senator's actions had crossed the criminal line. He didn't care what Dobson thought of him.

"I'm innocent," the senator retorted, "and I'm not letting this story spin out of control. Tim Hart is a drug dealer, and I'm going to make sure the public knows he's corrupting their children."

"You're behind the eight ball, Senator." No amount of backpedaling was going to influence Nick.

"Julie was a double victim here. A young, impressionable girl and first-time offender who was lured in by a convicted criminal." Senator Dobson was already spinning the story. "I'll have my press secretary send you a draft tonight, and your office will release it."

"You're the one I'm hunting here, Senator," Nick said. "I want to know every detail of your involvement in mutilating a poor creature for your daughter's gain. If I were you, I wouldn't go public with anything right now. I would lay low. Real low. Because you're under suspicion for bribery and cruelty to animals. Be expecting a subpoena," said Nick, rising. "Now if you'll excuse me, I have to finish up with a few things."

Nick stood there and waited as the senator rose coolly from his seat without a word. The senator knew better than to argue his case right now. It wasn't politically savvy. Nick could see the wheels turning in the man's head as he formed his last statement carefully, making sure to posture himself authoritatively in front of the glass separation window as he pointed a long finger at Nick.

"You have no evidence or reasonable witnesses from which to draw any accusation against me. Don't waste taxpayer money on trumped-up indictments, because I'll make sure the media gets that story too. And you won't be sheriff of Freeport County for very long."

"Good night, Senator." Nick refused to be intimidated.

"Good night, Sheriff," the senator said as he exited the lobby of the police station.

Nick was now sure that Tim's story had legitimacy. Tragic as Julie's death was, Nick took silent comfort in the fact that she would never know what her father had done to her beloved horse. He would definitely get Bodum's statement on this too. He wanted to make sure the senator could never get to Mercedes ever again.

Meanwhile, Julie's killer was still out there, and Nick was out of leads. He had forty minutes before the night secretary would arrive. He went into the kitchen and made himself a turkey and cheddar sandwich, grabbed a handful of potato chip pieces from the bottom of a nearly empty bag, and popped open a can of energy drink. He went back to his office and pulled up Julie's social media accounts for a third or maybe fourth time.

He kept trolling them for any comment, tag, photo, or emoji that might give him some clue.

Nick paused on a photo of Julie at a competition, sitting atop Mercedes. She wore a first-place medal, a huge smile and a...a riding helmet. Had Julie always worn a helmet when she was riding? And had she been wearing a helmet the day she died? The injuries she had sustained were located at the base of the skull, which would have been protected by a helmet. But Julie's helmet wasn't with her body when Farmer Gibbons drove her to the stable. It wasn't in her bedroom. It wasn't in Mercedes's pen or anywhere in the stable. In fact, no one had even mentioned it. So where was it? Or who had it?

Nick thought back to when Farmer Gibbons had showed him where he'd found Julie's body. It was lying next to a large rock on the bank of the creek. It made sense now. The killer had placed Julie's body near a rock to make it look like she had fallen off her horse and hit her head. Why hadn't he put this together before? He needed to find that helmet. Emily had not mentioned any method by which Julie had sustained her injuries. He needed to know exactly what had crushed Julie's skull.

THIRTY-EIGHT

A TEXT FROM BRANDON woke Emily the next morning. With sluggish fingers and a nagging stress headache that had cropped up overnight, Emily logged onto her phone and read his message.

Mom on board for a city wedding. What do you think of this place?

She clicked on a link from the Palmer House in downtown Chicago and scrolled through a series of images of ornate ballrooms. They were all huge. A small panic fluttered inside as Emily read his message, after first feeling a twinge of relief that he had reconsidered a city wedding. However, she had not yet thought about how big the wedding might be. She did a quick inventory of guests from her side. Her father. Aunt Laura. A few cousins. A small handful of peers. Dr. Claiborne and his wife. Now, of course, Jo and her family. Was that it? Maybe twenty-five guests? Of course, Brandon's family, his friends, and his parents' friends could easily fill a hall of three hundred plus. A Palmer House Christmas wedding could easily jump into the six-figure tab. It seemed outrageous. She still felt unsettled about not resolving their little argument from earlier. What should she tell him? Should she pretend like everything was okay? Deal with it when she was back in

Chicago? As she was trying to decide, a message from Nick pinged onto her screen.

Do you think Julie was wearing a helmet when she was struck?

What an odd question, Emily thought in her groggy state. Of course not. She didn't have a helmet on her. She swung her feet to the floor and slipped on her plush slippers. She never left home without them. She found floors, even carpeting, cold and dirty. She started a cup of coffee in the single-serve hotel coffee maker. While she was waiting for the water to heat up, Nick's question rolled around in her mind.

If Julie had been wearing a helmet, the fracture would not have been as pronounced. She might not have been killed at all. She could have been wearing a helmet when she rode out. But not when she was killed. And unless her attacker was also riding a horse, which was possible, her killer would have had to somehow get Julie off her horse to strike her at the angle at which she had been hit. Otherwise, there was a very, very likely chance that on horseback she would have outrun him. So, Mercedes hadn't been spooked at all. No. He'd fallen because he was attacked and struck in the leg. Blunt force trauma.

Emily grabbed her phone from the nightstand and pecked out a text:

Meet me at my dad's office. 20 mins.

THIRTY-NINE

EMILY JUMPED IN her car and sped to Dr. Lillen's to pick up a copy of Mercedes's X-rays. She then raced to her father's office, where Nick was already waiting for her. Her father had wandered out from the house too and was seated in the large leather swivel chair behind his desk. Emily remembered him filling the chair. In this moment, he looked shriveled and diminutive.

She dashed to her father's light box and slid on a set of X-rays from Julie and one from Mercedes. As Emily studied the images, it became immediately clear that there was a similarity in the patterning of both injuries.

"In both victims, the killer struck multiple times. See how these second lines stop at the first ones because they have nowhere else to travel? It's a classic blunt force pattern," said Emily.

"Same instrument?" said Nick.

"It looks to be," said Robert, turning toward his daughter, who was confirming with a nod. "Next step is to get this down to the state crime lab's tool specialist and see if they can identify the type of weapon."

"Only problem is, there's a huge lag time for the results," said Nick.

"How long are we talking?" said Emily.

"Months. The backlog is hundreds of cases."

Emily's face sank. "Maybe the senator could pull some strings?"

"We're not exactly on great terms right now," said Nick.

Emily searched his face with a questioning look but said, "It's his daughter. I think he'll do it."

"Here's the thing, Em: we don't just want to procure information for the sake of information. We want directive information," Nick said.

"I don't get it. Enlighten me here," she said.

"Okay, let's say the crime lab sends back a report in six months, indicating that the tool used on both victims was, for instance, a common crowbar. That's a very broad directional area for your investigation. Where do you even start with that? How would you go about finding *the* crowbar that was used in your alleged crime?"

Emily thought about it for a moment. Lots of people owned crowbars. She had one in the trunk of her car. Brandon had one. Her dad owned several. Every self-respecting Midwesterner with an ounce of common sense knew to have one. They would have to go digging through…

Nick finished her thought. "We can't just go digging through every car, garage, and shed in Freeport County to find it. Even if we could, it may be long gone. Buried. In a lake. A river? A field? In another county."

Emily saw the challenge here, but she countered, "We don't know it's a crowbar. It could be something more unique."

"It might. A little. But with no suspects, I'm still just looking for a needle in a haystack," he said.

"Right, but it's a smaller haystack," Emily argued. Her father remained silent, watching them spar it out.

"I need cause to get search warrants. I can't just go barging into any old haystack," Nick said. "And right now, I have no suspects. No cause. *Nada.*"

Robert finally spoke up. "It's great work, Emily. Very well done. But Nick is right here. It's a waste of county resources when you have no murder weapon to match it to and no suspects to search. Put it in your back pocket, and when the time is right, you'll know how to use it."

Nick left, but Emily could not leave it alone. She felt so helpless, and she hated feeling this way. They had so little to go on, and she understood Nick's point. But she couldn't get Sarah's, David's, or Dr. Lillen's faces from her mind. She would drown her exasperation in a bear claw from Brown's and try to focus on something else. Like wedding plans. *Oh crap. I never got back to Brandon.* Did he really need a decision right now about the Palmer House? She stepped outside to take a walk around the property and think things through. She felt they could be on the edge of having solid information about what type of tool was used in Julie's murder if only they could get the films analyzed. She checked her phone again. Another text from Brandon. And a missed call. She felt like their worlds were a universe apart right now. Him, looking at banquet halls and table settings, and her, trying to discover tool marks and murder suspects. She was nearing her father's apple tree when her stomach reminded her that it wanted that bear claw. Brown's Bakery. That was it! Emily spun around and make a dash for her Leaf. There was someone right here in Freeport's backyard who could help her identify the source of these fractures. Gratis.

FORTY

SHE PULLED INTO Delia's driveway just outside of Free-port and found her in her one-acre garden, gently snip-ping buds from a long, tall row of vines. The early autumn cold snap had turned edges of the leaves on the vine a golden, crinkled blonde. Delia looked up when she saw Emily approaching, and greeted her with a broad smile.

"Miss Hartford. Nice to see you again. Please don't tell me you're here to say goodbye and heading back to Chicago." Delia set down the snippers and gave Emily a hug.

"No, no, I'm not leaving yet," Emily assured her. "What are you growing in here these days?"

"Oh, these are my hops vines," she said. "It's har-vesting time. I grow them for a local brewery. And in exchange I get six bottles of their microbrewed beer every week," she said with a sly grin. "So far my fa-vorite is their carob winter stout."

"Since when did Freeport get a microbrewery?"

"Since two years ago. You should check it out. Just south of town," Delia told her.

"Maybe I will. Haven't had a lot of time to go ex-ploring. And honestly, I didn't think there was much to discover after twelve years."

"Right now they're featuring a pumpkin ale and a

summer squash IPA. I know it sounds awful, but it's an adventure for the taste buds," said Delia.

Emily laughed, remembering how Delia's unconventional ways and attitude had always breathed fresh air into this otherwise homogenous community.

"Looks like your garden is on its way out," noticed Emily.

"Yes, oh yes—we're supposed to get our first frost next week. I had a good crop of eggplant, corn, broccoli, tomatoes, carrots, peas, raspberries, and blackberries this year. Oh, and have you ever heard of purple beans?" she asked Emily.

"I have not," Emily said. "I think it might feel kinda fairy-talish eating a purple bean."

"Unfortunately, they turn green when you cook them," said Delia.

"I was hoping there would be more exotic fare," said Emily.

"I stick to the basics in the garden and save the exotics for my greenhouse," Delia said, pointing around back of the house to a large glassed-in structure.

"Wow, that's new since I lived here," Emily exclaimed.

"It's real nice in the winter. I can hole up there for months and feel like I'm in the Caribbean while it's snowing a blizzard outside," she said.

"Semi-retirement suits you," Emily teased.

"In all the best ways. So... I know you didn't come here to make garden chat."

WITHIN A FEW minutes Delia and Emily were situated inside Delia's large library, and she was paging through reference books. Both sets of X-rays were placed side by side, taped on a floor-to-ceiling, south-facing window. Delia examined them for a long time, sometimes with her naked eye and sometimes under a magnifying glass.

"You are right about the fact that the same instrument was used on both the horse and the girl," Delia finally concluded. Then she went back to work, concentrating in silence. She made a few measurements and sketched out a few drawings, then erased them and started over.

"It's a very unusual instrument. I've only seen it in one other case I worked on," she said after a while.

Emily listened, not wanting to break her flow of thought.

Delia logged on to her computer, scanned her drawings into a file, and then plugged the images into a software system that started to come up with possible matches. Emily watched in amazement.

Emily stared straight ahead as Delia continued to work. What a woman—what a role model! Emily had missed Delia. She noted that in just three days of being back in Freeport, she was starting to warm corners of her heart that had been chilled for a long time to this place.

"That's what I thought," Delia said as she turned the screen to Emily. "They were struck with this instrument."

The top part was sort of like pliers that pinched together. A large bolt clasped the two handles together. The handles were long and lean, at least a foot or more. The nose of the instrument came together in an elongated oval that could pinch something between its grasp. Emily recognized it immediately.

"Horse nippers."

"From what I can assess from both injuries, the oval hole that the pincers make when they are closed is about seven millimeters in diameter, and they have this angled tip that points toward the nose of the nippers," Delia explained. "That's a clue right there. That's what makes these nippers different."

"Is it specific enough to find my weapon?" asked Emily, Nick's words about a needle in a haystack ringing in her ears.

"It's quite specific. The one used on your two victims seems to be an antique version," said Delia, scrolling through the images in her reference books to find an example to show Emily. "I'm guessing somewhere around turn of the twentieth century. They made them from iron. Farriers kept them in many sizes, from six inches to fifteen inches or maybe larger. See here?"

Delia showed her an image on the screen. "The older ones have this pointy arrow-like notch. The newer ones today are just oval. No arrow notch."

"Seems like most of these don't have that notch," Emily said, examining the pictures on the screen.

"You got it. So in that sense, it makes your job a little easier." Delia made a copy of the nippers she believed might be a match. "So, go to it, girl. Or should I say, get the sheriff on it. From what I hear, you're pretty good at lighting the fire under Nick."

"Exactly what have you heard?" Emily asked. "Wait, are you talking about the Tim situation?"

Delia laughed. "Oh, don't worry. I'm proud of you for that. Nick needs some heat under him from time to time. Keeps him sharp and fresh."

"Speaking of Nick, I rushed over here so fast, I forgot to call him."

"You were just being resourceful. You can catch him up later. Okay, doll, let's get back outside and enjoy that beer," said Delia, shutting down the computer. "Head on out to the back porch, and I'll be out in a jiffy with a couple cold ones."

Emily settled into a rocking chair on Delia's back porch and took a deep breath of the fresh, verdant air. She was exhilarated that they had figured out what the murder weapon was. Now, to find its match. She was kidding herself to think that she could stay in Freeport until the case was solved. This could takes weeks, months. Possibly years. If ever. The thought of giving this all up to return to Chicago gave her an unexpected sad twinge. She was having a very hard time letting this go. She had promised Sarah. She had promised herself. And if she left, she would be a failure once again. Could she shoulder that burden on top of everything else?

Emily weighed what was waiting for her in Chicago. Surgery was just as challenging as crime solving. But let's face it. Surgical centers and technologies were so advanced these days. The risk of losing a patient was very, very slim. Especially for the kinds of routine procedures she was performing. Yet how could she deny that these kinds of medical mysteries shot exuberance through every neuron and cell of her body? She thought about heading back to Chicago, where her biggest decisions now would be if they should serve shellfish appetizers at her wedding and whether they should put a vacuum cleaner on their registry. And despite the fact that she had been planning her wedding with Brandon in her mind since their sixth date, in this very moment, living out his prescribed path for them, as amazing as it had always seemed before, now didn't seem nearly as fulfilling to her as being able to find justice for a vulnerable family and putting a killer in prison.

Delia came out with the glass mugs, beer and foam spilling over the lips. Emily studied Delia in the sunlight and noticed that she was more creased and frail looking than Emily had remembered. Was it the years, or perhaps the job, that had added this dimension to Delia? With all the awful things Delia had seen during her years at the FBI, how did she keep a fresh outlook on life?

"You look worried," said Delia.

"Do I?" Emily hadn't realized she was drifting off into her own thoughts. "It's just… Julie deserves justice, and it seems so…so impossible."

"You and Nick will get this case solved. I know it," Delia said.

"How do you know?"

"Because you're Dr. Robert Hartford's daughter," she said, smiling.

"I'm glad you're so confident," Emily said, wanting to believe her. "Thank you so much for your help." Emily lifted the cool mug to her lips again, and her diamond caught the sunlight.

"What does Nick think about that?" Delia pointed to Emily's ring.

"I don't think it really matters to him at all," she said.

"Oh, I doubt it doesn't matter to him. You were his first love."

"We were silly sixteen-year-olds."

"I know. But it's hard to let that first one go."

"It's been twelve years," she said. "Plenty of time to let go."

"Just be tender with him," Delia advised.

"Nick's over it. Moved on."

"I'm not so sure," said Delia, and Emily felt a slight irritation surfacing inside her.

"Why is that?"

"Hon, that man comes into Brown's almost every morning of the week. And this week, the morning after you got into town, he popped in for his usual custard long john, and he looked positively energized despite the fact that he hadn't gotten a wink of sleep all night. And I've never seen his face light up like it did when he told me you were back in Freeport and assisting on the Dobson case."

Emily took a swig of her beer. *Why was it that some people just couldn't let go of the past?* she mused. And then realized she was just as guilty.

"This is amazing brew," said Emily. Delia knew she was ducking the conversation, and just smiled. "What is it anyway?"

"It's a German kölsch," said a voice behind her. Emily turned and saw Nick coming up the porch steps. It was then that she noticed Delia had brought out three mugs.

FORTY-ONE

"Did you know I was here?" Emily asked Nick when Delia stepped inside to take a phone call.

"Delia texted me. Said you had made some breakthrough in the Dobson case and that I should come over and take a look."

Emily stared at him as he kicked back in his rocking chair and guzzled down half his beer in one chug.

"Looks like you're taking matters into your own hands again."

"It's not like that. I honestly didn't even think—"

"Exactly. I'm the lead detective on this case. You do understand that, don't you?"

"Don't speak to me like I'm a child. I was just trying to help. And it won't cost your department a dime."

Emily stewed in her annoyance with Nick. He might be lead detective, but he was certainly not displaying the type of investigative resourcefulness she had learned from her father.

"Maybe I should be asking why you didn't think of coming to Delia first?"

"If I didn't know you, Emily Hartford, I would say you're starting to take this case personally," Nick said, rocking forward and hopping out of his chair. "You were so eager to get out of Freeport, and now it seems like you're looking for excuses to stick around. Why is that?"

She hated that he had read her mind. Delia stuck her head out the screen door.

"Nick, come on inside. I'll show you what we found."

Nick held the door for Emily, and they entered. He followed her to the library, and together she and Delia showed him the new evidence.

"I'm impressed. Truly. But it's an impossible situation," said Nick. "I could waste hours chasing this and meanwhile risk missing a stronger lead."

"You have the tool identification when you need it," said Delia with a nod to Nick. "You know this investigation better than I."

"And I say, until you have a better lead, we start searching those haystacks," Emily announced with a determined tone. "I remember seeing Gary Bodum with nippers. Granted it was not an antique one, but maybe he has more out there."

Nick and Delia exchanged glances. "I saw that. And I know what you're thinking," said Emily, wagging her finger at them.

"You're as headstrong as your father. Maybe more so," said Delia with a warm smile.

"I'm not going to stand around here and do nothing." She gave Delia a hug. "Thank you so much for your help."

"Anytime, hon. Always here for you."

Emily took the X-rays down from the window and headed toward the door. She glanced back at Nick.

"Well, are you coming or not?"

WHEN SHE KNOCKED on Gary's office door and he looked up, Emily could tell he was surprised to see her and Nick. He waved for them to open the door.

"Sorry to bother you, but we were hoping we could take another look around the stables," said Emily.

"Sure," he said, rising and going to the door. "I'll join you if you don't mind."

"Thanks, Gary," said Nick. "This won't take long."

"Do you have anything new on Julie?" Gary asked.

"Gary, you know that if we did, we couldn't say anything," Emily replied, moving a few steps ahead of him as she scanned the stables.

"I assume you're going to her funeral this afternoon," said Nick, trying to smooth over Emily's brusqueness.

"I am. Not looking forward to it," Gary said.

"No one ever does," said Nick.

"No, I mean the part about being in the same room as the senator."

Nick nodded.

"Do you have a workshop?" Emily asked.

"Yeah, at the end of the barn, down past the last row of stables," he said, pointing.

The three made their way through the barn, past the empty horse pens.

"Where are all the horses?" asked Nick.

"Out in the pasture. It's horse 'free time,'" joked Gary.

Emily paused when they went by Mercedes's pen. Inside the pen was an easel board with a large picture of Julie in her riding gear, standing next to Mercedes. Surrounding it were other photos of her and newspaper clippings about competitions she'd participated in.

"Her parents had it delivered yesterday," Gary explained.

"It's beautiful. She's beautiful." Emily gazed at Julie's fresh face and perfectly white smile. A long blonde braid cascaded over her shoulder. Julie had one hand placed on Mercedes's neck, the other holding up a glimmering gold trophy. She looked like a graceful champion. Not a pressure cooker of college angst and ketamine.

Her eye caught a newspaper clipping she recognized. She stepped into the pen to take a closer look.

"Sarah showed me this photo. The guy's name is Vince, right?" She looked to Bodum.

"Vince Parelli," Gary said.

"Sarah said he and Julie competed a lot. Have you talked to him, Nick?" Emily asked.

"I don't really remember. Over the past few days, I've talked to over a hundred and fifty people. Who is this guy?"

"He's from Rock River. Farmer's kid with little formal training, but a really skilled rider. Probably Julie's biggest competitor," Gary said.

"Did you ever meet Vince?" asked Nick. Emily continued down the row of stables toward the workroom, and they followed.

"Just saw him here and there when we held competitions at Premiere. We're not a very big venue, but we're the only one in three counties. So we draw a pretty substantial regional crowd."

"What's he like?" Emily asked.

"Soft-spoken. Small in stature. But man, he has a great underdog story. He comes from a poor family. His parents have eight kids and counting. He's somewhere in the middle—maybe number five?" said Gary.

"What was he like in the ring?" Emily asked.

"A natural talent. I think he learned most of what he knows by hanging around competitions and watching

YouTube videos. His family doesn't have money for a trainer," said Gary, and then he paused for a second. "Well, that's not entirely true. His dad rode in high school. So he knows his way around the competition circuit."

"Where does Vince practice?" said Emily.

"Oh, at his farm. The Parellis own a hundred acres," Gary said.

"I thought they didn't have money," Nick said.

"They don't. They're land rich. Their farm was passed down from Vince's grandfather. The horses they own are work horses mostly," he said.

"Work horses on a modern farm? Are they Amish or something?" said Emily.

"No, just earthy. They run an organic farm and try to keep everything nonmechanized."

Emily nodded. Vince Parelli, son of a struggling organic farmer. There's no way he could afford college on his own. No way his parents could chip in. Vince had just as much talent as Julie. And he needed this scholarship even more than she did. *Was it a stretch to think that he would have killed Julie to get her place for the scholarship?*

Nick must have been thinking the same thing because he asked, "How was Julie and Vince's relationship?"

"They weren't friends, if that's what you're asking," said Gary.

Emily and Nick exchanged a look as they stopped at the closed workroom door. Gary unlocked it, and they followed him in.

"So, this is my work area. What exactly are you looking for?"

He flipped on the light. Bright fluorescent lighting hung from the fifteen-foot ceiling, and Emily saw they were in a twenty-by-twenty room lined with shelves holding horse equipment. On one side was a workbench, with tools hanging from a pegboard mounted on the wall.

"Is this where you keep *all* of your equipment?" asked Nick.

"It is. Picks, rasps, knives, nippers. All here." Gary pointed to the panel, bolted to the wall, where the tools hung in an orderly manner above the workbench. They looked much like the instruments she had seen at Dr. Lillen's stable.

Emily's gaze went to the collection of nippers on the pegboard. She studied each one, mentally comparing it to the image Delia had shown her. None of them were a match.

"You ever collect any antique tools?" Emily asked.

"No. Why would I do that? Those old things are a pain in the butt to use."

"Nothing's gone missing that you know of?" asked Nick.

"Not that I've noticed." Emily could tell this line of questioning was putting Bodum on edge. "Should there be something missing?"

"You don't have any in your office or at home? In your truck?" Nick kept at him.

"Sherriff, I'm not dim. You think Julie was killed with one of these tools?"

"I really can't answer that, Gary."

Emily pulled on a workbench drawer, but it was locked.

"Can you please unlock this?" she asked him.

"I wish you could tell me what's going on here," Bodum said as he reached for a set of keys in his pocket and unlocked the drawer. There was nothing of note in the drawer either, and Nick told him he could relock it.

"Listen, there's nothing more in here for you to look at," said Bodum, his voice rising. "I'd like for you both to leave. I have a lot of work to do."

Nick stepped back. She guessed they had crossed some legal line by the way Nick gently pulled her toward him. "We appreciate your cooperation. Thank you for your time, Gary."

"Next time, come with a search warrant," said Bodum, and he made sure they walked out first. He locked the workshop doors. "You can leave through the side door." He pointed to the right. Emily flanked Nick as they walked toward the exit, with Bodum following a few steps behind. Emily felt Bodum's eyes on them until they got into Nick's truck and drove off.

Disappointment permeated Emily's mood as they drove back into town. Haystack number one was a bust. *It would have been way too easy anyway,* she told herself. Maybe Nick was right. This could take a lifetime. They needed a stronger lead.

"I think I'll drive down to Rock River and pay a visit to Vince Parelli," said Nick. "Wanna come along?"

Emily checked the time. It was late morning, and she did want to come along, but… "I promised Cathy I would be over to help her pack up more office files."

"Okay," said Nick, the excitement dropping from his voice. "I'll drop you at Delia's to get your car."

But Emily wasn't ready to give up the hunt or more time with Nick. "Wait. I'll tell her I'm doing something case related and that I'll come by this afternoon."

Nick smiled at her as he turned the car around to head south toward Rock River.

She quickly texted Cathy that she would be there later. Just as Emily slid her phone back into her purse, a text pinged. She yanked her phone out to check.

"What?" she voiced at the screen.

"Everything okay?" said Nick, accelerating on the state highway.

Emily reread the text: I'm at the Pennington. Surprise!

"Is it your dad? Do we need to turn around?" Nick asked.

"It's Brandon. He's in Freeport."

Emily saw Nick's face fall as he slowed the truck and pulled into the nearest driveway to turn back to Freeport. And she knew for certain. Delia was right.

FORTY-TWO

NICK DROPPED EMILY off at the Inn and was headed out of town, toward Rock River, when something told him to stop off at Bishop's Funeral Home, where Julie's funeral was taking place.

Once he arrived, Nick parked the patrol car in the back corner of the parking lot and waited. He wanted to go in, but the pressure he felt from not yet having solved the case, and having to face the entire Freeport community, held him back.

Besides, he could justify being there on investigative grounds. It was a commonly held principle of investigation that sometimes suspects returned to the scene of the crime or attended vigils or a memorial service for their victim. Nick decided to stick around and see if there was anyone there who seemed out of place.

After a while, trickles of people started to emerge. No one caught his attention at first. Then, a family traipsed out, headed by the father, who plodded a few steps ahead of his wife, daughter, and teenage son. Nick didn't recognize the other three, but the son was definitely Vince Parelli, Julie's main competitor. They had come to him. How ironic and opportune.

Nick jumped out of his car and approached them. He introduced himself, and they willingly agreed to speak with him about Julie. He escorted them around the back, where there was a private sitting garden. He wanted to make sure they would be out view of the other funeral-goers.

"I understand you competed with Julie?" Nick said, and Vince nodded. "Tell me about that."

Vince looked to his father for approval to speak.

"Go ahead, son," said Mr. Parelli.

"Not much to tell. We competed against each other the last couple of years."

"Were you friends?"

"I guess. I mean, we only saw each other at competitions."

"I've heard the equestrian community is much like a family. It's nice to see you supporting the Dobson family during this time," said Nick with a warm smile.

"They were friends," said Mr. Parelli curtly, taking his wife's hand.

"I'm sure you've heard things about Julie's death," said Nick. "What have you heard?" Vince looked at his dad again. Nick found it a bit odd.

"We don't live around here, Sheriff. We live about an hour away," responded Mr. Parelli.

"Gossip travels," said Nick.

"We own an organic farm. Vince was working the fields the morning Julie was killed," said Vince's mother. "We were all so shocked to hear about it."

"I see," said Nick. "Were you all working the farm that morning?"

The little sister piped up proudly, "My job is to gather the eggs."

"That's right, honey," said Mr. Parelli. "And Mother was making us a healthy breakfast."

"That's right," added Mrs. Parelli. "If you're looking

for fresh organic produce, we do the farmer's market every Saturday in Rockwall Square."

"Good to know," said Nick. He noticed Vince dart his gaze to the ground. His left foot was making small circles in the dirt. *He's nervous about something,* thought Nick.

"What's your job, Vince?" asked Nick, trying to draw Vince out of himself.

Vince didn't look up. "Weeding and picking."

"What do you grow over there at the farm?"

"Everything." Vince didn't lift his eyes.

"He's pretty broke up about the Dobson girl," said Mr. Parelli. "You got any more questions for us? We've got goats and cows need milking."

"No, sir. Thank you for your time." Nick rose to shake Vince's hand. "And Vince, I'm very sorry for the loss of your friend." Mr. Parelli led his family out the garden gate, but Nick stayed behind. The whole interaction had felt stiff and unnatural. Nick believed that Mr. Parelli's controlling nature was probably the source of quite a few underlying problems in that family. However, there was certainly no indication that Vince had anything to do with Julie's death. Mr. Parelli had Vince pressed under his thumb. Nick was sure that Vince was working those fields during the time of Julie's murder. Yet, something was still off about the whole conversation.

As Nick drove away from the funeral home, his discouragement over the case grew. Any possible clue was dissipating before his eyes. He begin to doubt, really doubt, that he could solve this case. And now that Brandon was in town, Emily's focus would turn to him.

And to her father. And rightly so. She had gone above and beyond.

Nick pulled into his driveway. He usually loved coming home to sit on his deck and look out over the lake as he sorted through the events of the day. But right now, he dreaded facing his empty house.

FORTY-THREE

EMILY RUSHED OVER to the Pennington and found Brandon waiting for her in the lobby with a ginormous bouquet of red roses and towering white stargazer lilies. He handed her the flowers and greeted her with a long kiss.

"Why didn't you call?" chided Emily softly after his lips left hers.

"When you didn't text me back, I thought, this is ridiculous. Why am I not up in Freeport with my bride-to-be? And I figure being here will help me get to know you better. So, here I am," he said, going in for another kiss.

"I'm glad you're here. We need to talk. Face-to-face. Not like teenagers over text."

"Agreed." After Brandon let go of her, he took a good look at Emily and said, "There's a whole 'nother shade to the dark circles under your eyes that I've never seen before."

Emily laughed a little. "Is that your professional medical assessment of me?"

"You always look great to me."

"I'm exhausted," she admitted. "I wish you woulda warned me, though. I could have at least tried a little."

"I decided not to stress you out by planning some big visit," he said and drew her in for a hug.

His embrace melted her and all the stress she was shouldering.

"What about Dr. Claiborne and the research?" she whispered.

"He got called into emergency surgery."

She drew away and cradled her gorgeous bouquet, drawing in a deep breath of the lilies. "These are so beautiful. Thank you."

"What do you think of them for wedding flowers? Red. White. Christmasy, yet elegant. Maybe with some pine greens and cedar." She knew she should be grateful for his help. So many brides' fiancés skated by, doing only the bare minimum when it came to wedding plans. But she was having a hard time mustering up excitement for wedding talk.

"I like them. You have good taste," she said.

"Okay, I admit, they're not my idea," he said. "I mean getting you the flowers was, but the whole wedding theme—no."

"Your mom?" Emily asked, raising her brow in suspicion.

"Well, yes. Sort of. She suggested a florist."

"You already picked our florist?"

"I stopped by the Palmer House to put down a deposit, and the florist was just a couple blocks away. And since I was going to bring you flowers anyhow, one thing led to another, and I ended up with this bouquet."

"You put down a deposit?" Emily was still stuck on the Palmer House.

"You never texted back, but I know how much you love the Palmer House—"

"For drinks or dinner, yes." Emily felt the stress tighten in her gut. "Don't you have to have a date to put down a deposit?"

"I picked the date that was closest to Christmas, and actually, it was the only date available at the Palmer."

"So, when are we getting married?" The question felt like it was pinched out of her throat. Was this how getting smothered felt like?

"Saturday, December seventeenth," he said.

"December seventeenth?" she echoed.

"Wow, that's only the second time I've actually said the date out loud."

"Lemme guess: the first time was to your mom," Emily said with a displeasing tone.

"Yeah. I called her on the way up. It's a long haul."

"So your mom knew before me?"

"I wanted to make sure she knew to cancel the country club. And I wanted to tell you in person."

He had it all planned out. Emily was sure it made sense in his mind, but she was having a hard time adjusting to her life being planned without her. Emily waved her hand at him. It was no use getting mad. She managed to squeak out, "Are there any other plans afoot that I should know about?"

"I reserved the Lake Michigan Room. It's the one with the brocade curtains and massive chandeliers. And it faces the lake. Hence the name. The wedding coordinator told me that at that time of year, it will be decorated with three fifteen-foot Christmas trees."

"It sounds beautiful," she said. "There's just one thing. We already have a wedding coordinator."

"Oh, we do?"

"Yeah. My friend Jo wants to help."

"Jo that up until a week ago hadn't spoken to you in, like, ten years?"

"Yes. That Jo. We've sort of rekindled our friendship this week."

Brandon looked tweaked. "I guess it's no better or different than hiring a complete stranger."

"Except she's not a stranger. She's a good friend," said Emily.

"To you. I've never met her. Does she have experience in event planning?"

"You're talking in your doctor-giving-a-grave-prognosis voice."

"Fine. Fine," Brandon said, lifting his tone. "As long as she gets along with my mom," he added.

"Why?"

"Because they're going to be spending a lot of time together on the planning."

"They are?"

"Em, the train has left that station, and it's traveling at full speed. We're gonna need all the help we can get. And Jo doesn't live in Chicago."

Emily wanted to scream and pull the emergency brake.

"We should probably figure out our guest list this weekend because I'm concerned the Lake Michigan Room won't be big enough," said Brandon.

"How big is it?" asked Emily.

"It only seats four hundred."

"Four—zero—zero?" Emily gaped. "Do we know that many people?"

"My parents do," he replied. "They're already complaining because they have to figure out who to leave off the list."

Of course they are. They know everyone. Her throat was pinching closed again, and she took a couple of deep breaths and a few steps toward the couches in the lobby. As Brandon helped her sit, her flowers spread over her lap.

"My dad said he wanted to pay for the reception as a gift to us. But I don't think he was expecting to feed a small army brigade."

"My mom's already deposited thirty grand into my account. Have your dad pay what he can, and we'll get the rest."

"Thirty grand!" She gasped in shock.

"And there's another thirty coming," said Brandon.

Emily tried to hide her sticker shock. They could buy a couple of new cars or a small house in Freeport with that sum. And she knew that "paying what he can" would not sit well with her father. He didn't want to be some silent partner writing a check. He would want to be part of his daughter's wedding.

"Maybe Christmas is too soon. I don't even know if my dad will be well enough by then to make it down." She didn't mean to make her father the excuse for her cold feet. But it just came out.

"He'll be fine. And we can do this. We have plenty of help." Brandon broke into a confident smile. "And we can always get him a nurse or attendant if he needs help."

Emily closed her eyes and drew in another deep breath of her roses as she tried to center herself. She calculated today's date from December 17th. So much to do in just eighty-four days! A dress to create. *Four hundred* invites to send! Her father's house to sell. A practice to transfer. And a case to solve. Emily's thoughts drifted to Nick. She wondered how his visit with the Parellis was going. She caught herself wishing to be in his truck right now and immediately berated herself. How could that even cross her mind as she was sitting here with Brandon, planning her wedding day?

Her eyes popped opened, and she saw Brandon was no longer looking at her, but checking his text.

"Mom wonders how you liked the flowers." Brandon snapped a photo of Emily covered in stems. "I'll send her this."

"I wasn't even smiling," said Emily.

"You're adorable." He texted the picture to his mom.

"Why is it so important to try to please your mother all the time?" Emily blurted out.

Brandon gave her a puzzled looked. "I want to please you too."

"Do you have to tell them *everything*?"

"We're just close. That's what real family looks like, Em."

The comment stung sharply. And it wasn't the first time he'd made her feel bad for not having a good relationship with her dad. But come to think of it, what did a good relationship really look like? In the past few days, she had given little thought to Brandon and his activities in Chicago. She didn't know how his surgeries had gone or what the topic of his paper was even about. And conversely, he had not taken the time to talk with her at any depth about her father's conditions, the Dobson case, or how she was getting along up here in Freeport. Had they both been too busy, or too selfish, to take care of their relationship?

"Would you like to meet my father?" she asked him.

Brandon looked up from his phone. "I can't wait."

FORTY-FOUR

CATHY AND ROBERT were out in the yard when Emily and Brandon pulled up.

"He looks trustworthy. Doesn't seem like the kind of man who would want to hurt you," Brandon said. Emily gave him the evil eye. "I'm kidding. I'm kidding," he hastened to say.

"Are you nervous?" she asked him.

"Not too bad. Should I be?"

"We'll see," Emily said, her index finger poking at his ribs.

"Hey. I'm serious. What if he doesn't like me?"

"Then, he'll let you know." Emily winked at him and jumped out of the car. Brandon scrambled to follow her.

"Dad, Cathy. This is Brandon Taylor. My fiancé," she announced. Robert dove right in with a strong handshake. Cathy stepped in with a warm hug.

"Welcome to the family," she said.

"Well, not so fast. They aren't married yet," Robert corrected.

"Sorry to hear about your recent health scare," Brandon said.

"Oh, that bothersome incident," Robert said, playing it off as inconsequential.

"I thought it was a heart attack. Am I mistaken?"

"That's what they tell me. But what do they know. Doctors, right?" he said, and Brandon laughed. "Say, there's a project I need to finish up out back. Why don't you join me, and we can get to know each other better."

"Sounds great," Brandon responded with a side glance to Emily. She winked again and had a good feeling she knew what he was in for.

Robert stole Brandon away to the backyard. Emily and Cathy followed at a distance, safeguarding their conversation from the men.

"He's handsome, Emily, and has a very nice disposition," said Cathy.

"I'm not gonna disagree with you there," replied Emily. He was as good on paper as he was in person in Chicago. How would he fare here? Out of his natural habitat?

Emily glanced over at her dad, who was showing Brandon how to use a wood splitter. Brandon balanced a piece of wood on a block. Her dad placed an axe in Brandon's hands and signaled for him to wait. Then Robert raised his hands over his head in a chopping motion to demonstrate the maneuver and where to hit the wood. He indicated that Brandon should do a practice swing. Following Robert's lead, Brandon raised the axe above his head and nearly toppled over backward.

"I can't believe what I'm seeing," Cathy said, laughing.

"I feel a little bad that I didn't warn him."

"You do? Really?"

"Nah. You should see what I deal with on his family's side," she joked.

Brandon took a second swing, this time aiming for the log. He came down hard, missing the wood and gouging the axe deep into the chopping block.

"Try again, honey. You can do it!" Emily called out.

Brandon shook his head as he tried with all his strength to dislodge the axe. Robert stepped in and in one smooth motion released the tool expertly from the wood. He handed it back to Brandon, whose face showed a determination to whip this thing.

"So, how is my dad doing for real, Cathy?" Emily said.

"He sleeps in late, tires easily, and insists on a bowl of ice cream every night before bed," she said with a worried look. "Last night I found him passed out in the bathtub."

"Cathy, that's serious." Alarm bells were going off in Emily's head. "What do you think is keeping him from getting surgery?" she asked.

"Honestly? You."

Emily was taken aback. "I don't understand."

"He wants to reconcile. But he doesn't know how."

"Do you know what he's holding back?"

Cathy shook her head. "And I've never asked. That's between him and your mother and God."

"Well, I've tried already. Several times."

"Maybe you can reach out again?"

"I'm sorry you've been put in the middle of all this. You don't deserve it."

A loud crack shattered the air, followed by a celebratory whoop from Brandon. Robert broke into applause. Emily looked over and saw Brandon dancing around the wood block with two uneven pieces of log in his hands. Brandon held up his success for Emily to see.

"Good job, city boy," she called back and couldn't help but let a cheer slip from her mouth. Being out in the country like this, away from the constant striving to excel, was exactly the kind of thing they needed to reconnect. She liked seeing Brandon unwind and let loose. Emily had a strange but fleeting idea. Maybe Brandon would consider setting up a practice here, in Freeport County. There was always a need for good physicians in this rural community. Then she watched as Brandon brushed tiny wood splinters off his Italian wool slacks. Who was she kidding?

As DINNERTIME NEARED, Cathy insisted they stay for burgers and apple pie. They ate and then Emily pulled Brandon away to spend the rest of the evening with him. They returned to the Pennington and walked into Freeport so Emily could show Brandon where she grew up. The evening was cool and refreshing as they wove their way through Main Street and its bordering neighborhoods. Fall weather tipped the tops of the trees in red and yellow.

"That gray one with the white shutters was my where my friend Reena lived," Emily told him as they walked down a street lined with Victorian homes. "And my elementary school's only about four blocks from here, so after school, if my mom couldn't pick me up right away, I would go home with Reena and her sister. I was always so jealous of Reena living so close to town."

Brandon took Emily's hand, and they continued along the lamplit sidewalk.

"Did you ever take a bus to school?" Emily asked him.

"No, I was one of those kids you would've been jealous of," said Brandon.

"A townie," Emily joked.

"A townie?" he said with a laugh. "Yes, I guess I was a townie. I walked mostly. But sometimes my mom or

dad drove us to school if the weather was really bad."
Emily nodded.

"Living in a back-country town did have its advan-
tages, though. We had a lot of snow days. If the bus
couldn't get through the back roads, then no school,"
said Emily.

"I was expecting a much smaller town," Brandon
admitted.

"Really? Have you looked around?" she said playfully. "There's only one stoplight. We didn't get a Mc-
Donald's until I was a freshman in high school."

"No McDonald's! You didn't tell me you came from
a third world country," he joked.

Emily laughed and leaned into him, snuggling up
to his warm chest.

"Hey, I know this sounds crazy, but are you happy
in Chicago?" she asked him.

"Em, yes, you know I love it. Wait. Why are you
asking me this?"

"It's like we're on this one track, and we never enter-
tained any other options. Are we limiting ourselves?"

"I don't think so. I know I'm not. Chicago is a world-
class city. We have everything there. Family. Friends.
Careers. Opportunity." Brandon's bright smile damp-
ened. "Em, am I missing something?"

"I don't know. Maybe I'm just tired," she answered.
They walked for a few blocks in silence.

"Do you hear that?" she asked.

"Crickets. Birds. A frog somewhere," Brandon responded.

"And the wind rustling through the leaves, blowing
them to the ground. The sound of nothing but nature,"
Emily whispered.

"It's a little unsettling actually. Too quiet," he said.

"Nah, it's nice. I feel kinda detoxed from the city, you know? Like I'm not rushing around in a million directions. My mind is uncluttered. Like I'm removing years of boxes crammed in a tiny bedroom," she said.

"Let me remind you why we love the city. Watching storms come in over the lake. Walking through the city streets after a foot of snow has fallen. Marshall Fields windows at Christmas. Sailing along the lakeshore on warm summer nights."

"I…those are nice…but I don't know that I would miss any of those things."

"This may be nice for a few days. But living like this every day? Boring."

"I never felt bored when I lived here before," said Emily. "And I like that when I want to drive somewhere, I can actually find a place to park without circling the block five times. And there's never a line at the market. People here ask you how you are doing, and they actually mean it."

"I think you like the idea of a small town. And what you really needed was a good, therapeutic break."

"It's hardly been a break," she said. "I'm sleeping less here than I do on hospital rotation. There's just something comforting about being here. Like I don't have to prove anything to anyone. I just am."

"Well, you don't have to prove anything to me." Brandon drew her close again, and Emily smiled. "When are you coming home?"

Home. She had always referred to Freeport as home. And Chicago as…well, it wasn't *not* home. It was just… Chicago. Emily did not feel safe admitting to Brandon that she had mixed feelings about leaving and no idea when she was returning.

"As soon as I can."

"Oh. Good. Because I have one more surprise for you."

"You do? You sure you don't wanna save something for tomorrow?" she joked.

"I think this will make you want to hustle your butt back to Chicago sooner rather than later." Brandon pulled up a photograph on his phone and held it out so she could see the image on the screen. It was a four-story Chicago brownstone with a black iron staircase leading up to a dark green front door with a brass knocker.

"What do you think?"

"I think it's gorgeous," she said.

"I'm so relieved…because it's ours."

The comment hung there between them. Emily knew Brandon was waiting for a larger reaction, but her practical side surfaced.

"How can it be ours? I haven't even seen it."

"Yes, I know. But you will. And you'll love it."

"What do you mean exactly by 'it's ours'?"

"I made the down payment, and all we need to do is get your signature on the paperwork. I brought the papers with me," Brandon said.

Emily swallowed hard and tried to get a handle on the news.

"You bought us a house? When? I've only been gone a couple days."

"Yes. Yes, I know. But, I mean, we're getting married in three months. We don't have a lot of time."

"Where is it?" she asked.

"Lincoln Park. You'll love the street. It's right down from that Italian restaurant I took you to on our first date."

Whole sentences flew out of her mind and ended up all jumbled in her throat.

"It's been recently remodeled, but the old owners kept a lot of the charm. New kitchen, new baths, a marble fireplace. A small basement area, mostly just for storage. It's a bit musty. And a two-car garage off the alley. Can you believe it? Two cars. In the city. No more fighting for parking."

Emily finally managed to squeak out, "You've been pretty busy. Haven't you?"

"I can't sleep, I'm so excited."

"You bought us a house that I've never even seen. You didn't even tell me about it. You didn't even tell me you were *thinking* about buying a house." Emily felt like she was raising her voice, and she looked around, sure that people were staring from their windows. They weren't.

She let go of Brandon's arm and started down the sidewalk in a daze.

"I'm confused right now. This is exactly the kind of place we always talked about owning," Brandon said, trailing after her.

Emily's emotions teetered between seething and bewildered. Yes, they had talked, dreamed. But this was…real.

"Are you happy? Angry? Shocked? Disappointed? Help me out, Em," said Brandon.

"Maybe all of those. My brain feels white."

"Is this about not wanting to live in Chicago?"

"I didn't say I didn't want to live in Chicago."

"I'm confused. Do you want to live here?"

"I dunno. Maybe? I don't know."

"*Here* here? Freeport-here?"

Emily shrugged.

"We've literally *never* talked about this."

"And we've literally *never* talked about buying *that* brownstone."

"It's different."

"Is it? And what do you have against a smaller town? Somewhere on the water? With a lake view. And fresh air. And maybe swans."

"Swans?"

What was she saying? "You're missing the whole point," she said, running into a branch of a bush that was growing out into the sidewalk. It scraped her shin, and small beads of blood formed.

"Are you okay?" Brandon caught the branch with his left hand and snapped it off. "They ought to trim this off the sidewalk. It's dangerous."

"This is all moving too fast," she said.

"Enlighten me. Please. You're the one who wanted to bump up the wedding date," he said.

Emily spun around and faced him. "I was drinking wine that night."

"So you drunk texted me?"

"No. I wasn't drunk. I only had half a glass. But maybe I was too…"

"Too? Too what?"

"Hasty."

"So, you don't want a Christmas wedding?" he asked.

Or a wedding at all. She couldn't say it. She knew she wasn't being clear in explaining the thoughts and feelings that had been emerging in the past few days.

She hardly had a handle on them herself. The turmoil she'd stuffed away for so many years and thought she'd left behind was simmering up to the surface, along with an unexpected aching homesickness. Everything in her life seemed to be in question, even if she couldn't form those exact questions just yet. She was the prodigal daughter returning home, but she hadn't exactly asked for admission back into the fold. And she was still weighing whether she even wanted back. What would that mean? How could she even be a part of her father's life again with so much pain still scarring the distance between them? That had to be resolved first and foremost.

And then there was Nick. Nick was…well, she didn't know yet what Nick was. But she felt that there was something there. Wasn't there?

And this case. Even if the Senator had played a sinister part in this. Julie's mother needed to know how her daughter was killed. The whole town of Freeport was also depending on her, looking at her to come through like her father had time and time again. Further, she wasn't about to let anyone down the way she had been let down facing her own mother's death. Least of all, Sarah. She couldn't abandon her promise to Sarah. She wouldn't allow Sarah to suffer the way she had for so many years.

Emily's lips parted, and she turned to Brandon. "What if we waited to get married?"

"Until when?"

Until secrets are settled with Dad. Until things with Nick are explored. Until the balance of justice in Freeport is set right again. But she could say none of these things. She didn't have to. Brandon read them in her face. He stood there, looking at her in disbelief, his future draining away from him. She felt his despondency and wished she could ease it.

"Something's shifted in you. Something I can never be a part of," he said sadly.

She felt it too, but she didn't want to admit it. Emily looked down at her bleeding shin but made no attempt to wipe away the blood. *Why can't you be a part of this, Brandon? Because you don't know how? Or because you're not willing?* Emily couldn't form the questions into words. She was too afraid of the answers.

All she knew was that this time, she did not want to run to Chicago and sweep everything under the rug.

FORTY-FIVE

SUNDAY MORNING EMILY rose early, after a restless night's sleep, with a kink in her neck and a sore spine. She sat on the edge of her bed, kneading her neck with the knuckles of her left hand that no longer sported a diamond. When they'd returned from their downtown walk, Brandon had decided to go back to Chicago. Emily handed him the ring and told him to keep it in a safe place until she could figure some things out.

After a long, hot shower, Emily felt better. She curled up on the bed and tried to come up with a plan for the day. She wasn't even sure where to begin now that her life had shifted overnight. Visit Dad? Call Dr. Claiborne? Extend her hotel stay? How long would she be here? She grabbed her phone twice to call Brandon. Each time, she set it back down. The third time, she grabbed it and dialed Nick. She suspected Nick's talk with Vince Parelli had not yielded anything new, or he would have contacted her. But she wanted to hear it from him. Actually, to hear his voice. Nick's phone went to voicemail.

Emily decided she couldn't sit in that hotel room a minute longer. She threw on jeans and a sweater and jumped in her Leaf. On her way through Freeport, she picked up two hot cups of coffee and two hot cinnamon rolls from Brown's. She was glad Delia wasn't working because she didn't want to explain to her who that second coffee and roll were for.

NICK'S TRUCK WAS in the driveway, but when Emily rang the bell, he didn't come to the door. She walked around to the back of Nick's house and found him sitting on his back porch in an Adirondack chair facing the lake. He was unshaven and wore a baseball cap and a ratty pair of jeans. He looked as tired as she felt.

"It's really beautiful out here. I can see why you bought the place."

"Yeah." Nick kept his gaze straight ahead.

"Coffee?" She handed him a cup.

"Much needed." He took a long sip.

"I brought cinnamon rolls too."

"Thanks. Have a seat." He motioned to the chair next to him. "Where's Brandon?"

She shook her head and brought the coffee to her lips. She could feel Nick eyeing her hand.

"No ring?"

"Nope."

"You okay?"

"I will be." She handed him a roll wrapped in a napkin. "Don't wanna talk about it, though."

"I get it."

"You okay?"

"I will be. I sat outside Julie's funeral service yesterday. Don't wanna talk about it, though."

"I get it."

Emily looked out over the lake. Two swans surfaced from nearby and glided toward Nick's dock. Emily drank it in. In her head, she was comparing this view to her own dwelling back in Chicago, which was nothing even close to peaceful. Her back porch was big enough to fit a café table and two small chairs and overlooked an alley and dumpsters. Her front lobby door opened right onto the city street and deposited her into the bustle of commuters, bikers, and transients.

"Did you get a chance to talk to Vince?"

"I did. He was at home working the farm during the time of the murder. From what his family says. And how can I discount the eyewitness testimony of a mother and seven children? However, I went to a couple neighbors to corroborate."

"Sounds like a solid alibi."

Nick nodded. "This is the biggest case I've ever had, Em. And I'm screwing it up. And I'll probably lose my job."

"No, you won't. You're doing the best you can with what you have to work with," she said.

"My fear is that I'll never catch the guy who did this. And I don't know if I can live with myself if that happens."

Emily thought about the cold case section in the back of her dad's journal. "It may take some time, but I know you won't give up."

"I should have called in for more help from the state police," he added sorely.

"What could they have done that you didn't already do? Truth is, the physical evidence is paper-thin. No one claims to have heard or seen anything that morning. And you don't have a murder weapon. There's nothing in this investigation that you did wrong or missed."

"Some of it is thanks to you. We make a good team."

She glanced up and caught Nick staring at her with a longing look.

"I hardly recognize the girl I fell in love with back in high school."

Emily paused. Fell in love with? He had never said those words in high school. It shook her to the core. A million feelings and questions that she wanted to discuss sprang into her mind, but instead she took another sip of coffee.

"Just tell me one thing, Em. You owe me one honest answer. Why did you leave like that?"

"You shouldn't have thrown away my letter," Emily teased, but it fell flat against his pleading eyes.

"In that letter, I told you that it was hard for me to talk to you—anyone actually—about my mom's death. Everywhere around me, everyone was just going on with their lives. Jo, my dad, you...but I couldn't. I didn't know what to do because I just felt stuck. Paralyzed. I knew if I didn't get out, then I might not...survive."

"You were thinking of killing yourself?"

"No. Not that. But I felt so desperate. The only answer was to leave. And I didn't want anyone talking me out of it."

"Including me?" said Nick quietly.

Emily nodded. "Especially you."

"I've tried to forgive your silence, Em. I've hated this emptiness between us. It's driven me crazy all these years. I know we were young, but we had something. I wanted to..."

Emily felt him looking at her, but she couldn't meet his gaze.

"You wanted to what?" she asked.

Nick turned away from her and stood up. He gripped the top of the guardrail that ran along the deck and faced the lake. The sun was spreading across the water, betokening a beautiful day.

"I wanted to be there for you. But I didn't know how. I'm sorry."

Nick stared straight at the lake, his back to Emily.

She scrambled to collect the new feelings swirling around her. Her homecoming had definitely not turned out as planned. She'd expected to swoop in quietly, under the radar. Take care of her father and return to Chicago untouched. Unnoticed. Unscathed. Instead, the experience had been a bombardment of people, feelings, places, and memories challenging her present and influencing her future. Her whole life had been up-ended.

"We could still be a team," she said, surprised at her own answer.

Nick spun around. "What do you mean?"

Emily backpedaled. "The Dobson case. I'm…invested. I want to help you."

"No, Em. Your part is over. I should have never asked you to do more than the autopsy. I just didn't want you to leave. It was nice having you around again."

"What? This isn't about you. I did this for me. For Dad. And for Sarah."

"You've done your duty. You're free to go. The county has to move forward and hire a new ME. And I've gotta step up the investigation."

"But my signature's all over this case. I need to see this through. And there are people depending on me."

"No, on *me*. You don't live here. It's not your job."

Four days ago, his comment wouldn't have hurt at all. But this morning it felt like a sucker punch to the gut. A frustrated lump formed in Emily's throat. Her gazed pierce through him toward the lake.

"You understand what I'm saying about the investigation, right?" Nick looked to Emily for her response.

"Yes. Sure. I understand." But she didn't. Anger flashed through Emily. She wanted to kick and scream and pound him with her fists. This was completely unfair. Instead, she pulled herself together and eyed him coolly. He was only doing what was legal. She had taken it to a personal level. And she had to detach. At least until she could figure out another way.

"Since you're kicking me off the case?"

"I'm freeing you to go back to your life in Chicago," said Nick.

"Can you do me a favor before I go?"

"Depends."

"Julie's bracelet. Are you done with it?"

"Yeah. I guess so," said Nick. "There's nothing more we can do with it."

"Will you release it from evidence?"

"Yeah, I can do that."

She stood there facing him in an awkward silence, not wanting to go.

"So, I'm gonna take a walk now. Take care. See you." Nick carved a path around her and headed off the porch toward the wooden staircase that led down to the sandy beach.

Emily watched him descend toward the lake and travel along the shoreline. He didn't so much as glance back. In a few yards, he'd disappeared around a bend on the bank of the lake. Perhaps she had misinterpreted everything.

EMILY DROVE TO the Dobsons' house, grateful to see that the senator's truck wasn't in the driveway. Mrs. Dobson let Emily wait in the foyer while she went upstairs to get Sarah.

Sarah came down to the foyer, dressed in yoga pants and a sweatshirt, with a flat expression. She gave Emily a weak hello. Her mother stood a few feet away to observe. Her cold stare made Emily uncomfortable. And must have made Sarah feel the same because she turned to her mom.

"Mom, can you…go?"

"Ms. Hartford, could you please state your business with my daughter?" asked Mrs. Dobson.

"I just wanted to give her a gift." Emily tried to sound cheery and light.

"Mom. Please. Just go. It's fine." Sarah crossed her arms and shot her mom a nasty look that sent Mrs. Dobson from the room.

"How are you doing, Sarah?"

"Fine."

"You don't seem fine."

"They've grounded me. Indefinitely."

"Oh… It's probably just an overreaction."

"It's punishment. They say they don't trust me anymore." She let out a laugh. "They don't trust me, but I've never done anything. Meanwhile, Julie was doing drugs and sneaking around with David behind their back."

"It's not fair. I'll give you that. But my guess is that they're just scared."

"Of what?"

"They don't want to lose another daughter."

Sarah shrugged and let it sink in.

"So, why did you come here?"

"You trusted me to find something for you, and I

did," said Emily, handing Sarah a square cardboard jewelry box. "The police released this to me this morning."

Sarah opened the box, and a small gasp slipped from her lips. She slid Julie's charm bracelet into the palm of her hand.

"It's no longer being considered a piece of evidence in your sister's case."

Tears moistened the corners of Sarah's eyes.

"Where did you find it?"

"Doesn't matter. Put it on. Let's see."

Sarah stretched out her arm so Emily could fasten the clasp. She was glad she had taken the time to bring it to the jewelers to get it cleaned after she picked it up from the police station. Sarah smiled and hugged Emily. "Thank you."

"You're very welcome."

Sarah released her from the hug, and Emily noticed a worried look cross her brow.

"Wait. Does this mean you can't find Julie's killer?"

"The police are still working hard on that. It's in their very capable hands. So don't worry, okay?" Emily handed Sarah a piece of paper with her phone number on it. "I'm going to be heading back to Chicago. But if you ever need anything, just reach out."

Emily turned and faced the door to leave.

"Did you ever resolve that secret about your mom?"

Sarah's question drew her back.

"No. Not yet."

"Well, maybe someday."

"Yeah. Maybe." She mustered up her best reassuring smile for Sarah and then let herself out. When would the *whys* and *maybes* be over?

FORTY-SIX

HOPPING BACK IN her car, Emily checked the time. The Dobson stop had put her a half-hour behind on getting to Jo's kids' horse show. Arriving at Premiere, she noted that a decent-sized crowd had already gathered in the stands, and the junior horse show was getting under way. Making her way along the fence toward the stands, she saw that Jo's oldest two, Jeremiah and Jessica, were warming up their horses with the other junior equestrians in the ring. She made her way to the stands and found Jo in the bleachers a few rows up. She had saved a seat for Emily. A feeling of comfort flooded Emily as she sat down next to her bestie.

"Hey, I heard a rumor you were spotted with your fiancé in town last night," said Jo.

"You heard correctly."

"This is perfect. I'll set an extra plate for dinner, and we can talk wedding plans."

Emily stuck her hand out for Jo to see.

"Oh no. What happened?" said Jo, grabbing her ringless hand.

"I think I'm finally finding out who I really am. And I don't know if Brandon fits into that picture."

This was the crux of it all. Emily's life had been spiraling ever since she'd left Freeport. She hadn't been happy when she left. She'd been miserable. Searching. Grieving. Barely existing. Easing her pain meant running from it. And she had never slowed down long enough to examine that inner friction. She'd dealt with it practically, locking into the only path she had ever wanted: to be a doctor. Once on this path, Emily had slowly grown out of her misery. Time had tamped down the sting of grief. She'd studied hard. Worked hard. Pressed forward. Met Brandon. He became the object of her search and the sweet relief to all her friction. He knew how to live well, and he made life look easy and comfortable. She'd let herself melt into his world. His plans. His dreams. His future. Until there was little left of Emily Hartford.

Emily turned to Jo. "This is really uncharted territory for me. I'm scared, Jo."

"That's not a bad place to be. I know you can find your way."

"How can you be so sure?"

"You're here. That's a great first step."

As a line of riders entered the ring, Jo hugged her and then pointed to her son. "Oh, hey, Jeremiah's up."

Emily was so grateful for a friend like Jo. She settled in to watch the event, her mind and spirit relaxing as she decided that she wanted to do the hard work of repairing what she had severed so many years ago. It was the only way back to herself.

EMILY STAYED AT the show long enough to see Jeremiah and Jessica perform, and then told Jo that she needed to get back to her dad's house to help Cathy. She said her goodbyes and made her way down to the horse stalls, feeling drawn to visit Mercedes's pen again. She paused in front of the memorial tribute, which had grown considerably since she last saw it. There were fresh wreaths and vases of flowers filling the entire stall. People had left their medals, and there were dozens more photographs stapled to the wooden slates. Emily's heart sank, knowing that the case was still unresolved. Her thoughts wandered to the Dobsons and how desperately they needed answers.

She knelt to look at the pictures and articles of Julie mourners had left behind. Outside, in the ring, the crowd roared. The high school competition was in progress.

Vince would be out there competing for, and probably winning, the scholarship that had been favored to be Julie's.

She wondered which stall held Vince's horse as her feet took her into the south wing of the stables, where the older riders stabled their horses. The entire wing had been emptied into the ring. Horses. Riders. Trainers. Grooms. She went from stall to stall, looking at the name tags, until she heard two male voices arguing from a pen at the end of the row. It was then she noticed this stall held a large, caramel-colored mare.

"You owe me this competition," an older man was saying. "What the hell happened?"

"I'm sorry… I…fell out of the saddle," said the younger voice.

This was curious. Emily padded cautiously toward them, keeping out of sight.

"I lost my grip. It was my fault—not the horse's," said Vince. "Don't hurt the horse."

Emily turned a corner toward the last row of stalls. At the far end, she could see the silhouettes of two men, a teen and a grown adult. She crept a few steps closer and recognized Vince from the photograph. She assumed the other man was probably his trainer or coach.

"Did you score the shins like I asked?"

Vince didn't answer.

"Your entire future depends on this scholarship slot," hissed the older man. "Do you know what this cost me?"

Vince hung his head with a slight nod.

Why was this man so angry at Vince? The next comment caused a shiver to run through Emily's entire body.

"She's not standing in your way anymore. Do you understand that?"

"I didn't need you to do that," Vince whispered.

"And if I didn't, you wouldn't win. No win, no scholarship. No college."

"I can still go to college."

"Community college ain't no future. State university. Full ride. That's what I promised your mother."

Vince's father! Mr. Parelli leaned down next to Vince's horse and examined the shins. He shook his head, displeased.

"You didn't do it," he said.

"No, Dad. Please. Don't. I can still win," pleaded Vince.

Emily watched wide-eyed as Mr. Parelli reached into a duffel and retracted a long, thin pair of horse nippers. She focused on the instrument, noticing its oval opening and angled nose. It was the antique nippers. *Needle in the haystack. Murder weapon found!* She fumbled for her phone and pulled up Nick's number.

"Don't hurt him!" shouted Vince, pushing his father aside.

"Get out of my way," said Mr. Parelli. But Vince stepped right in between his dad and his horse.

Emily quickly pecked out a text to Nick.

Premiere. Now!

The nippers swinging at his side, Mr. Parelli warned his son again to step aside.

Vince remained in place, staring down his father. "You'll have to hit me before I let you get to him."

Emily pressed "Send" and watched the spinning icon in the upper left corner of the screen struggle to find a signal. She only had one bar and sent up a silent plea for the text.

"Don't test me, son," said Mr. Parelli as he edged closer to the horse. Vince wouldn't budge.

Emily glanced back down at the screen to see if the text had gone through. The bar line on the text was only a third of the way through sending. Emily waved the phone around in an attempt to get a better signal.

Mr. Parelli tried to circumvent his son, raising his arm to strike Vince.

"Move, Vince. I'm warning you one last time."

Vince shook his head and braced himself. Mr. Parelli swung the nippers back.

"You'll have to hit me," Vince said defiantly with fury in his voice.

Mr. Parelli inched closer, white-knuckling the nippers. "Vince, you bring this on yourself. I'm warning you one last time. Move out of my way."

Vince's hateful eyes met his father's. He stood his ground.

Emily buckled. She couldn't let this happen in front of her own two eyes. Leaping out from her hiding place, she yelled, "Wait! *NO!*"

But her voice was drowned out by the cheering crowd in the stands. The nippers came down on Vince's back. He dropped to the floor in anguish. Everything bottled up inside of Emily exploded in this moment.

Mr. Parelli froze for a second, waiting to see if his son would get up. Emily could hear the nippers drop from his grip and thump on the hay-padded stall. Mr. Parelli's anger never wavered as he stood over his son. "Vince. Son. Get up!"

Emily's eyes were glued to Vince, lying on the ground motionless. Outside, in the ring, the crowd reacted to some stunt taking place, drowning the silence of the stables in mounting applause. As the cheering soared, so did the adrenaline surging through Emily's system. She readied herself to lunge into the situation.

Mr. Parelli took a step in toward the horse and lifted his leg by the hoof. This time, Emily ran from her spot to stop him. "Get away from him!" she yelled.

Her efforts were thwarted as she tripped on a coiled rope hiding under a layer of hay. She fell, her phone sailing out of her reach and into a nearby, shallow grate about four inches below the floor's surface.

Mr. Parelli pivoted to see Emily recovering from her fall.

"Don't!" pleaded Emily, now on all fours.

"Miss, this is a family matter. You best leave us," said Mr. Parelli, stepping toward her.

Behind him, Vince peeled himself from the floor and yanked his horse out of the stall. He and Emily shared a quick glance. Vince understood her signal right away. He took his horse by the reigns, hoisted himself into the saddle, and galloped out of the stable.

Mr. Parelli dashed a few yards after his son, but they were gone. Emily crawled to the grate to search for her phone. Mr. Parelli then turned to Emily. She felt his gaze on her and looked up as he growled at her, "Who are *you*?"

Like a shot in the dark, it all came to Emily. Exactly what had happened on Julie's last day on earth.

Mr. Parelli was lying in wait for her, crouched in the bushes by the creek. When Julie and Mercedes passed by, he struck Mercedes first, bucking Julie off her horse. She tumbled to the ground, her helmet dislodging from her head.

Outrage boiled in Emily's veins. She rose to her feet, face-to-face with this murderer. She refused to back down.

"You killed Julie Dobson."

"I don't know who you are or what you're talking about, miss. I'm just a simple farmer minding my own business. I suggest you do the same."

Mr. Parelli inched nearer. Emily's feet were like trunks stuck in tar. He was now only two yards from her.

"You struck a teenage girl in the back of the skull and killed her with that," said Emily, noticing the nippers shaking.

"My son's been riding since he was three. My wife and I have scraped together every single nickel to get him this far. He deserves that scholarship. Not some spoiled senator's daughter."

Mr. Parelli lunged for Emily. She tried to back up but realized she hadn't left enough space for escape. Mr. Parelli attacked, the nippers coming down on her. Emily blocked the strike with her forearms, throwing Mr. Parelli off but sending her to a twisted heap on the ground.

In a flash, Mr. Parelli was standing over her, anger burning in his eyes. Emily's heart thumped inside her chest. Her skin prickled and her hands began to sweat. Emily opened her mouth to scream, but her cries went unheard under another wave of applause and cheers.

Mr. Parelli pounced on her, pinning Emily's arms to the ground with his boots. His hands encircled her neck in a death grip.

Emily's eyes grew wide. Fighting for her last breath, Emily braced herself, completely at his mercy. Her vision blurred...then the light closed in from the periphery, and in an instant everything went black.

FORTY-SEVEN

NICK'S SQUAD CAR peeled into the Premiere parking lot a little after five. He slammed it into park and ran to the main office. Gary Bodum had found Emily's phone buzzing in the drain grate. It was a text from Cathy, wanting to know when Emily would be around by the house. Then Gary had noticed Emily's car, still in the parking lot. Something was off, and he'd quickly alerted Nick.

"The text was up when I found it. But I can't get in because she has it passcoded," Gary said, handing Nick the phone.

Nick knew how to override the passcode on the phone. Soon, it blinked on. He immediately recognized the home screen as Emily's because it was set to a photo of her and Brandon in front of Buckingham Fountain in downtown Chicago.

"Do you remember the last time you saw her?" Nick asked as he scrolled through the recent phone calls.

"I don't know. I saw her in the stands earlier with Jo."

Nick noted that no calls had been sent or received since 8:42 am. Next, he went into the texts. The last one had been sent and failed at 1:24 pm. He clicked onto the message and saw that it was addressed to him.

Premiere. Now!

What was she trying to tell him?

"Have you searched the stable for her?"

"I did a quick walk-around."

"Gary, I need you to close the stables immediately," Nick told him.

"What? Why?"

"How many staff are still here?"

"Just a couple."

"Get everyone out of the stables and send them home. Touch nothing. Lock the doors. I'm sending over an officer to secure the scene. Don't let anyone near here or in here. Especially the press. Got it?"

"Is this about Emily? What do you think happened?" Gary's voice trembled. But Nick didn't answer as he fled into the stable. He had to find Emily.

WHEN HE DID find Emily in a crumpled heap in the back of Bodum's locked workroom, Nick rushed to her ragdoll body and dialed 911 with one hand. He put his hand on her neck and saw bruises. Her skin was cool to the touch, and Nick feared the worst. He checked for breathing. It was shallow, but present.

"Emily? Emily? Can you hear me?"

She moaned softly.

"Are you in pain?"

She nodded.

"I have help on the way. Hang in there, okay? You're gonna be fine."

She didn't answer.

"What happened? Who did this?"

Her eyes fluttered open, and he could tell she was trying to focus. Her lips parted, but no sound came out. Nick took her hand and squeezed it.

"Who? Please, Em."

Her lips pursed and she let out a guttural sound as she voiced, "Parelli."

FORTY-EIGHT

EMILY FAINTLY REMEMBERED Nick staying at her side while the sirens approached. He held her body off the damp ground as she drifted in and out of consciousness. Emily thought she heard him say, "Just stay with me. I don't want to lose you again."

At one point, when the paramedics took over and Nick had to let go, she was aware that she was lucidly dreaming, because one of the EMTs looked distinctly like Brandon in a white doctor's coat, coaxing her up the steps of their new brownstone in Chicago. Emily was standing on the sidewalk, looking down at her feet sunken into the hard cement. All she could see were the shoelaces of her running shoes. She couldn't lift her feet, no matter how hard she tugged. Brandon kept hopping the steps, higher and higher, farther and farther, leaving her behind. At one point, he looked back and shook his head at her, his broad smile fading. And then Brandon told her, "I'm going to arrest Parelli. I'll be back. You're in good hands now."

The dream grew dim, and she felt her muscles and bones settle into the gurney like weights into a soft, feather-down bed. There were voices. A lot of them. They kept asking her questions, slowly, which she couldn't answer because her mouth felt like it was filled with chewing gum. Soon, she gave up caring and didn't want to answer. None of it mattered.

Emily's body started to warm from the inside out, like a cup of chamomile tea. She thought she might have even been smiling, although she wasn't sure if the corners of her mouth were turning up. Complacency poured into her limbs. Her body grew lighter and lighter and lighter. The pain left. The fear dissipated. She drifted off to a deep, beautiful sleep.

As soon as the paramedics had Emily in their care, Nick hopped into his truck and sped off, terrified he would return and not find Emily alive. Nick prayed no serious harm had befallen her. When he'd left, the EMTs had no way of knowing the extent of her injuries or chances of survival. Nick was sick to his stomach for the entire hour-and-ten-minute drive to the Parelli farm.

Why had Emily been attacked? And how were the Parellis involved? And which Parelli? Father or son? Did they have something to do with Julie's death? What had Emily seen or heard? Questions pounded in synchronicity with his throbbing heartbeat.

On the way over, he alerted the Rock River Police Department about Emily's text and attack. He wanted backup ready to go. He informed them of his plan to visit the Parelli home and explained how he was going to play off his visit as casual. He was hoping for a peaceful arrest, but the Rock River sheriff agreed to keep a team on standby.

Nick pulled into the Parelli driveway and noticed Mrs. Parelli peeking between the curtains at him. As he turned off the headlights, she disappeared. Nick strode to the front door, trying with everything inside him to keep a professional demeanor and lower his pulse.

Mrs. Parelli came to the door, and Nick noted that she

had a dark bruise under one eye, and both were red, as if she had been crying. Had Mr. Parelli's control crossed a line? And how many times had it happened before?

"I'm sorry to bother you so late, Mrs. Parelli," said Nick with a false calmness. "Is your husband at home?"

"He is not," Mrs. Parelli said. Nick tried to sneak a look into the house. Through the sliver in the door, he could make out a line of four of the Parelli children, sitting silently at a long dining room table. Their heads were bowed over plates of food in front of them, but no one was eating. An unpleasant feeling crept over Nick.

"Do you know where he is?"

"I'm not sure at the moment," she answered slowly.

"I heard Vince ditched his big state competition. That seems odd since he was favored to win," said Nick.

"He wasn't feeling well," Mrs. Parelli lied with a quivery voice.

"Is he here?"

"He's not," said Mrs. Parelli.

"Where is he?"

"He's away for the night."

"What happened at the stables today, Mrs. Parelli?" Nick asked. "I thought Vince was going to ride and win.

"It didn't work out that way, I guess."

Nick thought he saw a flicker of light from the barn behind the house.

"Mind if I come in and wait for your husband?"

"You have a search warrant?"

"No, ma'am. I just wanted to speak with your husband."

"Best you leave now." She shut the door, and he could hear her locking the dead bolt.

So that's how they're gonna play this, thought Nick.

And he was quite certain that Mr. Parelli was still on the premises. There was a good chance one or both of the Parelli men were in that barn. Was Vince in danger as well? None of this added up.

Nick drove his squad car down the road and out of sight of the Parelli farm. Then, he pulled it off to the side of the road and hid his car behind a clump of large bushes. Cutting through the fields, he jogged back to the Parelli farm.

Nick started by searching the perimeter of the Parellis' barn. He found the large sliding barn doors padlocked but was able to jimmy a space between them big enough for him to slip through. As he entered, the horses moved in their stalls, standing, shaking their manes, and whinnying.

Nick let his eyes adjust to the dark, instead of switching on his flashlight. After getting a quick layout of the space, he crept toward the ladder leading up to the loft that covered about half the length of the barn and contained about two dozen hay bales. He searched them and then climbed back down the ladder.

He moved slowly through the barn, checking each stall. Along the back of the barn was a long workbench. Nick strode over. His inspection soon yielded a pair of antique nippers hung beside other nippers of varying sizes and shapes. He recognized the tool immediately as the one Emily had shown him in the pictures.

Silently, Nick removed his cell phone from his pocket and texted for backup. Rock River texted back that they were en route, with an ETA of five minutes. The pressure was mounting inside of him. Nick continued his search, creeping through the barn, sifting through equipment, stacked crates, stalls, and feed bins. He was about to enter one of the horse pens when he heard a rifle cock behind him.

In a singular motion, Nick reached for his sidearm. Out of the corner of his eye, he spotted the shadows of three hay bales stacked near a horse's stall. He dashed for them the moment the rifle shot exploded near him, barely missing. Crouching behind the bales, Nick knew that he had only seconds to react. The horses started to stamp and whinny, startled and panicked by the gunfire.

The rifle cocked again as Mr. Parelli moved closer.

"Don't come any closer, Mr. Parelli. Put down your gun or I will shoot," Nick warned.

Mr. Parelli fired at the sound of Nick's voice. Nick ducked as a hole blew through the top of the bale. Nick had no choice now. He aimed his handgun toward the direction of fire and shot two rounds into the dark. Both missed. The shooter shuffled to the side of the barn.

"Mr. Parelli, a team of police is on its way to your home," Nick warned. "You are under arrest for the murder of Julie Dobson and the attempted murder of Emily Hartford."

The rifle cocked again.

"Mr. Parelli, put your weapon down!"

Nick crouched off to one side as the shell blew a second hole just below the first. He gripped his weapon, planted himself belly down across the floor along the bottom of the hay bales, and started firing, praying he wouldn't hit any of the horses.

Nick exchanged several rounds of fire with Mr. Parelli until he realized no shots were being fired back at him.

The ringing in his ears deafened him. He waited

for the gun smoke to clear, then slowly emerged in a slight daze to find Mr. Parelli's body bleeding out on the barn floor.

FORTY-NINE

EMILY AWOKE IN a hospital bed. She blinked her eyes open, and the overhead light immediately made her sneeze.

"Bless you," said Nick, who sat eagerly at Emily's side.

"How long have I been here?"

"You've been sleeping for about a day and a half," he said with a smile.

"That explains why my stomach is trying to eat itself," Emily said. "What day is it?"

"Tuesday. How does a pudding meal sound?"

"Terrible." Her hand went to her jaw, and she realized that part of it was bandaged. "That's why I'm talking so funny?"

"It's badly bruised, but thankfully not broken," said Nick. "Your shoulder was dislocated. And you have a few cracked ribs and some bruising on your neck. But otherwise, you're in good shape considering you almost died.

"Your dad was here earlier. I promised I would call him as soon as you woke up."

"I think I might have died if you hadn't shown up."

"I don't wanna talk about *ifs*... I'm just grateful you're okay."

"I'm a little confused about one thing," said Emily. "How did you know where to find me?"

Nick pulled up a newsfeed on his phone, where he

was crushing an interview with the press. In it he explained how Gary found Emily's phone, how he discovered Dr. Emily Hartford in the workroom, and how that led to the shoot-out at the Parelli farm.

"Mr. Parelli's dead?" Emily asked in a hushed voice. "Are you okay?"

Nick nodded. "I'm under investigation. Police procedure. Not worried. It was self-defense in the line of duty."

Emily reached out and took Nick's hand. "Thank you."

"I can't believe how close I came to losing you. Again."

At those words, the image from her lucid dream of being stuck in the cement in front of her and Brandon's brownstone flashed across Emily's mind.

She knew in that instant, she wouldn't be going back to Chicago.

Emily smiled again through the pain, then realized her head was throbbing. "Is it time yet for another pain reliever?"

Nick pushed the nurse's button. Emily gazed around the hospital room that was overflowing with floral arrangements.

"Where did all these come from?"

"For not being here the last twelve years, you sure seem to have a lot of fans in Freeport," he said. "Let's see. The lilies are from your dad and Cathy. That one with the red, white, and blue carnations is from the Freeport Police. Jo and her family sent the practical philodendron. Delia brought in that huge field flower bouquet, insects and all."

"What about that one?" Emily pointed to a vase that

held two-dozen salmon-colored roses. Nick went over
to retrieve the card and handed it to Emily.

She read the card aloud. "Get well soon. Love, Brandon."

"He's called and texted at least a dozen times." Nick
handed Emily her phone. She pulled up a string of texts.

I wanted to come up the instant I heard. But I didn't
know if that would complicate things. I will always cher-
ish what we had. I am trying to understand. Please let
me know if you need me there. I love you.

She sat with the message for a moment. Brandon was
big-city born and bred. She could not hold that against
him any more than he could hold Freeport against her.
She realized it went deeper than geography. She still
had things to work out. Things to prove. That untapped
part of her she had hidden away long ago was not going
to stay hidden any longer.

Emily pointed to a white, flowering orchid on the
windowsill.

"It's from Sarah," said Nick. "She delivered it to the
front desk downstairs herself."

"Read me the note?"

Nick turned the card on the plastic stick. "Dr. Hartford, thank you for being there for me. I will never forget you. Sarah Dobson."

She had succeeded. Satisfaction stretched across her
face.

"You can't imagine how grateful the Dobsons are.
The senator wants to do something to honor you."

"Publicity stunt. They just want to pivot the eyes of
the press away from his abuse accusations."

"I'm sure you're right about that." Nick moved over to her bedside.

"Make sure he doesn't do a thing," said Emily. "My involvement was purely happenstance. Right place. Right time."

"Own this, Em. You're a town heroine."

A heroine. Writing her own story. Making choices out of instinct and passion, not practical duty. Carving her path. Not running and hiding.

"I'm glad the Dobsons have some sort of answer. Even though everything that's happened is just awful and unnecessary."

"I know this is going to sound weird, but you're radiant right now," said Nick.

She didn't feel radiant, but she did feel more at peace than she had in a very, very long time.

"I have to admit," she said with a lopsided smile. "I like this Emily."

"She scares me a little. Please don't ever try to stop a killer again."

Emily laughed. "A heroine makes no such promises."

She fell quiet for a moment. The silence between them was comforting.

"I suppose you'll be going back to Chicago as soon as you're well enough?"

"No. Actually," she said softly, "I feel like there's a purpose for me here. And I want to see it through."

"You gotta get things right between you and your dad first," Nick said.

"I'm ready." She hoped he was too. With her father's faltering health, she knew it was a conversation she couldn't ignore much longer. There would be no lasting peace without forgiveness.

"It's gonna be okay. You're home now."

Nick slouched back into the chair next to her bed. Emily felt there was more he wanted to divulge. But she didn't press. For now, it was enough that he was here.

FIFTY

THE NEXT MORNING, Emily woke up feeling less sore and less stiff and quite eager to get out of the hospital. She was hungry for a bear claw and exhausted from staying up half the night chatting with Jo, who was coming off second shift. She wanted to get a good night's rest in her bed at the Pennington.

Before the first shift nurse could come check on her, Emily wandered out to the nurses's station to make sure she was on the discharge list for the day. She informed the nurses that she needed the doctor on duty to release her by noon. *Yes, it's true what they say,* she thought. *Doctors make the most obnoxious patients.*

At 12:17 pm, the nurse wheeled Emily out of the hospital's front doors to Nick, who had volunteered to drive her home and was waiting with her Leaf in the pickup area.

As they zipped to her dad's house, Nick informed her that he had investigated a single-car fatality early that morning. The victim had been brought into the morgue.

"Guy wrapped himself around a tree. Found half a case of empty beer cans scattered on the interior. So, should be a simple case."

"Is this your coy way of asking if I'll do an autopsy?"

"Only if you're feeling up to it."

"I'll need an assistant," she said and smiled at him. Ten minutes later, they pulled into the driveway.

"That's odd," said Emily, looking with dismay at the overgrown grass. "I hired a service to cut the lawn."

"Your father probably thought he could do it himself."

"No doubt," said Emily as Nick shut the car off.

"I can cut it while we're here. You head on inside and see your dad." They exited the Leaf, and Nick made his way toward the barn.

Emily stood at the front door for a minute to collect herself. She had rehearsed this in her mind a thousand times. Could she remain gracious and respectful? Could she weather the results? Could she believe her father? All remained to be seen.

Emily rapped on the door and waited for an answer. When none came, she rapped again.

"Dad, hey, it's me," she called out. "Dad!"

She cracked the door open. In the backyard, she could hear Nick start up the lawn mower.

"Dad, are you in there?"

Maybe he's out in the garden, she thought. Cracking the door open a little farther, Emily was accosted by an acrid whiff of smoke that wafted out from the crack in the door.

"Dad, it's Emily. Are you in here? I'm coming in!"

She rushed to the kitchen to find a smoky haze clouded the room, making it difficult to see whether her father was in there. Emily rounded the kitchen counter and spied him slouched against the cupboards, his head hanging over his chest.

"Dad? Are you all right? Dad!" She knelt quickly at his side. "Oh my gosh, what happened? Dad!"

Dr. Hartford's eyes cracked open, and he tried to focus.

"Em. Thank God," he muttered.

Her medical training kicked in as she reached for his wrist to check his pulse. Scanning his face, she noted his pallor, his face gray and his forehead wet with perspiration.

"Your pulse is really weak," she said. "Can you hear me? Dad, what happened?" Emily leaned in so she could hear her father's feeble voice.

"The pot. On fire."

Emily gazed up and saw the ceiling covered in dark soot and white foam. A used fire extinguisher lay at her father's feet.

"Dad, did you pass out while you were cooking?" she said, raising her voice so he could hear her.

"I think so," her father said.

"I warned you this could happen," she said with fright in her voice.

"I'm fine. Just need meds," he panted.

"No. You're not fine. Your heart is dying," she said, reaching for her phone and dialing 911.

"Don't call...no ambulance," he wheezed.

Emily jumped up to the sink and filled a glass with water. She cracked opened the kitchen window and searched quickly for Nick in the yard. She could hear the mower, but he was nowhere in sight. He must have started with the front lawn.

"Nick! Nick!" she yelled, her futile cry getting lost in the distant roar of the lawn mower motor. She gave up and knelt back down next to her father.

"Dad, this is why you can't be here alone," she said, chiding him out of fright and frustration.

"I'm not alone. Cathy lives here," her father mumbled argumentatively. "I'm not alone."

"She's not here right now," said Emily, kneeling back down by his side with the glass.

The 911 operator answered, "Hello, what is your emergency?"

"Yes, I need an ambulance at Dr. Robert Hartford's home address. He's conscious now, but he needs immediate medical attention. I'll stay on the line."

"Where are your heart meds?" Emily asked. Her dad pointed to a lazy Susan on the counter. Emily found the right pill bottle and crouched down next to her father as she pressed the pill between his lips, onto his tongue.

"Swallow this," she instructed, handing him the water. Dr. Hartford drank.

"I need more time," he said.

"More time for what?"

"More time with you," said her father, whose skin had an ashen look to it. "I want the surgery."

"You do? For sure?" Emily said.

"Yes."

"That's great. Yes, we'll do that right away," she replied.

"Can you stay for it?"

"Of course. Yes. I'll stay," Emily said with great relief. "That's what I came here to tell you. I'm staying in Freeport for a while."

"Good. Good." Her father slid to the floor and lay on his side.

"Dad, hey, talk to me," Emily said. "Don't pass out. Keep your eyes open."

"Your mother...we need to talk about your mother," he said in a whisper.

"Yes, I'd like that." Emily felt a wave of relief.

"She died, you know…" He trailed off, and Emily's heart sank.

"I know she died, Dad." Was the diminished supply of oxygen making him delirious?

"No. You don't know."

"Yes, I was there, Dad. But we don't need to talk about that right now. Conserve your energy. The ambulance is on its way. Focus on me. Eyes open."

Sweat was running down Dr. Hartford's forehead now. He continued to pant for breath.

"No. The real reason…how she died…"

Emily froze at the mention of it. She fixed her eyes on her dad as his eyelids drooped down over his pupils. He began to drift toward unconsciousness. Emily frantically searched for a pulse.

"What happened, Dad?" She pressed her ear closer to his mouth so he wouldn't have to strain his voice.

Robert panted out his answer in staccato phrases. "It. Was. My. Fault." He struggled to inhale.

"What's your fault? Dad?"

"Mary… Mom…" He couldn't catch his breath.

"Okay. Don't talk. Just breathe. Breathe, breathe, breathe," Emily instructed.

Robert found the strength to utter two words. "She had…"

"Dad…shh…"

"Cancer."

"What?"

"I didn't know…until the autop—"

He slipped into unconsciousness.

"No. No. Dad. Come on. Stay with me."

Emily leaned in toward his chest, listening as each breath became more prolonged than the one before it.

She agonized over his last words. *What did he mean, she had cancer? Surely, that's not what killed her. Why didn't he know? Why had Mom kept this from us? And what did all of this have to do with her accident?* It still didn't explain the blue slipper. His news churned in her gut with a sick sensation. *Where is that ambulance?*

Emily kept her fingers on her father's dwindling pulse. She closed her eyes, pinching out a tear, and with all her being willed him to live.

* * * * *

ACKNOWLEDGMENTS

THANK YOU TO Julie Gwinn. When we first met, this novel was just a script and a prayer, but even in that two-minute meet-and-greet in that noisy line at Starbucks, you recognized the potential in the story and me. You stuck with me as I wrote it into novel form and then pitched it relentlessly until it found the perfect home with Crooked Lane. My deepest gratitude for being with me on this journey and for believing in me. I'm pretty sure I still owe you a coffee. Your Starbucks or mine?

Thank you to Anne, Jenny, Jennifer, Matt, Sarah, and the amazing staff and editors at Crooked Lane. It was worth the wait to find you all! You have been a dream to work with and have helped me shape this story into something I'm proud of. You were the perfect finishing flourish on this marathon project. I don't mean this to sound trite, but let's be honest: our relationship is the youngest on *The Coroner*'s literary journey, and you all still need to pass one more test…posing for a selfie in my body bag.

To Barbara N., Chris and Kathy R., Sheryl A., and the many other mentors and writers at the Act One Program in Los Angeles who saw the earliest drafts and the potential in this story when first started as a feature script in 2002. You all did your best to nurture the seed of this story and to nurture me as a newbie writer to tell it. Even after a couple dozen drafts and lots of rejections, I held on to your advice that truly great stories never die. There are not a finer bunch of storytellers that I've come across. You are a part of *The Coroner*'s story. Thank you.

Thank you to Ronald E. Graeser, D.O., and Gail Graeser, the real coroner (ahem…medical examiner), and his wife. Dad, thank you for being part mad scientist, part absent-minded professor, and full-time fan of your family. Mom, thank you for embracing Dad's quirkiness while showing the utmost level of grace and composure as he de-thawed that dog in the oven and ruined your Tupperware with his experiments. I only hope people don't read this story and think it's autobiographical because life in our coroner's house was sure a lot grittier, messier, and less dramatic than it is depicted here, wasn't it? I could not be more grateful for the oddities and unique experiences of my childhood. They inspired my imagination. They made me aware of the utter dependence we have on faith, family, and community. And they have stirred me to try to live each day with fullness, gratitude, and vigor…because tomorrow is never guaranteed. Love you both forever.